Consigned to Oblivion

B.C. Hedlund

B.C. Hedlund

Copyright © 2020 B.C. Hedlund
All rights reserved.
ISBN: 9798629325116

CONSIGNED TO OBLIVION

To my mother
Thank you for everything

"We are all broken, that's how the light gets in."

- Ernest Hemingway

Prologue

You know that feeling when you're falling? When you take a step onto what used to be solid ground and suddenly it just falls out from under you? You start to spiral slowly, gathering speed until you know that you are within seconds from hitting the ground, and you're praying that you'll hit it, that everything will just disappear, that everything you've been fighting to escape will just consume you and everything will be over. But then the ground doesn't come and you just keep falling and falling and falling, trapped in a nightmare that will never end. A nightmare that slowly becomes your seconds, then your minutes, then your hours, then your days, then your weeks, then your months, then your years, as it becomes the never ending eternity of your life. At some point you start hoping you hit the ground, you start looking for a way out, but the harder you look the more desperate you become, the more trapped, the more lost, and the more you want to escape, no matter which way out you have to take.

The longer you fall, the darker the world becomes, and every time you catch a glimpse of light you reach for it, but you keep falling, and you have to watch as it slowly fades back into darkness. It doesn't matter how much you want to stop falling, you never will.

Once an object is in motion it will remain in motion.

I'm falling.

Until something stops me, I will be forever falling.

My toes hang over the edge, and a few stones tumble down into the water far below me. The world is spinning, the whole world appears to shake, but my hands are suddenly steady. My movements no longer reflect those of the girl who used to walk through life scared of everything that could hurt her. They're sure, still.

I'm no longer that girl.

I'm still that girl in the sense that, when she stood in front of the mirror, there was no face reflected back at her. Just a figure staring back at her in fragments, darkness blotting out the reflection in places where the light had ceased to reflect. She had become so obscured by darkness that there were no more refractions of light to show her form in its entirety.

That part of me, the dark part, the part that makes my reflection cease to exist, will never fade.

But there are so many parts of me that have faded. Bad parts, and good parts.

I look down. The world tips for a second, and when it steadies itself it's a blur, still spinning, still shaky, but it's still there.

I can feel the spray from the waterfall on my skin, reflecting the colors dancing against the horizon, painting the body of a girl so darkened by the world that she had lost all color.

The water below me glitters in the waking sun, a silent elegy seeming to glide across the surface, disrupting the calmness of the water.

The quiet wind sneaks through my hair, blowing it around my face, obscuring the scene in front of me. Voices of those I left behind whist past my ears, parts of the past that will never resurface.

Maybe, if I had some sort of alter life, and I hadn't run away like this, things could have been different. I would have graduated high school, kept my friends, my family, my life. But going back now was never an option. Because of the choices I made in my life, this is the last one I get to make.

And *I* get to make it.

Not the damaged part of me, not the desperate part of me, just me.

It's my choice.

I've stood atop this cliff so many times that I feel like I know how far down the drop is, even though I've never jumped before. I know the breezes that float through here, whispering coaxing words of remission into the ears of the damned. Trying to get them to step away. I know the colors that shine against the horizon in the morning, and how they fade once the sun rises just enough that there is no need for any colors to manifest its arrival.

I know that the stones beneath my feet will not be what gives way first.

I turn my back on the world.

The world gives way beneath me and I stretch my arms out like wings, feeling the wind tear through my fingers as the elegy roars in my ears. The colors are ripped from my skin and stay there, suspended in the outline of the girl that was standing on the cliff edge.

She's not there anymore.

Chapter One

A car alarm went off outside.

"*Damn it*," the zipper on my backpack split as I picked it up. "You've got to be kidding me," I swore under my breath as the alarm continued screeching in the background.

"Cassandra!" Mom called from the kitchen.

I grabbed a paper clip and unbent it, holding it between my teeth until I wrestled the zipper back into place and stuck the clip in it, keeping it from popping again.

"Sandra!"

"Mom, I have to go," I said quickly, pushing open my door and bypassing her in the kitchen.

"Do you want breakfast? I made toast," her eyes followed me to the back door.

"I know, I'm sorry. I've got to go, I'm going to be late."

"Oh, okay, well have a good day," she gave me a thin smile.

"You too, tell Grandma I'm sorry if the alarm woke her."

"Okay."

"Bye, I love you."

"Bye."

The three unsaid words hung in the balance as the door slammed shut behind me.

The alarm was still ringing, echoing in the silent neighborhood.

"Maddy! I thought I told you I lock it when it's out of the garage!" I unhooked my keys from my lanyard and chucked them.

"I forgot! Oh- *shit*," she fumbled at the keys, missed, and watched as they clattered to the ground.

"Since when can you not catch?" I rolled my eyes at her, getting down on my hands and knees to fish them out from under the car.

"Since when did you forget that I can't catch *anything* to save my *life*?"

"*Including* a boyfriend."

Maddy spun around, face reddening, "Hey!"

"Aw, come on, Gabi, that was mean," I unlocked the car.

"Yeah, yeah, so I've heard. Please make that noise stop, I could hear it a block away," she walked up the driveway, pulling her hair up into a messy bun.

"Considering you only live three houses down, *funny*."

"Well, let's wake up the people a block away and ask them if they heard it- wait, they're *already* awake. I wonder *why*."

Maddy huffed, "Leave me *alone*, thank you very much."

I turned the alarm off, "Stop bitching and get in the car."

"Someone's in a bad mood," Gabi pulled open the passenger side door, Maddy glaring at her as she crawled into the back.

"I haven't had coffee yet, I woke up late."

"Well, we still have to pick up Rachel, we can get some on the way."

"*We?* You assume that I'd let you guys get coffee?"

"Oooh, can I get a chai latte?" Maddy leaned forward between the two front seats.

Gabi turned around, "This early in the morning?"

"*What?*" Maddy said defensively.

"No one cares what crazy thing you get," I said, "but we aren't going to Starbucks, we're stopping at Dunkin, just so you know."

"Aw, why?"

"Because I'm broke and Dunkin is cheap. *Plus* it's on the way, Starbucks is on the other side of town."

"Cass, school doesn't start until 7:40, can we *please?*"

I looked at Maddy in the rearview mirror, "Are *you* driving?"

"That's not *fair*, I don't have a car."

"I don't either, this is my Grandma's, you know that."

"Okay, but you still get to drive it!"

"Oh, and what was that, *who's* driving?"

"Fine. *Fine.*"

We pulled up to Rachel's house. "Well, guys, what do you think, should I give her five minutes or use the lovely car horn?"

"If I had to *wake up* to that *stupid* car alarm, she can be notified by you honking that damn horn," Gabi threw Maddy a glare over her shoulder.

"You woke *up* then?" Maddy shot back.

"Like you never wake up and leave within a span of five minutes."

"I *don't*, it takes me at least twenty minutes!"

"What the hell do you do in the morning?"

"It takes me a long time to find an outfit!"

"God, and look what you end up wearing every day. The same jeans and a college sweatshirt." Today it was Harvard, yesterday it was Princeton, the day before that it was NYU.

"The jeans are different!"

"What, are the rips in different places?"

"*For* your information, yes, but they're also different colors and styles and-"

"If you say so, Maddy, *if* you say so."

"Cass, are you going to get Rachel out here or not?" Gabi reached over to press down on the horn, but I swatted her hand away.

"*Yes*, I am. I'm sorry, your debate over Maddy's clothing was just *too* distracting. I think that might just be all I think about for the rest of the day. On my chemistry test I might just draw little college sweatshirts instead of noble gas configurations."

"Make sure they're *crew*neck college sweatshirts."

Maddy rolled her eyes, "*Haha*, very *funny*."

The front door opened and Rachel appeared, tying a plaid button down around her waist.

Gabi rolled down the car window. "Hurry up! We want coffee!"

"I see we're all in a sunny disposition today," Rachel grinned, shooing Maddy to the other side of the car.

"Why couldn't you just go around?" Maddy complained.

"It was quicker, quit whining."

"I'm not!"

"Sure you're not. Why the sudden, overwhelming need for coffee this morning, guys?"

"Well, *I* was up late studying for my AP chem test," I glanced back at her, "Gabi got woken up by my car alarm going off, and I don't know what Maddy's excuse is."

"I just want coffee."

"You *always* want coffee," Gabi undid her seatbelt and kneeled on her seat to talk to them. "Get coffee at home, then maybe you won't set anymore car alarms off."

"I *do* have coffee at home, but my dad weakened it."

"I wonder why."

"Gabi! Sit normally, *please*," I glared at her.

"Fine, fine, you're such a kill joy."

"*No*, I'm such an *illegal* driver. I'm not even supposed to be driving you guys around yet! I *just* got my license. All of you've had yours for at least eight months! You guys should be driving, not me."

"Your point?"

"That last thing I need is to get pulled over because you're fucking around in the passenger seat!"

"No one's going to pull you over," Gabi rolled her eyes.

"Yeah, and if they do, she can just fuck around in the passenger seat and get us out of it."

"Hey!"

"Just saying," Rachel shrugged.

"What if it's not a *guy* that pulls us over?" Maddy asked, smirking.

"Well," I pulled into the drive-through line, "then Rachel can fuck around in the passenger seat."

"Hey!" Rachel said, annoyed. "I don't appreciate that!"

"Yeah, but we know what you *would* appreciate..." Gabi coughed.

"I swear to god I will fight you."

"You will, will you? Square up."

"What are you, *five*?"

"Can I take your order?"

"Yeah, um, a medium coffee with cream and three *decaf*," I answered.

There was half a millisecond of dead silence, then an uproar exploded behind me.

"What was that?" the voice asked from the speaker.

"A medium coffee with cream," I turned around, "what do you guys want?"

"Medium latte."

"Large coffee with espresso."

"Small coffee with cream and sugar."

I repeated the orders into the speaker, denouncing Maddy's large to a medium.

"What'd you do that for?" she pouted.

"You'll thank me in thirteen years when you've reached thirty without dying from a stomach ulcer. Pass up your money."

They passed it up, and I handed them their coffees.

"Remind me why we have to get to school so early?" Maddy blew on her coffee, took a sip, and cried out.

"Rachel has some music meeting, Gabi wants to meet *John*, and I have to print an essay."

"And why do *I* have to go so early?"

"Because, if we don't take you to school, you'll never get there on time," Rachel said.

"Cass, do you want to study after school?" Gabi asked.

"I can't, I'm sorry."

"How come?"

"I have to get home, I have some sort of appointment or something."

"Ew, fun."

"Yup."

"Maddy?"

"I have to take my cousin to driver's ed."

"God," Gabi said, "can you *imagine* the people learning to drive this year?"

"Don't remind me, I'm already terrified," Rachel rolled down the window and stuck her hand out, letting the wind dance through her fingers. "Cass, hit the gas, there's no one around."

"Rachel!"

"Aw, come on, live a little!"

"I would like to *live*, period."

"Thank you, Maddy."

* * *

I parked the car and everyone climbed out. We made our way inside and split up; Rachel to the band room, Gabi to the fourth floor, Maddy to the cafeteria, and me to the library.

I sat down to print my essay, scanning it over first.

"Hey, James."

An extra space appeared in the middle of the sentence I was fixing. "Hey, *Taylor*."

"Anyone sitting there?"

I hesitated, then shook my head, and he sat down at the computer next to me.

An awkward silence followed before: "How was your summer?"

"Fine." I deleted the space. "How was yours?"

"Too short, band camp started in August which *sucked*."

"Yeah, I got to hear all about that from Rachel," I clicked print.

"What class is that for?"

"English," I logged out.

"I finished my essay at like midnight, it was so bad-"

"I've got to go."

"Oh, okay, see you."

I grabbed my paper and left.

Rachel met me outside the band room, sorting through a new stack of scores.

"More work?"

"It's never ending. Did you print your essay?"

"Yeah. And guess who talked to me."

"Who- *oh*, what, did you run away from him?"

"*No*, I talked to him a *little*."

"Oh, really? So at band tonight I won't be hearing about how you abruptly jumped up and walked away, or made some vague excuse?"

"Well..."

"I don't get what your problem with him is!"

"There's not really a problem, I don't know, we just don't talk much anymore."

"*Much*?" she shoved a stack of papers into my hands, "Cass, you don't talk to him at *all*. You guys used to be friends."

"Used to be as in like three *years* ago. We barely even see each other anymore. The last time we had anything resembling a conversation I was standing in my neighbor's driveway with their dog in my PJs without makeup or a bra!"

"Yeah, and I get it, but it was freshman year, let it *go*, at least be civil to him, he does *try* to talk to you."

"I am civil to him!"

"Sure you are."

I rolled my eyes, "He calls me *James*, Rach, no one calls me that."

"So? You call him Taylor!"

"I call him Taylor because he calls me James!"

"Isn't it ironic, you both have first names as your last names."

"*Rachel*."

"Cass*andra*."

"*Fine*, I'll try a little harder."

"*Thank* you."

"I still don't get why you care so much."

"Because! He and I are friends, you two used to be friends, and I swear to god if I have to hear him going off about how you don't talk to him anymore even though he tries to talk to you, *one more time,* I'm going to kill both of you!"

"*Alright*, alright, I'll *talk* to him."

"Good."

"It has been three years though."

"Yeah, but it'll only be four if you let it. It's up to you. If you want to hang on to the past, hang on to it. Your call."

I avoided eye contact, even though I could feel her eyes on me.

"I still don't get exactly what he *did*."

"It's... it's complicated."

"*Everything's* complicated. It's always a complex simplicity or a simple complexity, there's no middle ground."

"Yeah, I guess."

Just another irony of life.

*   *   *

"So, Cassandra, how are you doing today?"

The silence echoed through the room like a gunshot.

"Cassandra?"

A bullet whizzed over my head.

"Fine."

She nodded. "What did you do today?"

It glanced off a metal vase in the corner.

I shrugged.

She twirled the pencil between her fingers, tapping it against the clipboard.

It pinged off the mantle.

Her: "Did you have any tests?"

Me:

Her: "How are your friends?"

Me: "Fine."

Her: "How's your family?"

Me: "The same."

Her: "As in?"

Me:

Her: "Cassandra?"

Me:

She sighed as the bullet flew over her head, missing her brown curls by millimeters. "Cassandra, I can't help you if you don't let me. The whole point of this is to talk about your feelings, this is a safe environment."

My fingers drummed against the couch. "I'm aware."

"Do you want my help?"

I looked up at the ceiling. Smoke peeled off of the bullet hole embedded there. "Not particularly."

"Then, may I ask, why are you here?" she leaned forward. I leaned back.

She sighed again. I shrugged.

"Cassandra, we still have forty five minutes left in the session."

I shrugged sarcastically.

"Cassandra, what do you suggest we do?"

"I don't really care."

She rubbed her head, applying pressure to the bridge of her nose between her eyes. "Cassandra, I know you've done this before, so let me rephrase the question, why are you *here*?"

"My mom wanted me to come."

"How come?"

"I don't know."

"I believe you must have some inclination."

"Nope."

"Cassandra..."

I know how this works. The questions, the tricks, the games, the false sense of security. I've done it all before.

"Cassandra, can you at least try?"

I set my eyes on her, shifting my weight to the edge of my seat. Another bullet flew past my face as the old one fell back through the ceiling. A third bullet lodged itself in the pillow next to me.

The truth is, I'm here because my grandmother started getting worried about me again, even though it's been years. My mother couldn't spare enough energy to notice even if she wanted to.

She broke eye contact and looked back down at her clipboard, sighing.

I watched the clock hand as it made its way around the face. I could hear it tick. With every minute that ticked by another bullet whizzed past my face, ricocheting around the room.

Each one a reminder of all the things I've tried not to remember.

* * *

I parked the car in the garage, leaving a note for Maddy on the garage door to avoid another incident like this morning.

Mom looked up from her computer as I locked the door behind me. "Hey."

I glanced over at her, "Hey."

"How are you doing?"

I shrugged.

"How was it?"

I shrugged again. She turned back to her computer.

"Hey, Cassie!" Grandma wandered into the kitchen. "Do you want anything to eat?"

"No, thanks, I picked something up on the way home."

"Okay, well there's leftovers if you want any, I made lasagna."

"Alright, thanks, Grandma."

"How was your day?"

"It was good."

"Did you finally get that car alarm off?"

"Yeah, Maddy forgot that I lock the car when it's outside the garage."

"Why wouldn't you lock the car outside of the garage?"

"I don't know. We're talking about *Maddy* here."

"*Right.*"

"Okay, well, I still have work to do, I'll see you in the morning."

"Okay, goodnight," she kissed me on the cheek.

"Goodnight. Goodnight, Mom."

"Night."

I took a deep, inward breath, turning away.

With my door shut tightly, I pulled open the window and sank to the floor against my bed, watching as the world fell asleep.

I don't know how long I sat there. I fell asleep for a little, and when I woke up my room sparkled with fragments of silver light. It was so long ago that that was my only companion, my only solace. The days when I was called a "freak" for being the "mute girl".

Days that were so long ago, days that were just yesterday. Is the difference of a year really that different from the difference of nine years?

Taking into consideration the multitude of events nine years ago verse the multitude of events now. The multitude of events nine years ago that have had enough impact to stretch over the course of eight years, the final ninth in which the shockwaves took over to carry it to me now.

Taking into consideration the path of oblivion we are so consigned to along the course of our lives. We don't travel an obscure distance, but loop around the perimeter of a circle. A never ending line that repeats itself until we manage to break it.

Taking into consideration the fact that oblivion is simply that, oblivion.

Everything is quiet at night. Perfectly still. Undisturbed.

I shifted my eyes to the stars the moon is never seen without.

I was alone with nothing but them. The stars and the moon. The simple patterns and figures etched in the sky by their light. Alone with nothing but them and the echoes that strained against the walls, with the ghosts that hid in dark corners, under the bed, behind furniture, in the closet, in all the dark places that remain even in the fragmented light.

One of the floorboards below me was loose, and I popped it up, pulling out the topmost piece of paper stuck between the slivers of wood. I read it, tore it into shreds, and let it fall back into the floor, trapped.

My phone buzzed on the table next to my bed, the screen blinding me as it glared to life before dying again. It took another nineteen times before it finally fell silent, and stayed that way.

"How are you doing today?"

One bullet.

"There are no words. There will never be any words."

"Why are you here?"

Two bullets.

"Because, it's like living in the wake of disaster. One that swept away everything. Everything you had: your home, your family, your sanity. Your life. Everything until you had nothing."

How do you put that into words?

"Do you want my help?"

Three bullets.

"No."

"Then why are you here?"

Four bullets.

"Because it's like being in chains."

Five bullets.

"Chains that you know you can never escape, trapped in a world where your attempts to escape go unnoticed."

19

Six bullets.

"Your tears fall on the cold floor of the bathroom at three am and no one can hear you."

Seven bullets.

"You're drowning, but no one can see that you're drowning because your clothes aren't weighed down and your hair doesn't drip."

Eight bullets.

"You see the life everyone else has knowing that you'll never have a life like that."

Nine bullets.

Chapter Two

I woke up to violet light streaking across the horizon.

I checked the time. *5:00*

In the mirror to my left a girl stared back at me, hair sticking up on the back of her head, face indented with fabric marks from her sleeve, mascara streaks dried under her eyes.

The girl looked away, and it's as though she was never there.

No one will remember her, someday.

Isn't that what we're all living in negation to? The idea that everything we say and everything we do will someday be forgotten? Who cares what happened in her life? Who else cares about the disaster that was left behind in her life when everything else left? Who, someday, will care about her and how she lived her life? Who will care about how she died or when she died or when she did anything? Sure, they'll remember her for a little, they'll talk about her, they'll laugh about her, they'll cry about her, they'll do all that. But in the end, who cares?

Someday there will be nothing left to substantiate her existence.

No one will remember her.

I looked back at the mirror, where the glass reflects all the refractions of light. My reflection is barely visible, with so little refractions to reflect. Hidden in the back of my closet, behind dresses and shoes, where I used to hide from the world. I spent so much time in the dark that part of me got lost in it. Now the face of a ghost looks back at me.

The messy brown hair. The pale face, hollowed cheeks, sleepless eyes.

A ghost.

I got up and crept down to the kitchen. The coffee maker was off. I coaxed it to life, and sat down at the kitchen table holding an empty mug tightly between my hands. The cold of the ceramic seeped into my skin. The world outside the window was dimly lit, the streetlights flickered off, and the first signs of life began to materialize.

Mrs. Erin Collins next door, opening her car door and throwing her briefcase into the backseat, balancing her coffee mug on top of her car until she found her keys again. Mr. Jones slipping out his side door, hobbling down the driveway with his cane and pink slippers to pick up the morning newspaper before his wife woke up, waving at Mr. Davis next door, sitting on his porch with his coffee, cat on his lap, white hair sticking up messily, who waved back, grinning before hiding behind his newspaper. The lights of each house flickering on; a succession in which everyone believed their actions were strictly their own, failing to scrutinize the succinct progression of events in which every action is linked to another. The succinctness of a world so individualized by fabricated individuality.

The coffee maker bubbled to a stop, and I filled the cold mug.

5:30

I sat there for a while, watching the mundaneness of the world roll by, and with it, time, until the clock hit 5:40, and then 5:45. I slipped back into my room and sat down on the bed, holding the coffee close to me, pleading with the ceramic underneath my fingers to retain the warmth. My phone buzzed again, a reminder of everything I'd ignored last night.

10:00. Rachel: Heyyy what's up

10:05. Rachel: Cass where are youuu

10:07. Rachel: What was the English homework?

10:08. Rachel: Ugh fine, I'll text the group chat later

* * *

12:37. Rachel: Hey, anyone do the English homework?

12:38. Maddy: I have Trin we're on a completely different book

12:38. Gabi: Rach, we had to read the rest of chapter five and answer the study questions

12:39. Rachel: Shittttt ugh

12:39. Gabi: Rach just do it tomorrow during lunch

12:39. Rachel: I willlll. Also, I texted Cass and she never responded

12:40. Gabi: When'd you text her?

12:41. Rachel: 10 o'clock!!!

12:42. Maddy: why the fuck are you two still up go to sleeeep

12:43. Gabi: Maddy please, we're in high school no one goes to sleep before two a.m.

12:43. Maddy: I do!!!

12:43. Gabi: then put your phone on do not disturb, *honestly*

12:45. Rachel: Isn't Cass usually up this late?

12:46. Gabi: Yeah, I think so

12:47. Rachel: Where is she?

12:48. Maddy: Probably *asleep*

12:49. Gabi: oh my *god* Maddy

12:50. Maddy: *Fine*

12:52. Gabi: Rach, maybe her phone died

12:53. Rachel: Maybe... I don't know.

12:55. Gabi: She'll read this in the morning and you can yell at her then

12:55. Rachel: Yeah, okay

I scrolled through the rest of the conversation, which continued into a number of tirades all looping in numerous, unending circles. I put the phone back down on the table and just sat there, staring at the blank wall in front of me.

A girl, maybe five or six years old, materialized on the gray paint, a door next to her. The door opened and a man stepped out, scooping the girl up into his arms and spinning her around. She made whooshing sounds like an airplane, giggling and screaming. A woman stepped out behind the man, wrapping her arms around his neck and smiling at the girl.

No one would have guessed that the demons in his mind were destroying him.

No one would have been able to tell how many tears she was holding back.

I'd rather have those two unhappily happy people, than the broken frame of one of them and the distorted memories of the other.

*   *   *

"Cass! You're late!" Maddy waved at me from the side of the garage. "Gabi and Rachel already left, they took Rachel's car."

"Yeah, sorry, Maddy. I woke up late."

"You haven't answered any of our texts, is everything okay?"

I got in the car and turned the key in the ignition. She scrambled to pull herself into the passenger seat after me. "Yeah."

"Cass?"

"What?" I looked over at her. She looked down at her hands, fiddling with her ID.

"I- nothing."

"What, Maddy?"

She shook her head.

"Cass! Where've you been! You've been MIA for the past like ten hours!" Rachel jumped me the second I walked into the cafeteria.

"We thought you died or something, oh my *god*, Cass," Gabi shook me, waiting for my playful response and vague, apologetic excuse.

"Yeah, sorry I guess I fell asleep," I forced a small laugh, pushing past them.

"Where are you going?"

"Class."

"It doesn't start for another twenty minutes!"

"I have to study."

They watched me walk away.

I headed up the main staircase to the fourth floor, ducking into the bathroom. The stalls were all vacant, the only noise derived from the automatic sinks that periodically turned on at random.

Hand braced against the edge of the sink, I looked up at myself in the mirror.

Pale face hidden behind a layer of foundation. Washed out cheeks masked by faint pink. Sunken eyes given the illusion of life by layer after layer of mascara.

A mask to hide a ghost. An embellished coffin to hide the faces of the dead.

The door opened and I jumped, pretending to be washing my hands in the sink. I glanced over at the door. I didn't know her, just a freshman or sophomore, a face I recognized but couldn't place.

She gave me an awkward smile before disappearing into one of the stalls. I slipped out of the bathroom, averting my eyes.

"Cassandra!"

I turned a sharp corner and went down a flight of stairs. I heard the footsteps echo through the stairwell, stopping as I disappeared through the doors onto the third floor.

"Cass?"

Turned left. Walked straight. Ascended another flight of stairs.

"Cassandra-"

Left again. Straight. Up a flight of stairs.

"Hey-"

Right. Down. Left. Down. Left. Up. Right. Up.

Up. Up. Right. Up. Left. Down. Down. Down. Down...

Until voices no longer called my name, no longer tried to get my attention, no longer said 'hey' or asked questions.

Until no voices said anything at all.

I pressed myself against the wall inside the Area of Refuge by the elevator on the fifth floor. I held my breath for ten seconds, twenty, thirty, forty, forty-five, fifty, fifty-five, fifty-seven, fifty-eight, fifty-nine... and then I took a breath, listening to the pounding of my heart in my ears and the gasping of my lungs after forgetting how to breathe.

My legs gave out beneath me but I refused to let myself collapse.

As long as I stood, I didn't fall. As long as I didn't fall, I stood.

The bell rang. The sea of footsteps had faded about ten minutes ago. I closed my eyes, opened them, and then made my way to class and slipped inside.

No one paid me any attention as I took my seat next to Jamie Lorry. She spared me a quick glance, complete with raised eyebrows and speculation before returning to the more interesting contents of her notebook. My phone was alive with text messages, and I glanced at them. Aside from Rachel's quick "where are you" from thirty minutes ago, there were just a lot of random messages about various assignments and work they didn't want to do.

I slipped the phone into my backpack and let it sink to the bottom.

*   *   *

When I left school, instead of driving home, I picked a road and just drove. No turns, no distractions, just straight into nowhere. I ignored the phone buzzing from the bottom of my bag. It wasn't anything important, it never was. Their attention spans didn't allow for lengthy worry or serious conversation. If there was a problem, they addressed it briefly and then just let it disappear. Always just under the surface, always there but never acknowledged.

I pulled off onto a side road, the tires complaining in the rocky dirt. The car rattled down the road for about a mile before turning into an outlook and rolling to a stop. The ignition quieted as I opened the car door and stepped out.

The iron railing guarding the edge of the outlook was cold in the warm air. The wind unrelenting, the sky a dimming gray above me, all things dreary and distant, cracking along the edges, spider webs of doubt appearing in the middle.

The air grew thick as the clouds penetrated the perspicuity of the sky. I looked down, shifting my weight against the rusty railing. The world slanted down steeply, threatening to send everything set in stone down a landslide into anonymity. Everything shifted and I took a deep breath, steadying myself. It righted itself in the same moment. Unless someone was watching, it would have been impossible to notice it. Its gravity was lost in the gravitational pull of oblivion.

Pluto got pulled into oblivion. It was my favorite planet. Dad would point it out to me, close to the "teapot" of Sagittarius. After it got pulled into oblivion, people forgot about it. It was too far away to be noticed. Once no one notices anymore you become invisible. First to them, then to everyone else, and then to yourself.

I turned my face upward to the sky as the first signs of breakage made their way into being. Then, it shattered. An ocean of everything the world wanted to clear from its surface, to wash away from existence.

I let the water drench me, washing away the layer of foundation over the pale face. Washing away the color in my cheeks. Washing away the mascara that hid the sunken eyes. Washing away the human and exposing the ghost.

I let the water wash away the dirt on my skin, the lies, the pain. The remainder of yesterday, of last night, of the last nine years... of everything. I let it seep into my clothing and weigh it down. I let it weigh down my hair. I let it anchor me to the ground, my hands to the rail, myself to reality.

I let it wash away the tears.

It washed away everything. Just like it did all those years ago. The way the water washed her away, and then him. And then us. Everything.

Until no one remembers that it was there.

*   *   *

The back door opened quietly, and I slipped inside. *7:30*

"Cassie!"

I winced as the silence splintered, sending shards into my skin. "Hey, Grandma."

"You've been gone for a while, school stuff?"

"Yeah, I was studying with a friend."

"Who?"

"Rachel."

"Okay. Do you want something to eat? I made mac n' cheese."

"Yeah, thanks." I followed her into the kitchen, glancing at the papers and notebooks scattered across the table. "Where's Mom?"

"She went out to the store, she'll be back in a little bit."

"Oh, okay," I set my stuff down on the counter as Grandma busied herself at the stove, and started to tidy up Mom's papers, straightening them and gathering her pens and papers into different piles. I made four piles of papers, leaving them in the same relative place they were before, no change in order. She always complained about how she couldn't keep anything in one place.

Grandma set a plate down on the counter and I sat down across from her. She didn't say anything for a while, watching me push my food around my plate.

"How was school?"

"It was good."

"How're your friends?"

"The same; crazy, as usual. Gabi's almost got a boyfriend, Maddy's grade obsessed, and Rachel's still gay."

She chuckled, "Sounds about right."

"Yeah," I grinned.

The side door opened and Mom walked in, tossing the car keys back and forth in her hands. "Smells good, Mom."

"Do you want some?"

"Yeah, thank you," she set the keys down on the table and adjusted her glasses, "did someone mess with my papers?"

I looked down, fiddling with my necklace. "I did."

"They're all out of place! Cassandra..."

"Sorry, just trying to help."

"It's fine, just please don't do it again."

"Okay."

She took a second, rubbing her head, and composed herself. She sat down at the counter next to me, "How was school?"

"Fine."

"Classes?"

"Fine."

"Friends?"

"The same."

"How's Gabi's 'almost' boyfriend?"

"Still not her boyfriend."

"And Rachel? Still-"

"Fine. I have work to do, sorry. Night, Mom," I got up and scraped my plate.

"I can get that-" Grandma reached for it.

"I got it," I put it in the dishwasher, "goodnight, Grandma."

"Goodnight, Cassie."

I glanced at Mom. She didn't look up from her plate.

* * *

I sat and watched the rain falling outside my open window. My fingers twitched, nails inching closer to the skin. I have no sense of time in this world. An hour can feel like eternity. A minute can feel like eternity. A second can feel like eternity. They're never just hours, just minutes, just seconds. They're just eternity.

In that span of eternity, I draw up a list in my head. The list I made years ago, now hidden between the words torn up and scattered beneath loose floorboards and cracks in the foundation.

A list of reasons.

The reasons to live.

And all the reasons to die.

Chapter Three

October 1st.

That's what day it is today.

Not September 30th. Not October 2nd.

October 1st.

I sat up in my bed, gripping the sheets tightly, because maybe if I hold on tight enough to this one window of reality, none of the others will open. The floodgates won't open and I won't be swept away.

But that is not how reality works.

I feel it hit. The weight crashes over me, knocking the wind out of me and sending all the pieces of my shattered world into the irretrievable but unforgettable depths of oblivion.

6:17 am.

The same as every year.

Every year since I was seven.

My grasp on reality has been shook loose, and I am lost in the flood that swept away all the things in my life that once were concrete pillars, but have been knocked down by the sheer force of it all.

The floor is hot beneath my feet, but becomes cold as my bare skin touches it. With each step ice spreads, spider webbing out across the hardwood surface, frozen in place.

One step. Two steps. Three steps.

Everything I touch darkens underneath my fingers, losing color until the world becomes black and white.

Like watching an old film on replay.

Four steps. Five steps. Six steps. Seven steps.

I see the door and my heart stops.

Eight steps, nine steps.

I am standing right in front of it.

Ten steps.

I pass it.

Ten steps. And slowly the color fades back into the world, and the water around my feet disappears as the floodgates rebuild themselves and reality shifts back into place.

Like nothing ever happened.

"Cassandra?" Mom looked up at me, "you're up?"

"Yeah," I stood in the doorway, watching her carefully.

"Happy official birthday," she smiled, but her eyes were blank and distant, her mouth twisted in a fine line between indifference and a forced smile.

I am officially seventeen today.

I looked down at the ice creeping over my toes and up around my ankles. "Thanks."

I was born at 11:59 pm on September 30th, seventeen years ago.

Dad was declared dead at 7:17 am, at the same hospital, October 1st, seven years after that.

"I-" I hesitated, "I was wondering, if maybe... you'd want to visit him today?"

Her eyes met mine. She took a deep breath, paused, then shook her head, "I'm sorry, Sandra, I just- I can't. Not today."

"It's okay. I'll tell them you said 'hi'."

Her voice cracked, "Send them my love."

"Okay."

She got up. "I'm going for a walk, leave a note if you leave before I get back."

"Okay."

I watched her disappear behind the door, and the temperature dropped ten degrees as it shut.

I stood in the doorway, my feet frozen just in front of the kitchen, frost creeping up my leg, solidifying into ice as it went.

Everything was still.

A dead sort of stillness.

The mundane world was quiet, no one up this early on a Saturday. On Saturdays, the mundaneness is broken, at least until eight when everyone finally has to carry on with their mundane lives.

But it's funny, everything stops for a bit, until someone hits play again and it all starts. Never paused for too long. A perfect succinctness to the clock-like mechanism of the world.

I left without leaving a note.

The world is the same today as it is any other day. The changing leaves twisting in the wind, the air beginning to grow colder while at the same time retaining its warmth. The sky turning blue in the wakening of the sun. The stars dissolving back into nothing.

At the same time, everything is different. The colors are faded, the blues not as resilient, the reds not so bold, the yellows and greens a dull, sickly color.

It was a forty minute drive, but it felt more like forty hours. Forty hours and forty minutes and forty seconds.

A lot can happen in forty seconds.

No one was there when I pulled into the parking lot.

Why would anyone be here? It's not exactly a place everyone wants to spend their Saturday mornings.

Just the unlucky ones.

Just the *really* unlucky ones.

I stepped over haunted flowers and decaying grass, trying not to think about all the ghosts I was treading over.

There are too many ghosts here.

The ghosts of all the people who have no where else to go. No one else to haunt. No one else who cares. Nothing but the headstones that list their name, date of birth and date of death, and nothing more. No funny anecdote, no meaningful, philosophical quotes, just name and life. And some of those have faded or been so carved out by time that they are no longer visible.

No one cared, so they faded back into oblivion with the rest of the forgotten.

I stopped in front of a headstone. The wreath of flowers from so many months ago was brown and lifeless.

"I should have gotten something to replace them," I whispered, kneeling in the grass in front of it, "sorry."

The sun glinted off the polished stone, illuminating the words.

Kenneth James

August 13, 1971 - October 1, 2009

"Never regret anything that made you smile"

Thank you for your service

"Mom says 'hi', she just didn't think she could handle coming... not today. We miss you. We miss both of you." I glanced at the headstone next to his. Smaller, older. The angel carved in it smiled at me.

I looked away.

I let the silence wash over the world, carrying whispers of things never said, of regrets, and sorrow, and happiness. None audible, but quite plainly there. Melancholy and quiet.

I can't believe it's been so long.

I get lost in the silence. All the words I could say wandering in endless spirals in my head.

All the words I could never and will never say.

I haven't been here in a while. The last time I was here there were people milling about in the shadows. Flowers peeking out from the dirt, all things bright and lively in a dark and dying place.

Today, it's just me.

A cold breeze knocked some of my hair loose from behind my ear.

A group of people passed me, heading toward another grave. Another mound of dirt, another cage of mahogany and veneer. Another stone to substantiate and ample existence.

I guess I'm not the only one, the only *really* unlucky one.

I turned back to the grave, ignoring their sideways glances, the sad, pitiful looks, the quiet whispers.

My eyes scanned the ground in front of me, then traced the engravings on the stone and lingered there.

There are so many things you're not supposed to ask.

The elegant font almost makes you think it's not as bad as it is. Like the words on a plaque for some award, a congratulatory engraving.

A congratulatory engraving for being buried six feet under the ground.

Every year, the same time, that clock turns. It never stops. No extra seconds in between. No extra time. Every year, 11:59 to 12:00. And it's another year. It's been ten years.

It's been *ten* years.

And every year I ask myself the same question. Every year I let myself stray deeper into wondering, into blaming everyone. Making excuses for him. Blaming everyone but him. How could I blame him? He's gone. You can't blame a dead person. It's not morally right. So you blame the living. You blame the living because they're still alive, because blaming them doesn't make you as guilty. They can say they're sorry, they can beg for forgiveness, they can apologize for everything they didn't do wrong.

You're not supposed to ask why.

So you don't.

And you think it will get easier. But it doesn't. Not even after ten years.

I never got to say goodbye.

I sat there, the grass cold and dying under me, watching the shadows switch places along the headstone.

Somewhere in my head someone keeps pressing rewind and replay. The same forty seconds. Over and over again.

40 seconds. 80 seconds. 120 seconds. 160 seconds. 200 seconds. 240 seconds. 280 seconds. 320 seconds. 360 seconds.

Four hundred seconds.

"Hey," a hand appeared on my shoulder, fingers hovering just above the fabric of my shirt. I didn't jump. I heard his footsteps.

I glanced over at him, "Why are you here?"

"I know- I know you don't want to talk to me, okay? I saw you, and it looked like you could use some company."

"I'm fine, but thanks." I forced myself to my feet. His hand fell away from me. I crossed my arms, calculating the situation. "What?"

"I- look, I'm sorry. I know that's long overdue, but- but I'm sorry. And, I know- today... you shouldn't be alone."

"I'm *fine*."

"Are you sure? I mean- that's my uncle," he nodded his head at a funeral behind us. "I hated him, didn't talk to him for years, and I'm not okay. There's no way you're okay."

"I'm sorry about that. And I'm fine."

"James... can I- can we- do you want to go get a coffee or something? I know I'm completely out of line, but..." he avoided looking at me, fixating on a spot on the ground.

I inhaled slowly, and then exhaled. "Yeah, okay."

"Did you drive? I came here with my mom, and I really don't want to deal with her right now."

"Yeah, I drove. My car's over there."

"Okay, cool."

We didn't talk until we got to the car, and we didn't talk when he got in the passenger seat next to me, and we didn't talk all the way to the café, and we didn't talk when we sat down on a bench in the park by the coffee shop, and we didn't talk until he stopped stirring his coffee and looked up at me.

"James?"

"Yeah?" I kept my eyes on the steam rising in spiraling tendrils from my cup.

"Cassandra..." his green eyes flickered around the setting before resting on my face.

I looked up at him. "What?"

"I-" he looked back down at his coffee, "I don't know."

"Taylor... what are we doing? It's been-"

"A couple years, I know. Trust me, I know."

"Why now?"

He shrugged, "I- I honestly don't know. I just know that something clicked, and I miss talking to you. I've had to watch you live your life without me in it, and I miss you."

"But why *now*?" I didn't take my eyes off of him.

"I was too scared. I tried- you didn't let me. I was out of your life, and you didn't let me back in."

"No, I didn't."

I made sure to keep my words in check.

"At this point in my life, my philosophy is, if you want to leave, get the hell out."

When you get hurt over and over again, eventually you have to figure out how to not let yourself get hurt anymore.

"Rachel said-"

"Rachel and I, what happened with us, it was different. I'm not going to explain how, because I don't know. It just was. We forgave each other. It took a *long* time. But we did it. It's not the same with us. Friendships aren't things you can just tape back together."

"Can you just listen to me?"

I remembered Rachel's words before I had a chance to say no. "I- okay."

"Look, Cass. I *know*, I know all of that. But I was younger then, I was stupid, and all I'm asking you right now is to listen to me. I'm *sorry*, I've said that, I don't how many more times you want me to say it. I'm not expecting things to go back to normal, but I want to try. I want *us* to try. Cassandra, I love-"

"Don't," I looked away, breaking eye contact. "Don't say it. You should have said that three years ago. Two years ago, a year ago, maybe, but not now. Look, I'll talk to you. I'll try, okay? That's the most I can do. Anything past that... just no. Okay?"

He took a deep breath and pushed his blond curls out of his eyes, "Okay."

Okay.

"Taylor?"

He glanced sideways at me. "Yeah?"

"Why'd you do it?"

"Do what?"

"Why'd you leave like that?" I kept my eyes locked on a piece of gum stuck to the sidewalk under the bench. I heard him exhale slowly.

"I don't know. I wish I did. It was three years ago, I just don't remember. It was a long time ago, Cass."

"Taylor?"

"Yeah?"

I stared straight ahead of me, watching the faint outlines of two children playing in the park, chased by their parents, their father laughing and making them scream as he picked them up and spun them around. "My dad died ten years ago today."

"Cass..."

"I can remember everything. *Everything.* Every word, every sound, every smell, every person, every piece of clothing, every facial expression, every thought. Everything. That was ten years ago. Ten years is a long time. *Ten years* is a *really* long time."

Ten years is an eternity. Every year, every month, every week, every day, hour, minute, second, is an eternity within itself. I'm still living every year, month, week, day, hour, minute, and second of the past ten years.

Because the thing about eternity?

It never ends.

Chapter Four

By the time you turn seventeen, there are two things you know.

1. You're graduating in a year.

2. Everyone who's in your life is going to stay, and everyone who's not isn't coming back

At least, they aren't supposed to come back. If they do, you have two choices. You can let them in, or you can keep them out. At that point, there's no middle ground. No going back, and no going forward. Just there and then, one choice. No one telling you what to do. Just you. Whichever choice you make, and there's no going back.

After so many years, I don't know why anyone would come back. After that there's just a void, and nothing anyone can do to fill it. There's this empty space, and in it all the hurt and all the wounds have already resolved themselves and healed. After so many years, there's nothing to mend but scars.

By the time you turn seventeen, there are two things you realize.

1. You're running out of time.

2. Soon the past eighteen years of your life will be mostly irrelevant.

I mean, think about it. Eighteen years. For most of us, that's eighteen years growing up in the same town, with the same parents, in the same house, the same neighborhood, with the same people, the same streets, the same schools, nothing changes. For eighteen years. And for the kids that don't grow up surrounded by the same faces every day, the same street signs, they still don't have complete control over their lives. Until we're eighteen, we don't get to live. But after we're eighteen, we don't either. Our lives are a stop and start, with no pause. No rewind. No flash forward. We have to live through every grueling second, every painful minute, every long hour. Every painstaking day, week, month, year. But after the first eighteen years, everything changes. We go to college, we leave town, we leave our friends, our family, the street signs, the schools. Everything changes. For the most part, the past eighteen years no longer matter. We won't talk to half those familiar faces. We won't even see half those familiar faces again. We won't walk down those familiar streets longer than the time needed to say goodbye, tape up boxes, and leave. We'll remember most of it, but we'll forget a lot of it. The stupid mistakes we made, the places we grew up, where we learned how to be people, we'll forget that. Nothing was made to stick, and nothing is built to stay. It'll all disappear as we continue on with our lives, making a place for ourselves in the world.

The first eighteen years are irrelevant.

And by the time you turn seventeen, you only have one more year before everything changes. Before everything you built over the last eighteen years just crumbles, the foundation kicked out from beneath you, the walls knocked down by a wrecking ball.

By the time you turn seventeen, you better have some idea what you're doing with your life. Otherwise, you better figure it out.

By the time you turn seventeen, you start waiting for the day when everything becomes obsolete.

When you can turn your back on the world and let the past die, when you can bury the ghosts once and for all.

But until then, you have to watch them every day, hiding in their corners, flitting in and out of sight, returning when you almost forget. You can't forget what you always remember. Just like you can't remember what you always forget. There are some things in life that you can't forget, that you'll never forget.

No matter how hard you try.

*　　*　　*

"I can't study anymore, I'm done. If I fail, I fail," Rachel closed the textbook and leaned back in her chair.

"Are you sure?"

"Cass, my brain is fried. Dead. Obsolete. It's not functioning anymore."

"Alright," I put the textbook back in my bag, laughing, "if you say so."

"If I have to look at one more equation or fact, my head is going to explode, so yes, I say so."

"Are you going to stay?" I glanced around the library. It was quiet, not very many people working this late in the afternoon.

"Naw, I'm going home. *But*," she leaned toward me as I started to get up, "you owe me information."

"What?"

"What happened with Taylor?"

"What do you mean?"

"Cass, remember, I *talk* to him."

"Did he tell you?"

"Part of it, but I want to hear what you have to say."

"There's probably nothing you haven't already heard from him."

"Is it true you agreed to try to be friendly with him again?"

I shrugged. "Yeah, I guess."

"Why didn't you tell me?"

"It's not a big deal."

"Cass, you haven't talked to him in *how many* years, what the hell?"

"It's not a big deal, okay? Plus, he just- there are just some things he doesn't get."

"Like what?"

"Just... things."

"Well, I hope you figure something out fast. Look who's coming over here."

I looked over my shoulder, "Oh my god, seriously?"

She checked her phone, "Sorry, I've got to go, my mom's asking where I am."

"Rachel-"

"You'll be fine!" she mouthed at me, already at the door.

"Some friends I have," I muttered.

"What?"

"Nothing," I didn't look up at him.

"Can I sit here? The other tables are taken."

I turned my head toward another very obviously empty table to my right before turning back to him. "Sure."

"Thanks."

I grabbed the textbook out of my bag and opened to a random page.

"How's it going?"

"Fine."

"Cass..."

"What? How am I supposed to elaborate on that?"

"I don't know, I'm sorry."

"Stop saying that."

"Saying what?"

"Stop saying that you're sorry."

"Why?"

"Because- because I don't want to hear it. It's not true. You've said it so many times that it's lost all meaning. And you know what? I don't *care*. I don't care if you say you're sorry."

"Cass..."

I shoved the book back into my backpack and wrestled with the zipper. "If you were sorry," I gave him a long, steady look, I didn't break eye contact, I didn't look away, "you would have said it a long time ago."

And I left, ducking behind bookshelves so he can't find me when he comes after me. My breathing quickened, and I ducked behind the fiction shelf to catch my breath. My head was spinning, and soon the world was spinning with it, breaking into pieces that chased each other around in front of me.

Footsteps.

I gripped the shelf behind me. Faster and faster and faster...

"Cassandra?"

I turned away from him, "Please, just go."

"Cassandra..."

"There's nothing you can do now. Okay? I'm sorry, I want to- I want to try, but I can't. It's too late. There's nothing left. I let go of you years ago. And you know what? It took me a long time. Okay? And then I did. And now you're back... what the hell. What do you want? It's been three years and you don't even know why you're back. Do you? If you do, I'm listening, but until then, just leave me *alone*, please," I closed my eyes, trying to steady my breathing. My heart was sprinting at a hundred miles a minute. The world still spinning and spinning and spinning...

"Cassandra."

I forced my chin upward. "What?"

His eyes met mine, green verse brown, and held me there, locked in the stare. That stare. Those eyes that I used to fall asleep thinking about. Those eyes that I used to look at every day knowing that they'd always be there. Those eyes that I tried so hard to forget.

He kissed me.

My body went numb, every inch paralyzed.

Then he stepped away. "You wanted a reason, well that's it. See you around, James."

I watched him turn his back on me, the gray fabric of his backpack growing blurry, then disappearing behind the door, around the corner, into the street, until I couldn't see it anymore.

*   *   *

"Can you tell me a little about your friends?" the pen scratched against the paper.

"What about them?"

"Their names, what they're like, how close you are, things like that."

"I guess I could."

"Alright, that's good."

"If you say so."

"So, can you?"

"Can I what?"

"Tell me about them?"

"Um... alright. Sure, yeah. Okay."

She stared at me intently over her clipboard.

"Well, there's Anne. She's two years older than me, in college you know. It's insane. She always tells me these *crazy* college stories. I stay in her dorm with her sometimes, she sneaks me into parties. But she's your typical nerd, coffee, party obsessed, popular girl. But she's smart, like really smart. I've known her for the past three or four years."

"Okay..."

"Then there's Carly, she's a foster kid. She's a couple years younger than me, I haven't known her for very long. But she's nice, kind of quiet, she's got all these parent issues. I don't hang out with her too much, just when I can.

And then Jane, who's got a ton of sisters. She's the second oldest, and she has to take care of her younger siblings because her sister just got engaged. She likes this one guy, but he's like all mystery, and he's been flirting with another girl even though we all know he's in love with her. She pretends to hate him, but we all know *she's* in love with him too. They're a bunch of idiots. I love her, though. She's always been level headed, does what's right, and usually doesn't screw up."

"Alright."

"There's Colin. He's one of my only guy friends, really. He has this thing for girls named Katherine. Kind of broke his streak last year, so that was good. I don't see him much anymore, he moved. We weren't ever super close though, so I don't mind much. Now Quentin, I miss him. He went off to college with his girlfriend, so I don't see him much at all."

"You guys were close?"

"Oh, yeah, really close."

"And most of your friends seem older?"

"Yup. Not all of them, though. Simon's my age. He's gay, so we usually have a lot to talk about, guy wise. I'm basically the only one he's come out to so far."

"And having a gay friend, what's it like?"

I stopped and stared at her. "It's no different than having a straight friend, he just likes guys... are you homophobic or something?"

She bit her lip, backtracking, "No, no, of course not, just asking. It's my job to ask questions."

"Sure."

"Continue, please."

I pretended to be scratching a spot above my eyebrow as if thinking. "Then there's Violet. Her sister died last year, it was terrible. She hasn't recovered quite yet, but we're close. She's my age. We grew up together. She's friends with me and Hazel. Hazel has cancer. It sucks, really. She's probably not going to get better. But she just met this guy Augustus and-"

"Cassandra," she leaned forward, her glasses slipping down her nose. "Have you been naming off fictional characters the entire time?"

"Anne wasn't a fictional character."

"Other than Anne?"

I shrugged. She sighed, capped her pen, and looked at the clock.

"Our time is up, so I'll see you next week."

"Okay."

She got up and herded me toward the door, holding it open for me.

"Oh, and I forgot," I turned back to her.

"Yes?" her eyebrows disappeared into her bangs.

"Anne lives in an attic behind a bookshelf."

"Cassandra, is this some kind of joke to you?"

I stared her down and mimicked her eyebrow movement, "Of course not."

"I'll see you next week, Cassandra."

I stepped out into the waiting room, "Did I tell you about Holden?"

She shut the door.

I grinned, turning on my heel. There was a girl sitting on the couch, waiting. She kept her head down, hair covering her face, and fidgeted with her sleeve, pulling it down over her hands, covering the length of her arm, her knee shaking against the floor. At the sound of the door clicking back into its closed position, she glanced up. A grin flitted across her face before she looked back down.

I felt myself smile as I turned away.

I spared her a second glance before I closed the staircase door. Instead of her, I saw another girl, a little younger, maybe seven or eight, sitting just like she was. Long brown hair shading her face, split ends where she pulled at it or tossed and turned when she couldn't sleep, when her dreams were plagued by nightmares. When there was no one at her bedside to comfort her. Sleeves pulled down at far as possible, hood pulled over her little head. A woman sitting at the other end, staring at her hands, never looking up, barely blinking. An older woman sitting next to her, arm around her, looking up at the younger girl every now and then. The girl didn't move, she didn't so much as flinch. She might as well have been dead for all the movements she made. In some ways, I guess she was. When you've lost all will to live, when you've trapped yourself in a world where nothing exists, where everything hangs in a balance, when the only reason you breathe is because your body makes you, you might as well be dead.

When a part of you dies, it dies. For a while, you die with it. Your life support is your lungs, those god damn lungs that won't stop breathing. Your life support is your body, that won't stop functioning no matter how much you beg, how much you ask, command, or plead. Your life support is everything but your actual will to live. Like when the only thing keeping you alive is your will to live, when your body is telling you to die. Instead, the only thing keeping you from dying is your body telling you to live, forcing you to live.

You never had a choice.

Then I looked away, closed the door, and left. And she disappeared, fading away back into oblivion.

I wanted to forget. I've wanted to forget for ten years. Why don't we ever get a chance to forget when we want to. Sometimes people block out the worst parts of their lives, the things they physically can't remember. What about the things you mentally can't remember? What about the things that cause you more pain than they would physically? Why don't we block those out? Why don't we get just one time, one moment in our lives when we can choose to forget everything? Start fresh. A clean slate. No past, no future, just now.

Everyone should get one clean slate. A second in which they can close their eyes and breathe, one breath in which everything is cleared from their lungs and they have a chance to start over. To rebuild the shattered walls, to reset the cracked foundation.

Everyone deserves that.

But life isn't fair. It's never been. We don't get what we deserve. We get what we don't deserve, our worst fears. We get the darkest version of the impossible.

Life isn't fair.

That's another thing you realize by the time you turn seventeen.

Nothing's fair.

Fair is an ideal. Not a reality. If fair was a reality the world would be a lot different. Nothing can be fair because everyone has their own idea of fair, their own morals. Something that's fair for one person isn't fair for another.

By the time you turn seventeen, you realize that not everyone is always going to be happy. It's part of the equilibrium of life. In order for there to be equilibrium, some people have to be unhappy when others are happy.

Some of us just compensate for more than our share of happiness.

And that's what's not fair.

My phone buzzed in my pocket, and I pulled it out.

Taylor: Hey, I'm sorry. I know I probably crossed a line. And if you want me to leave you alone, I will. Okay? I get it. I'll go, if you want me to.

Me: Don't apologize.

Taylor: Cassandra?

Me: What?

Taylor: Do you want me to leave?

Life is strange. There are things we can control and things we can't. That's common knowledge. Just like the fact that there are people that you let back into your life and people you don't.

And of course, there are the people that you try not to let back in, but they fight their way back in anyway.

When they fight their way back, let them. They've made the decision for you. And it doesn't happen often. Those people are rare. Those are the people you won't have to fight to hold on to.

So when they fight, hold your breath for a second, and close your eyes.

Then breathe. Open your eyes. Forgive them.

And let them.

Me: No.

Let them stay.

Chapter Five

I drove until the sun rose, blinding against the dark skyline. Light years away, the stars died. Light years away from the stars, my car died.

The engine sputtered for a mile or two, then gave a soft purr and went silent.

"Dammit!" I slammed my hands against the steering wheel, pummeling it, "dammit, dammit, dammit!" My forehead made contact with the leather. It hit harder than I meant it to. "*Dammit.*"

After five minutes of fuming, I opened the sun roof and climbed out on top of the car.

The morning was crisp, sunny, no clouds above my head. A soft breeze, no chill; just a typical fall morning. A perfect day.

Irony is a fickle friend.

The wind tangled my hair around my face and I pushed it away, watching the world shift into existence, dragging me along with it. The hours of forgetting and being forgotten far behind, and the hours of remembering and being remembered not far ahead. A bird took flight from a tree in the distance, growing smaller and smaller as it faded back into the sunrise.

My heart had begun to race, moving from a walk to a jog to a sprint in one, two, three beats as my fingers rattled against the car.

I closed my eyes, and opened them.

Five things I see.

A tree. The one maybe ten, twenty feet away, across the road, neighbored by other trees, taller trees. Sheltered and trapped at the same time. It's branches almost bare, but not quite. A few withered leaves, golden and orange and crimson, fighting to hold on. Bark a deep, aging brown, like dirt drying after the rain.

The pavement, under the car, stretching across to the wall of trees on the far side. Cracked, broken, fading in the sunlight, potholes dotting the surface. The washed out yellow line forming a divide between the two sides, the right side and the left side, the left side and the wrong side, the right side and the wrong side.

The car beneath me. Light blue shining against the rising glow of the sun. Windows rolled down, letting the fall air in, sun roof open behind me, waiting to catch me if I fall back in.

A squirrel darting in and out between the tree roots, scrambling up the side of a sapling, jumping across to another, and scrambling back down. Tail twitching as it scrambled for nuts in the cold, not yet frozen ground.

My shoes. White converse stained brown from years of wear. Soles scratched and peeling, but managing to hold on regardless. The red line wrapping around it faded to a pale pink. Paint peeling along the flowers painted there too many years ago.

Four things I feel.

The cold of the metal car roof beneath my fingers. Warming in the sun, but still cold. That metal feeling of forever being cold, the one that never goes away.

The clothing against my skin. The faded navy skinny jeans with rips at the knees. The plain black crew neck t-shirt with a pocket on the right over my chest.

The necklace. The simple pendant hanging in a circle against the black backdrop. The warm metal between my fingers as I fiddled with it, rolling it back and forth, back and forth, back and forth.

The warmth of the sun against my face.

Three things I hear.

A bird, a sparrow, maybe, whose song echoed through the silent sea of trees and endless sky and splintering light along the horizon. The music fading back into silence for a time before awakening again.

The wind in my ears, howling and whispering, soothing and taunting, carrying the bird's song in and out of sight until it left and didn't come back.

Silence. No cars, nothing for miles, the air still in the early morning. For a second, no wind rustling the remaining leaves, no birds singing, nothing as I held my breath and waited for the worst of the storm to pass. The worst of the storm at present. The part where trees are uprooted and roofs torn off and cars flipped over; the part where streets are flooded and electricity goes out and people panic. The part where you just have to sit and watch until everything goes still in the wake of the disaster.

Two things I smell.

The lavender from my conditioner wafting up from my hair.

The fresh fall morning surrounding me, no distinct smell, necessarily, just that feeling, the sense that it's fall.

One thing I know.

I know that I don't know where I am.

Five, four, three, two, one.

One, two, three, four, five.

Six, seven, eight, nine, ten...

Five. Four. Three. Two. One.

I laid back on the roof, staring up at the sky. It's the same sky as always, just no clouds, a pure blue, but otherwise the same. It's the same sky I look at every morning and every afternoon and every night. Some things never change, and the sky is one of those things.

I slid off the car, locked it, and started walking. I know I've been here before, but I can't place a finger on it. I can't match the trees to a specific location. If I have ever been here, it hasn't been for years.

A trail head came into view a couple feet ahead, and I followed it into the trees, wrapping my arms around me to block out the cold. It stretched on for a while, moving deeper and deeper into the woods, until the rest of the world just faded away. Back into oblivion. I kept looking around, trying to find something recognizable in a world I didn't recognize. The logical thing would be to turn back. But my feet wouldn't stop. They were set on a course, on one unknown destination, and there was no stopping them.

The path began to narrow about a mile and a half in, and I pushed through the trees, ignoring the branches that clawed at my skin, the more aggressive ones leaving gashes where I'd fought to get away.

It's not like one or two more scars decorating my skin will matter. Maybe a few more would complete the ornamentation, make it come together as something, like a few streaks of paint on a canvas to complete a work of art.

A sick, twisted image, but an image nonetheless.

Up ahead the trees fell into a wall of wood and branches, a small, roughly marked path clearly visible up ahead, though it narrowed into an abandoned sliver maybe a foot wide at most. I stumbled through it, pushing away branches until they veiled the world behind me, leaving nothing but the one ahead.

It's a clearing. Wide, bordered by high trees, mostly maple, a couple oak and a few pine, dotted with flowers. Only a few remaining, the cold having chased away the majority. A lake, surface glistening in the sunrise, and a waterfall cascading down to the surface from a small cliff, neighbored by a wall of stone built into a small stone structure, elegant, strong, but dissipated with years, decades of wear and erosion. A couple other trails emerged into the setting around the clearing, but there was no other sign of life. Just me.

It looked like something out of a storybook, some sort of lost realm that I found. *I* found it.

Bits of ivy crawled up the side of the stone, invading into cracks and openings in the surface wherever it could.

The waterfall. The steady stream of water, unwavering. Ripples expanding in the surface, echoing across until they faded back into the still surface of the lake. The surface glittering in the sun like all the stars that had disappeared.

I made my way to the water's edge and kneeled, letting my fingers brush against the surface. It was cold, but refreshing. A warmth in the concept rather than in the actuality.

It's so isolated. There are no other sounds except from the ones issuing from the world around me, the twigs breaking under my feet. No other breathing besides my own. No other hearts beating but mine. No life but my own. Just me. Just me, alone in this big world that fits into such a small place. A small fraction of the entirety within which it is contained. A world in itself, and a world within a world. A world of its own, within a world, within a world, within another world, within a bigger world, within a more immaculate world, within an infinity of worlds. An oblivion of worlds.

An oblivion of everything.

I pulled off my shoes and socks and left them a couple feet away from the water with my phone. There were several large rocks jutting out into the water and I climbed out onto one, letting my legs dangle off the edge, my toes submerged in the water. I looked down over the side of the rock, staring into the bottomless void below me.

What would it be like? To just sink, straight to the bottom? To watch as everything faded away?

What would it be like? To never resurface?

But that's part of wondering.

You wonder because you don't know, and you might never know.

And if you ever do, it might be the last thing you get to know. Or at least, one of the last.

The sun had taken post at a higher place in the sky, and every sign of sunrise was gone, all the colors, all the calm, all the serenity had vanished. I let the sun rest on my face, making no effort to shield my eyes. Instead, I looked into it, straight ahead, the blinding light no one dares to look at. The brightest thing in our world. No one looks at it because it's a lot to take in, regardless of the strain it puts on your eyes, it's the brightest thing in our world. The brightest things hold secrets, most of which are the things we hold closest to our hearts, and those are, most plausibly, the most secret things. The things we are so scared of losing, because once we lose them, we never get them back.

The brightest things are often the darkest.

In the light I see everything I'm missing.

It's so much. So much of my life. So much of my past, my future, my world... everything.

We may be blinded by the light.

But there's a reason we can't see in the dark.

* * *

Around maybe eight or nine o'clock, I got up. The sun had shifted again, and no longer infiltrated my line of vision. I only remembered the car sitting, dead, on the side of the road when I saw my phone and keys sitting on top of my shoes. I sat down next to them, picked up my phone, dialed, and listened to it ring.

"Hey, Cass, what's up?"

"Hey, Rach, um, quick question. Can you come help me? My car broke down."

"Ahh, Cass, I'm sorry I have to help out with band stuff until twelve. Maybe someone else will be able to, I'm sorry, I have to go. Love you!"

"Love you too, see you later." I hung up and stared at the phone.

I dialed again.

"Hey! What's up?"

I cringed at my sporadic choice. "Hey, um, my car broke down, can you come help me? Or do you have band stuff, too?"

"Actually, I can, just give me like thirty minutes and I'll call you again."

"Oh my god, thank you."

"No problem. Where are you, anyway?"

"No fucking clue."

"Great."

I paused before responding and listened. Footsteps. Dim, but there.

Footsteps that weren't mine.

My voice dropped to a whisper, "Um, okay, I've got to go, I hear footsteps."

"Cass, wait, where are you?"

"I don't *know*, let me get back to the road."

"Wait-"

I froze. A voice. Not through the phone, but the same voice. I looked up.

*   *   *

He waved at me from the edge of the woods, from one of the other trails leading here. To my isolated world. *My* isolated world that *I* found that *I* feel comfortable in, that *I* feel safe in.

My world.

He paused, a confused half grin etched on his face, then took a couple tentative steps toward me.

"Did- did you know I was here?" I said.

He shook his head. "Nope. Coincidence, I guess."

"Weird coincidence."

"Yeah."

"What are you doing here? Don't you have other stuff going on like band or whatever?"

"Not at the moment."

"But- but what are you doing *here*?"

"What, am I not allowed to be here?"

"I... No- it's just that- I don't know."

He stepped closer to me, "I've been coming here by myself for the past year, and before that I used to come with my dad."

"Oh."

"Yeah."

"Okay."

"Can I join you?" he nodded at the rock I'd climbed back onto.

"Okay."

He kicked off his shoes and slid next to me, leaving less than two inches between us.

I moved a couple centimeters to the right, widening the gap, but the more I moved away, the less spaced there seemed to be between us. Until I ran out of rock and my head went underwater.

It was still surprisingly warm compared to the cold air, but my lungs went numb with lack of oxygen and too much exposure to water.

I opened my eyes.

It was a different world. Not different as in slight changes, but extreme contrast, something different in its entirety rather than its part.

I hung there, arms above my head and hair floating around me, and sunk to the bottom like a stone. It wasn't as deep as I first thought it was.

My lungs screamed as my feet hit the sand. I sprang upward.

I wanted to sink. Back to the bottom. And stay there. Never moving. Never thinking. Just there, on the bottom, never breathing.

My head broke the surface and my lungs gave way, gasping for air.

"Are you okay?" he leaned over me.

"Yeah," I said, coughing. He offered me a hand and I took it, but before he could pull me back onto solid ground, I pulled him off of it.

"Hey!" he was already laughing as his head broke the surface. I let myself grin slightly. "What'd you do that for?"

I shrugged the best I could while treading water, "I didn't mean to, it was an accident!"

"Sure it was."

"You don't believe me?"

"Not particularly," he splashed me and I shrieked. "My clothes are soaked!"

"So are mine!"

"I didn't push you off though!"

"Mhmm."

"I *didn't*."

"So!"

"So?" he pushed the wet curls out of his eyes, which shone emerald green against the blue of the water.

"Nothing."

"Okay," he shook his head, laughing.

For a second, it was like no time had passed, and all the years between us disappeared. All the years in which we became different people evanesced, and it was just us. The *old* us.

"Okay."

*   *   *

We sat on the edge of the water, and while the air was still cold, the sun had already dried my clothes. Owen's hair was still dripping and he kept pushing it out of his eyes.

He caught me looking at him, "What?"

"Nothing."

"Sure."

"Taylor?"

"Yeah?"

"You're not going anywhere, right?"

His hand slipped into mine, and I fought the impulse to flinch away, letting his fingers intertwine with mine, "I'm not going anywhere."

"Okay."

"Why are *you* here, of all places?"

"Just because," I shrugged.

"Just because why?"

"Just because."

"Nothing's ever 'just because'."

"What if there's just not an explanation? What if it's *just* because?"

"There's always an explanation."

"Do you really believe that?"

He looked over at me, "Yeah, I do."

"Why?"

"Because, there are too many things in this world for anything to be 'just because'."

"Too many things?"

"Too many things."

We sat there for a while, and I could feel the mist on my skin, radiating off of the falls. My fingers loosened in his grip, and I pulled my hand away.

He turned his head toward me as I looked away. I went to tug down my sleeve and turned my arm away when I remembered I was only wearing a t-shirt.

How could I be so careless?

"Are you okay?"

"Yeah, I just should go. I have to figure out what's wrong with my car."

"Do you need help?"

"No, no I'm fine."

"I know *you're* fine, but your car's not."

I looked down, grinning.

"What's funny?"

My face reset, "Nothing."

"Um... okay."

"But no, my car doesn't need help either."

"You sure?"

"Yeah."

"Alright, well I'm going to stay here for a while. If you need me, just call. See you later."

"Bye."

I didn't look back.

I took my time walking back to the car, stopping every once in a while to let the petrichor air fill my lungs and leave them, taking a part of me with it every time. Taking a part of the ghosts that plague my past. A part because the whole will never leave.

Never in a million years.

The car was still there, in the same place I left it, the roof open, a couple leaves having fallen into it. Otherwise, undisturbed. I climbed back in and tried the engine a couple times, and finally, it turned back on.

I started driving, opening all the windows and letting the wind roar in my ears, everything else fading away. No other life, no other sound, no other anything.

I drove until the sun fell back to Earth and everything was blanketed in gray, the median before the darkness.

The car sputtered back to silence again in the middle of a wide, empty field. I didn't try to restart it. There was still no one around, it was around midnight, and everything was quiet. A silence rarely seen among the living.

A silence I know too well from spending so much time among the dead.

I saw them, then, the man lifting up the small girl while she screamed with laughter, the girl that used to be me. The woman yelling at him, telling him he'd be late for work even though she didn't want him to go. He put the girl down, scooping her up in his arms again when she raised her arms above her head. He cradled her in one arm and hugged the woman tightly with the other as she wrapped her arms around him, tears in her eyes. He kissed her, and then the girl. He took the day off work that day, and the girl stayed home from school. The woman had already called in sick. He fought back tears, the unshaved hairs on his face and dark circles under his eyes saying everything he couldn't.

It's all blurred, now.

I didn't try hard enough to remember.

I should have tried harder.

But I never thought I'd have to forget. I never thought I'd have to forget any of them.

I still don't know why he was going to try going to work that day. Maybe he thought that, by then, he'd be able to get through the day. I think we all thought that, until the week started. By Wednesday, we all knew we couldn't. Then Thursday came. It had been a year. She would have been four. I was seven.

All of them, the people who were there that day, they don't exist anymore.

I climbed back onto the roof of the car, pulling my jacket on. In the cold air, I rolled up my left sleeve, running the fingers of my right hand up and down the ridges engraved there. So many questions, unasked and unanswered.

Light years away from the stars, I sat there, watching everything fall back into place.

And, light years away, the stars came back to life.

Chapter Six

"Cassandra!"

"Coming!" I locked the front door, pulling my jacket sleeves down over my hands.

"Hurry up, we're going to be late!"

"It's a party, no one's ever late," I climbed into the passenger seat.

"Very true, but I told Julie I'd be there around eight and now it's nine, so..."

"Oh, I see, you told *Julie*," I grinned, giving her a shove.

"Hey! I'm driving, no hitting!"

"*Sorry*," I propped my feet up on the dashboard, "so, how are things with Julie, anyway?"

"Same as always," she glanced over at me, "and feet down, please!"

"*Okay*. Why don't you drive everyone to school in the mornings? You have your *own* car, and it *works*."

"Okay, but *because* it's *my* car, everyone else will treat it like you do, and I put up with you, but the rest of them, yikes, I'd go ballistic."

"Okay, fair enough."

"Yup."

"So, who else is going to be there?"

She shrugged, "No idea."

"Lovely."

"We'll find out soon," she pulled into the driveway, glancing over at me as she turned off the car, "why, anyone you're hoping to see there?"

"No, of course not!"

"Sure, I believe that."

"*Rachel.*"

"*Cassandra*," she mimicked me, "I'm not judging, don't worry."

"You should be."

"And why's that?" she locked the car and we headed up to the front door. Music was blasting from inside.

"I'm being stupid."

"How come? He's not a bad guy, Cass."

"He's *him*, though. He's Owen *Taylor*, which, one, is a weird name as it is, and it's just... him. I didn't talk to him for three years. I was practically *in love* with him. I got over it. I just... I don't know."

"Cassandra," she opened the door, grabbing my arm and pulling me through the crowd of people, "tonight," she found the beer keg and handed me a cup, "don't think. Don't think about him. Don't think about school, just don't think."

I looked down at the cup, swirling the liquid back and forth, then I looked back at her, and nodded, "Okay."

* * *

"Cass!" Maddy tackled me, the contents of her cup almost spilling everywhere, "when did you get here?"

"A couple of minutes ago. When did *you*," I eyed the cup.

"About an hour ago, when you were *supposed* to get here."

"Where's Gabi?"

"Talking to *John*, maybe talking, maybe something else, I don't know."

"*Okay* then."

"Did you get a drink already?"

"Yeah," I held up my cup and she nodded, giggling.

"I'm going to go find Rachel, want to come?"

"No, sorry, but Maddy... Rachel's probably upstairs with Julie..." I trailed off as she bounded away, stumbling a little.

I glanced around the room, and did a double take when a sandy haired head turned toward me, grinning from the other side of the room. I froze, and then I turned and pushed my way through the throng of people. Someone called my name, and I ducked down to hide my face. Rachel was in the kitchen, talking to a group of friends with Julie hanging on to her, giggling stupidly.

She saw me and waved, "Cassie! Rach, Cassie!"

Rachel grinned, supporting Julie around the waist, clearly more in control of her actions and speech than her girlfriend. "Cass! How's it going?"

"Give me another drink."

"Yikes, that bad?"

"Not yet, but it will be."

She glanced behind me, then looked back at me and raised her eyebrows, "*That* bad?"

"I don't want to hear it, Rach, just give me another drink, *please*."

"*Fine*, but this is the last one for you."

"I've only had one!"

She shook her head, "And look at you, you're a mess."

"I'm not *drunk*."

"*Good*, keep it that way," she handed me back my cup.

I downed half of it in one sip, "Two and a half," I held it out.

She rolled her eyes, taking it, "Two and a half."

"Thank you."

"Now, here, go out that way, up the stairs, and hide in the bathroom in Julie's room until he's gone, third door down the hall on the right. No one'll be in there."

"Are you sure?"

"Oh, *I'm* sure."

"Rach!"

She shrugged, "Or, you could go that way, toward the guy staring at you waiting for you to turn around and acknowledge him."

"*Fine*. But you *owe* me."

"*I* owe *you*?"

I nodded at the beer cans sitting next to her on the counter.

She shook her head.

I lunged forward and grabbed a six pack, ducking under her arm, "Haha!"

"You're an idiot."

"I'm aware."

"Alright, now go, get out while you can."

"I'm going!" I disappeared through the door into the hallway, watching him approach Rachel over my shoulder, her barring him from following me and keeping him locked in what must have been a lengthy conversation on something the average person would find incredibly boring, such as the fantastic alignment of the planets and constellations and the various conspiracy theories circling them, most of which she developed within the same second she thought of them.

She caught my eye and raised her eyebrows. I grinned and made my way up the stairs and down the hall. I wandered down the hallway, counting the doors on the right, ignoring the sporadic giggling and screams coming from behind various closed doors.

People always forget that a closed door doesn't mean complete isolation. People always forget that a closed door doesn't mean you're alone in the world. People always forget that a closed door doesn't mean no one's watching.

People always forget that a closed door always has to open.

I closed Julie's bedroom door and looked around. It was a cozy room, pictures of her and Rachel scattered across the walls along with sketches and various quotes. A stack of books on her desk, a camera teetering precariously on top. An organized appearance with a messy undertone.

The bathroom wasn't much different. I sunk down onto the tiled floor, gripping the alcohol tightly in one hand, cradling my head with the other.

Everything from the past ten minutes was rattling around my skull.

Everything from the past ten hours. The past ten days. The past ten weeks. The past ten months. The past ten years.

It doesn't feel that long ago.

In retrospect, it's not.

I'm seventeen. In ten years, I'll be twenty seven. Ten years after that, I'll be thirty seven. Ten decades after that I'll be dead.

A rotting corpse in the ground.

I took a sip from the cup, wincing as it burned my throat.

I don't think I'll be buried. I'd rather be cremated. Less messy. Less for people to have to deal with. Easier to let go and forget than a body rotting away under the ground.

I stared up at the ceiling, counting the various spots there from god knows what. Childhood tantrums involving soap and shampoo, water stains from the floor above, cracks in the paint, peeling of the paper from years of neglect.

Cracks in foundations set so long ago in stone that seemed so strong. The initial appearance throwing all reality and fact into an abyss, sheltered by the simply complex understandable. Ignoring the complex simplicity of the unexplainable. So many years of pressure and strain managing to tear away the screen of security and definition, of purpose and ill restraint, of possibility and innocence. The abstemious remarks of those left to themselves, fooling themselves into a sense of security, of fabricated safety and sanity in a world where no such thing could ever exist in the entirety of which people long for.

Peeling of paper from layers and layers of self assurance and secrets buried under mountains made of boulders that disintegrated into mountains made of sand.

A game of cards dealt without looking to see what was already laid out on the table.

Life.

Simple in retrospect.

Death.

Simple in retrospect.

I'm alive.

Simple in retrospect.

My father is dead.

Simple in retrospect.

I am breathing.

He is not.

Everyone in this world is breathing.

She is not.

Everyone in this world has a chance to make something of their life.

They do not.

Simple in retrospect.

But oh so complex in these cracked foundations and peeling papers and games of cards.

Simple.

Simple is better.

Less chance of misunderstanding. Less chance of mistakes. Less chance of hearing echoing refrains of worlds left so far in the past. Less chance of waking dead ghosts.

Simple in retrospect.

Oblivion is simple in retrospect. Like so many complex things, it is simple solely for the fact that no one wants it to be complex. People want to make it understandable, to act as though they have the ability to hold it in their hands, study it, balancing it in their clumsy fingers, and see it. To see it past the blindness that clouds their vision. Scraping away all the layers that make oblivion just that, oblivion. Scraping away all the layers until it is simply time in the mask of the unknown. Until it is an ideal representation of the time with which they have left of their lives. Something that, when all else falls away, they can turn to, something they can blame when all else fails, when their lives become an endless spiral of unknown and unforeseen and falsities.

Of fabricated facts and fabricated reality.

Scraping away the layers.

One by one.

All it does is create a shadowed, mutated figure that used to exist as a beautiful, complicated component backstage in all aspects of humanity.

Scraping away the magic in something so completely unable to be understood that it is understandable and leaving a bare, broken object so completely able to be understood that is requires no thought, no contemplation, just observation. Leaving something that doesn't stretch the barriers of human intelligence and tears at the boundaries between morality, ideology, theology, and everything else that plays a role in keeping the Earth spinning on its forever teetering axis.

There's no magic in something like that.

Facts. Hard, stone cold facts.

Facts born from the deepest and most hidden places of thought that only those bold enough to brave the divide could discover to turn falsities into realities.

So many cracks spiraling away and within one another in the mirror. Another accident from childhood.

I laughed quietly, taking another swig from the cup. Then I threw my head back and laughed; I laughed until my face turned red and tears rolled down my cheeks. I laughed until the alcohol took full control of my body and I laughed until I could no longer tell if the tears were a result of the insane hilarity I'd been hit with or a long suppressed sorrow.

It's funny how things like that make their way around at some point.

All the tears you never cry find a way out eventually, one way or another. No one is immune to the irony hidden under every footstep, buried in every footprint, until you stop and turn around and there is all is, staring you in the face.

The irony.

Everything you ever tried to escape never really disappears.

And one day all you have to do is turn around.

Life is just one shit hole of ironies.

The irony of life.

A door creaked open somewhere outside the room. A voice. My lungs froze, my breath catching, the laughter dying.

"Cassandra?"

Of course, it wasn't Lily. Or Maddy. Or Julie. Or Gabi.

Because of life's many ironies, when it gets bored of watching us laugh at it and instead decides to find humor in our twisted plot lines, we get hit with the blunt end of the sword. I had my laugh. Now life gets its.

"Cassandra?"

I climbed into the bathtub and sunk down, hiding myself within the small, makeshift fortification.

"James, I know you're in here." Footsteps getting closer, then a shadow.

I closed my eyes, only opening them when I knew he was there and escape was a distantly abstract possibility.

"What are you doing?" he looked down at me, eyebrows furrowed at the red cup I was clutching as though it were an anchor in a riptide.

"Hiding."

"From?"

"You," my loosened tongue gave way to superficial thoughts and words, ones that a more adequate sense of control and stiffened tongue would have prevented.

"Cass, come on."

I made a face as if thinking it over, "Um... no. No, thank you."

"Please?"

"No."

"Why?"

"I'm perfectly comfortable where I am, thank you very much."

"Sure you are."

"I *am*," I sipped the contents of the cup, realizing shortly that there was no more there to consume. "Give me that," I gestured to the beer cans.

"Come out, first."

"*Fine*," I hauled myself out, back onto the cold tile floor. He sat down next to me and I glared at him. He didn't look at me, just took a can, handed me one, and popped his open.

Neither of us spoke, not for a long time. A concatenation of seconds and minutes, concatenations in which we spoke a thousand words in a thousand silences.

"I don't know what to say to you," I said finally, breaking the thin layer of glass. He looked over at me, but I kept my eyes on the doors to the cabinet under the sink. I waited for him to say something. He didn't.

"I don't know what to say to you," I repeated, "I keep... I keep thinking about it, replaying it, and the thing is, I don't even know what I'm replaying. It's a mix of things, really. Some from so long ago I don't even know when they happened or if they were real. Some from so recent that I don't know if I made it up in my head or if it was a cruel trick of the light. I keep trying to find a middle ground, some way to move past everything, because I did. I moved past it. But usually when you move past something you don't stop to think about the possibility of it popping back up in your face when you least expect it." He opened his mouth, but I kept talking. "I don't know what to say to you, because I keep thinking you're the person you were before, the person I used to know. I knew that person so well. Like the back of my hand. The boy I used to walk to school with every day, the one obsessed with his various weekly interests, the one who changed his career every day. The boy who used to smile at me when I walked past him. The boy who didn't know how to walk away from someone as if they'd never known them. And three years, I know, is a long time. We were younger then. We were children. We were naive, innocent, convinced that there was good somewhere in the world. We were children. We've changed since then. But the thing is, we didn't change together. And, I mean, we can't do anything about that now. We didn't change together. I don't know you. You're as much of a stranger now as you were thirteen years ago when we met. I don't know *how* to know you. And I don't know what to say to you."

I turned toward him, watching his face in the dim light as it twisted, a million different emotions displayed for a split second before being replaced by the next.

"We changed apart."

"We changed apart."

"We can't do anything about that, now."

"Nope."

He paused, "We could change together."

"What?"

"Well, we can change together, now."

"I guess."

"Yeah." I could feel him watching me, scanning my face for a reaction, for anything that gave away details in place of my short, clipped responses. "Have you been crying?"

"No."

"You have mascara streaks under your eyes."

"Oh," I reached up to wipe them away, "must just be the alcohol, it makes my eyes water."

"Cass, what's on your arm?"

"Nothing." The sleeve fell back down over my forearm and wrist.

"Cass..."

"It's *nothing*, okay?"

"Cassandra."

"What?"

He turned his arm over, "I have them too."

I stared into his face, exhausted hilarity and irony washing over me. I shook my head, grinning, fighting the insane laughter bubbling in my chest. "Great, so we're two fucked up kids. Great team, really top notch."

"Cassandra..."

"I'm sorry, I'm sure *you're* not fucked up. But me? Well, I'm pretty fucked up. I've been pretty fucked up. And you know what? You really, *really* shouldn't care."

"Why? Doesn't everyone deserve to have someone who cares?"

"Are you saying that I don't already have someone who cares?"

"No," he said quickly, "but I'm assuming that all of your friends out there getting drunk off their asses have no idea that those exist."

I shrugged, "I'm sure they know. They just don't want to admit it. It's easier to pretend they don't exist."

"Easier for them or easier for you?"

"Easier for everyone."

"Easier for everyone else?"

"Easier for everyone." I don't look at him.

"Everyone but you."

"Easier. For. Everyone."

"You don't count yourself in that 'everyone'."

"Of course I do."

He raised his eyebrows. "Really? So when you say everyone, you include yourself because you truly feel like you fit in with that 'everyone'? You don't count yourself out because you don't feel like you deserve to be included? That as long as everyone else in the world is happy it doesn't matter whether or not your happiness exists?"

I hesitated for half a second longer than I should have.

"Yeah, exactly."

I shook my head. "Easier... easier for everyone." I popped open my can and took a sip, trying to drown the words in the silence.

He mirrored my movements, and we just sat there, drinking in silence. The loud, busy kind of silence.

His fingers began to intertwine with mine. I jerked my hand away, moving a couple inches away from him.

"Sorry," he muttered.

"You should go."

"What?"

"You should *go*."

"I don't think so."

"I think so."

"Do you want me to?"

My head was buzzing. A chorus of different buzzing. Multiple choirs all buzzing at different frequencies in different rhythms and different dynamics and different pitches.

"Cassandra, what do you want?"

I laughed, the insane, maniacal laughter that gets people sent to insane asylums. The laughter finally breaking free from its superficial cage of sanity. "What do I want?"

"What do you want."

"I want to fucking die."

* * *

A detrimental silence. A storm that had finally broken, at least in part. A tidal wave that left everything deserted and quiet. The eerie sort of quiet. The sort of quiet most people don't survive to hear.

He seemed to be fighting words, discarding and replacing nouns and verbs, sorting through them until he could find the right ones. I broke the silence before he could.

"I'm sorry."

"Why?" he didn't look at me.

"I'm just sorry."

"I'm sorry too."

"We say that a lot."

"We really do."

"We say that *too* much."

"I think that, in some cases, there's never too many times you can apologize."

"I think that, in most cases, when you have to apologize so many times there's no point apologizing anymore."

He looked down at his hands, fidgeting with the tab on the can. He didn't say anything for a while. The splintered glass resealed itself.

"Are we one of those cases?" he said slowly, twisting off the metal tab and rolling it back and forth between his fingers.

"I don't think so," I swung my can back and forth, watching the liquid inside spiral. "Not yet."

"But we might be?"

"We might be."

Chapter Seven

I woke up with my head against the bathtub next to Rachel, my head buzzing with all the words of the previous night.

I shook Rachel's shoulder and she groaned, keeping her eyes shut, "What, Cass?"

"Wake up."

"Why?"

"Because it's morning."

"And I have a hangover, I don't give a shit if the sun's been sober all night and I haven't."

"What?"

"What do you mean, *what*?"

"The sun's sober?"

"Yes. It's sober. It gets drunk at night sometimes, and the next day it's cloudy because it makes up not being able to do its job by making the clouds come in and give us the illusion that it's there because people put so much shit and hope on the sun."

"Are you still drunk?"

"Maybe."

"Where's Julie?"

"No fucking clue. Probably downstairs. How are you fine?" she rubbed her head, reaching over and turning the shower on. Cold water rained against the back of my neck.

"I'm not."

She pushed herself up, climbing under the cold water. "You seem like you are."

"When did you come up here?" I followed her in, the water soaking my clothes.

"Taylor came down and told me you'd passed out, so I came up here to check on you and ended up passing out too."

"Did he-"

"Tell me anything? No. But let me just say, he's a good guy. You've got a good guy, there," she shivered, gasping in the freezing water.

"Yeah," I said quietly.

"Are you going to tell me?"

"Tell you what?"

"Tell me what happened."

"Oh, um," I shrugged, "I mean, it wasn't really anything."

"Cass, come on."

"We just... we talked. I just don't know if it's worth it, Rach."

"Why not?"

"Just- we're going to try, I think, but there's baggage there. There's so much we have to ignore."

"So ignore it."

"It's not that simple."

"Cass?"

"What?" her eyes shifted from my face to my arm, practically bare in the drenched, white sleeve.

I turned my forearm toward the ground.

"Cass," she grabbed my arm, twisting my wrist upward.

"It's *nothing*, Rach."

"Cass..."

"Rach, I promise."

She looked at me, eyes searching for something she couldn't find. Something she knew she was missing but couldn't see. Her fingers loosened. "Okay."

The water drumming against the sides of the tub filled the silence of the room. A room already so burdened by silence it was a miracle it could hold anymore.

Things have a way of surprising us. Miraculous occurrences that are unthinkable, miracles of which are usually not miracles but percentages, categorized as miracles because the percentages are so small that their chance of occurring are almost impossible. Almost.

People have a way of surprising us. People we thought were different than ourselves turn out to be the same. People we thought changed have changed in ways we didn't imagine.

We have a way of surprising ourselves. We overlook things that should be obvious and make them transparent against an opaque backdrop.

The world has a way of surprising us. In ways that show us things in people and ourselves that we would have missed. Often, it's the worst parts, the worst parts of the world that bring out the worst parts of ourselves.

Often, it's the parts we don't want to remember.

*   *   *

"So, do you want me to read you the story of Hercules again, Cassandra?" Dad asked, already sitting me down on his lap. I said yes, but when he opened the mythology book and began to read, I just focused on his voice. I already knew the story by heart. By the time he finished reading and closed the book, I had memorized every zigzagged stitch on his clothing and every dot of stubble on his face. I never wanted to forget him. Never in a million years.

I wish I'd tried harder to remember.

But I didn't think I'd ever have to forget.

There are a lot of things I never thought I'd have to forget.

I never thought I'd have to forget having someone to share dolls with and wrestle in the snow with and watch a movie with during a road trip when Mom and Dad were busy talking in the front seat.

I never thought I'd have to forget hearing his voice every day, singing, reading stories, laughing, talking to Mom, talking to me, starting little conversations with people he saw in stores, old friends, perfect strangers. Waving if anyone flipped him off on the road. He was a terrible driver. But he didn't care, and because he didn't care, neither did anyone else.

I never thought I'd have to forget what it was like to be part of a family, to have people who could care about you and love you. Instead of having broken parts of it, knowing what it was like to have unbroken parts.

*   *   *

Taylor and I don't talk much over the following weeks. It's a good kind of silence, though. One of the relieving kinds. One where all the bad things can be washed away into a sea of unspoken words. I don't mind the distance.

But I hate it.

I hate it because I find myself missing him.

I'm not supposed to miss him.

I haven't talked to Rachel much, either, or anyone else. I've withdrawn into my own little bubble, my own little section of the world.

It's like flying on a plane, flying by yourself. When you're surrounded by people but you put in your earbuds, turn on your music, and ignore everything else. When you're surrounded but alone. A bubble of individuality in a world where nothing is individualized.

People look at people alone like a red light, a label that says you have something wrong with you, but people who are alone are the smart ones. They're the ones who know how to avoid getting hurt.

Once you let anyone else in, once you think you have something to be scared of losing, once you think you have everything... that's when you lose everything.

If you're alone, the only thing to lose is yourself.

Sometimes we lose that too.

I pulled up one of the floorboards, the one under my bed, hidden by the sheets I never bothered to tuck into the bed frame. I had to fish around in it for a couple minutes, sifting through shredded papers and objects. Stupid objects, really. Stupid objects and stupid words on stupid papers. There are so many things I should burn, just erase from existence completely.

"*Shit*," I jerked my hand out, putting pressure on the finger sporting a good sized slice. I held my hand out in front of me, studying the cut. It's only bleeding slightly, and after a minute the stinging and throbbing dies down, and it goes numb.

I forgot I put those there.

I used my other hand, being more careful this time, and finally found it. I know it by touch, the paper is different than the other papers that have congregated there. I haven't held it in months, but I know the touch from the days when I would take it out and study it religiously. I have it memorized.

The date. *June 29, 2014*.

The author. *Caroline Regan*

The title. *Twelve year old hospitalized after suicide attempt*.

The words.

A newspaper clipping from five years ago.

A story that should never have been written. Confidentiality was not taken into consideration when Caroline Regan decided to write this article.

My hands used to shake as they held it.

They never said the girl's name. Never referred to her as anything that tied her to anything more than a girl who tried to overdose when she was twelve. The girl whose body they found ridden with scars. Mostly her thighs, her stomach. Only one on her left wrist.

They didn't say all that, of course.

But they didn't have to.

There was no address, no picture, no name; it was hardly a story. But it was there. In plain sight.

Everyone knew.

Even though no one knew.

The talk about the article died down before the girl was out of the ICU, and by that point she'd been admitted to psych. And everyone forgot about her.

Stapled to the back of that article, a shorter clip, cut out of a newspaper, the only whole version of the countless, shredded pieces strewn across the bottom of the floor.

An AMBER alert for the same girl, now thirteen, a year later. The alert disappeared within hours, just as quickly as the talk did, and within that time span she was back in psych.

The first time she'd been in psych for two months. They decided that it hadn't been a serious attempt, just an accident- she was only twelve. What do twelve year olds know of death and dying? Twelve year olds only know what they've seen. But of course they overlooked the fact that she'd already seen more than most twelve year olds.

The second time she was in psych for three months. It wasn't a suicide attempt, but she had a history.

The third time, after the third AMBER alert, it was three weeks.

By that time, she knew how to hide.

Of course, no one else knew that. It wasn't in the article. No one traced the articles on the girl back to the ones dating six, seven, eight years previous, the ones where the same girl was mentioned, this time by name, regarding the death of her grandfather, then her sister, and then her father.

No one knew that.

They only knew the simple words they read, the ones on the torn, dirty pages I now hold in my hand, so many years later.

The wrong words.

The words binding her disappearance and hospitalization to obscure reasons and potential child abuse, rather than to the troubles of her childhood. Words ignoring the secrets hidden in her floorboards and walls. The truth.

All the wrong words.

I can't hide from the rest of the world.

They don't know. But they know.

I still can't deicide which is worse.

Is it worse to have everyone know your deepest, most terrible secrets?

Or is it worse to have everyone know your deepest, most terrible secrets, and be one of the only ones to know that they're yours? To hear people talk about them, years after. To turn away and act like you didn't hear the words. To maintain your composure until you can make it to the nearest bathroom stall.

Even if no one else knows who it is, it's always going to be there, haunting garbage dumps, recycling bins, archives, neglected piles of crap, hoarded 'historical' shit.

It never comes back.

But it never goes away.

And no matter how many times they read it, no one understands. No one reads the words that aren't there.

How could I make anyone understand that I'm not what they made me?

They made me a monster.

And I'm not a monster...

I never *wanted* to be a monster.

Maybe I'll tell someone, someday. I'll tell someone when the words no longer send chills down my spine. When the words no longer make me see the girl lying helpless in the hospital bed with her grandmother sitting in a chair next to her, her mother gone. When the words no longer reflect the parts of the past I keep trying to forget. When I finally forget the words I keep trying not to remember.

Maybe I'll tell someone.

Then again, maybe not.

Maybe I'll tell someone when the floorboards are no longer loose.

I'll tell someone when I no longer see myself in the words I keep reading, over and over and over again.

Over and over and over and over and over...

Over and over without changing.

I'll tell someone when the nameless girl is no longer me.

* * *

I went back to the woods, to that secluded area hidden in the middle of nowhere. Taylor didn't make an appearance, and I sat by the water, watching the world shift in and out of consciousness.

I don't know how long I sat there. I don't know if days passed. Or weeks. Years could have passed and I wouldn't have noticed.

I just stared at the glass surface of the water, waiting for it to change. Waiting for the glass to break. Waiting for everything to shatter and all the pieces to fall back into oblivion.

Unlike the silence, this glass doesn't reseal itself.

Once it's broken, all you have are pieces. You're lucky if you even have that.

* * *

The water was cold that day. It was in the first few months of fall, between the end of September and the beginning of October. The flowers had barely started to disappear, the birds returning to warmer places down south.

We'd been begging to go since August.

Dad said it was finally warm enough, so we went. She wasn't in school yet, and he took the day off of work, calling me in sick at school. He said it would be a little trip, just the three of us. Mom couldn't afford to miss work, anyway, she had some big meeting or something.

The lake had a dock a couple yards out, at the edge of the shallow end and the dip where the water became too dark to see the bottom.

Dad took us out to the dock, making sure our little life vests were securely tied. We weren't allowed to jump into the deep side, only the shallow one. We were little then.

Dad got into the water, waiting to catch us when we jumped to help us climb back onto the dock. I, being older, jumped first.

When I did, the dock rocked.

As my head went under, before my life vest or Dad could catch me, I heard a small scream. It echoed in my ears, only fading when my head broke the surface.

Dad was swimming as fast as he could to the other side of the dock. I scrambled on top to watch.

A little purple and green life vest was floating on the surface.

I couldn't breathe. I felt like it was me, stuck under the water.

I felt like someone had hit me right between my ribs, knocking the wind out of me.

I was only six.

But I was old enough to know what was happening.

I was old enough to know I couldn't do anything about it.

Dad's head broke the surface, a little body cradled in his arms as he swam back to the shore. I followed as quickly as I could.

He dropped to his knees in the shallows, laying the girl down on the sand and trying to breathe life back into her. He tried to get her to open her eyes. He kept waiting for her to cough, the water leaving her little lungs. He kept waiting for her little chest to start rising and falling again.

I could see his fingers shaking.

Her chest rose, her sandy curls shifted on the sand.

I saw his hands steady.

And then it fell.

And didn't move again.

I'll never forget the sound he made that day. It wasn't a scream, or a sob. It was a guttural sound, like a dying animal, shot in twenty places before it was finally shot in the heart.

I stood behind him, my ankles still in the water, unable to fully process what had happened.

I turned around.

The wind had carried the life vest out from behind the dock.

It looked so small and innocent, so far away. So simple.

No one would have been able to see the ghosts it held.

The wind shifted, blowing it back toward the dock. It hit the edge, and rested there, pressed against the algae covered wood.

A little purple and green life vest.

* * *

The glass shattered.

But there wasn't much more to shatter, anyway.

I felt the tears before they fell. Once they start, it's a cascade. I can't do anything to stop them. At least, I couldn't if I tried.

I feel weak and vulnerable as my walls begin to crumble, pieces of the stone smashing and leaving gaping holes in the armor that once held in the demons that haunted my past.

The walls that held them in because I couldn't keep them out.

There was no one there to hold me, to tell me that it was okay. Just their soft, sweet voices whispering in my ears. The way they used to.

"If you want to leave, you know the way out."

"You know what you have to do."

"It's easy."

There is no way out. The only way out doesn't even guarantee an out. The "better world" might just be another version of hell. It might be worse.

There are so many reasons to live.

There are too many reasons to die.

They might follow me when I die.

The fear. The voices. The ghosts.

People talk about suicide like it's a crime. But it doesn't affect them. They don't rely on that person to keep living. They can live by themselves. They're still breathing. Their hearts are still beating. They can still feel.

Sometimes keeping a person alive kills them more than dying.

Suicide is not a side effect of depression.

Suicide is an escape route, a way out for people like me.

The most extreme desperation seen even in people who know that there isn't an escape route.

Nothing is one sided.

The only shape with one side is a circle.

There is no way out.

* * *

I'm alone. But I like being alone.

I can't handle being around people, not when I'm surrounded by so many ghosts. Ghosts that are still alive and ghosts that are dead.

The ghost of a little girl stands in front of me, but she disappears, fading away into nothing.

All that's left is a little purple and green life vest.

But then, it was just a little purple and green vest.

Chapter Eight

They were nice to me, the first couple weeks at least. The nurses were nicer a lot longer than the doctors. They didn't get a lot of kids as young as I was.

The doctors were gentle at first, the questions were simple, the evaluations were easy enough, and I "passed" most of them. They couldn't find anything wrong with me. I was there mostly for observation, because they couldn't figure out what would possess a twelve year old to steal her mother's bottle of antidepressants and down the whole bottle, clearly prepared for all of the effects that would ensue.

The second time, they pressed me more. I was thirteen, but still young. Now they couldn't just say it was nothing. They looked into child abuse, but I denied the allegations and showed no signs other than the fact that I had snuck out of my house in the middle of the night on July 7th and tried to hop a bus ten miles away from my house the next morning. Someone called the cops after they saw the AMBER alert, and then me.

Some people can't mind their damn business.

The third time, I left school and didn't turn back. I don't know how far I got, I never checked. A town called Brookstone or something. I don't remember.

That time, they kept me for three weeks. By that time, I'd learned the protocol. I'd learned how to answer the questions and how to act so they didn't think there was anything wrong with me. So they'd think it was just a fluke or me being a 'teenager' and let me go. It worked.

It's funny how they think all that stuff works. All the evaluations, all the questions. Like we really tell the truth when we know there's something wrong with us. Like the surveys they make you fill out at the doctor's office once you turn thirteen.

I lied on every single one of those.

But the third time, I got out after three weeks with nothing more than a requirement to attend one therapy session a week for a year.

I didn't talk through those.

I've learned since then. When we learn, people like to say that we're better, because we no longer show symptoms, we no longer apparently hurt ourselves or are outwardly depressed. We learn.

It's the best way to hide.

*   *   *

"Your grandmother said you haven't been home for the past couple of nights." The pen tapped against the clipboard.

"That would be true."

"Where were you?"

"Not home."

"And instead of at home, where were you?"

"Places."

"Cassandra-"

"You said my grandmother told you?"

"Yes."

"Not my mother?"

"Yes."

"Oh."

"Is there a reason you ask?"

My face hardened, "No. No, just wondering."

Her eyes lingered on my face, "Are you sure?"

I hesitated, "Yeah."

"Cassandra, please, this is a safe space."

"It's nothing."

"Please, try to talk about it. It might help you."

"Help me?" I leaned forward, "*help* me? Okay. Fine. I'm assuming you know my history, so I'll skip the replay. My mother is distant. She's been distant since my sister died and since my dad died. She hasn't said 'I love you' since I was seven. She doesn't pay attention to me. *I* can't *be* helped. I'm a lost cause. Childhood trauma. Childhood trauma that led to acting up in older age, leading to feeling neglect or something similar. A mother who doesn't show emotion because she's scared of losing me. I'm all she has left. I know all of that. I don't need you to explain why my life is what it is. I know why. It's not hard to understand."

"Everyone's life experiences are different."

"But the outline is the same. There are the same explanations for everything. You push me to talk and whatnot because you know I'm more likely to lie and hide from the truth. It's a defense mechanism. My sister died when I was six. My dad died when I was seven. My childhood ended when I was seven. I tried to kill myself when I was twelve. I ran away when I was thirteen, and then when I was fifteen. Childhood trauma. Difficulty trusting people. Refusing to replay the past," I watched her face, "but you'd know all that, wouldn't you? It's textbook."

"It's not textbook."

"It *is* textbook. My life is textbook. *I* am textbook. Anything you could tell me I'd have already read online or in a book."

"You're not textbook."

"Sure."

No one in this world is special. We all fit one generality or another. We're all textbook.

I'm not any different.

"Cassandra?"

"What," I didn't look at her, not this time. I could feel her eyes drilling into me, trying to further break the surface.

"Is there anything you want to talk about?"

I took a deep breath, then looked up. "No."

She put down her pencil, "Okay."

The bullet fired into the ground and lodged itself there, silent.

*   *   *

"That's it!" Maddy threw herself forward onto the table, almost knocking her head against it. "I'm done! I'm done, I'm quitting."

"You made it this far, you'll be fine!" Gabi flung her book down on the table, "me, however, I've been struggling since freshman year."

"I'm going to fail this test and then I'm going to fail this class and then I'm going to lose my class rank and then my GPA is going to drop and then I won't get into college and then I'll have to work at a fast food place for the rest of my life!"

"Maddy," Rachel rubbed the sides of her head, "would you please, *shut* up."

"I'm *sorry*, I'm freaking out."

"We're *all* freaking out. I'm working on a college application I need to focus."

"Already?" I looked up from my paper.

"Yeah," she glanced over at me, "prescreen."

"What school?"

"Manhattan School of Music. I have to get an audition video done within a month."

"Wow, someone has to flex on how talented they are," Gabi grinned.

"Oh, shut up," Rachel shook her head, "I'm never going to get in."

"*You* shut up," Maddy chucked her pencil at her, "you're fifth in the class, you practice 24/7, you do sports, you have like twenty thousand extracurriculars, you'll be fine."

Rachel caught the pencil, "This is *audition* based, if I blow the audition I'm done."

Maddy stared at the pencil, "Why can you *catch* too?"

"You can't compare yourself to her, Maddy, she's a freaking god," Gabi tapped her pen against the table.

Rachel fixated on the pencil, "Gabi, *please*."

"We're all too stressed out, we need to do something *fun*. Like go somewhere or do something."

"I don't have *time*," Maddy groaned.

"It's senior year, you have time."

"When would we do this 'somewhere or something'?" I asked.

She shrugged, "I don't know, like this weekend."

"Can't," Rachel said, "I have music stuff all weekend."

"Of course. Well then, we'll pick another day."

"Gabi..."

"Rachel, this is senior year. We're not going to spend it stressing. We need a break."

"I'll take a break once I get into a college."

"You've been saying that since seventh grade."

"And I mean it."

"*No*, because once you get into college you'll have to keep busy so you don't get kicked out of college and then you won't be able to take a break because you have to get your masters and then you won't be able to take a break because you have to get your doctorate and *then* you'll have to get a job and keep that job and who knows what else."

"Gabi-"

"You're never going to take a break. It's not what you do. I get it, I admire that. But you need to actually take a break once in a while. You're going to drive yourself crazy."

She messed with her hair, pulling it up into a bun, "*Fine*, I'll take a break."

Gabi grinned, "*Good.*"

"Hey," Maddy nodded at something over my shoulder, "look who it is."

"Who?" I turned around.

"Lauren Foster," Maddy whispered.

"Ew," Gabi made a face.

"Anybody talked to her recently?" I watched her disappear behind a bookcase.

"Of course not," Maddy glared at the spot she vanished.

"She's not that bad," Rachel said, watching Maddy carefully.

Maddy gaped at her, "What do you mean, 'not bad', she's terrible."

"She's a bitch, to *you*, and I get it, you guys were close, but that was like a year ago, let it *go*."

Maddy huffed, crossing her arms and sinking down in her chair.

My eyes lingered on the place where Lauren Foster had disappeared, and darted away when a sandy haired head appeared around the side of the bookcase. Rachel glanced at me but didn't say anything. No one else noticed, Maddy still ranting about Lauren and Gabi nodding and interjecting to add her own comments here and there.

"Um," I glanced back up, the head was gone, "I'll be right back, I want to go find a book."

Rachel raised her eyebrows. I ignored her and made my way to the opposite side of the bookshelf, trying to look like I was busy scouring the shelves for a book. He wasn't in the first row. I turned into the second, no one. I looped through row after row of books until I turned a corner, and there he was, back turned, trying to reach a book on the top shelf.

"Need any help?" I said. Why am I so *stupid*?

He turned slowly, "No, actually, I've got it," he held up the book.

"Oh, um... okay. Good, that's... good." I spun on my heel, face going red.

"Cass..." he trailed off.

I stopped, staring at my shoes. "I-" I forced myself to lift my head and look at him.

"Cass, I'm-"

"Don't, don't say it, please."

"But I-"

"Just- just don't say it. Please..."

"Okay."

We stood there, six feet apart, staring at each other. Words hanging in the balance between us, so many words. Words that would never be spoken and words that would never be heard. So many things we wanted to say, but couldn't. The words I wouldn't let him say, hanging in the balance. If he says them, it'll be over. There won't be any point. We'll have reached that point...

We can barely look at each other. We don't smile. We don't laugh. We don't talk. I can barely look at him, and he can barely look at me.

Twelve years ago: us playing in his yard, jumping on his trampoline, trying to do flips and failing; running after each other, racing. I was always faster than him. Putting on stupid little plays; wrestling in the snow; splashing each other in the pool; sitting together at lunch.

Ten years ago: him sitting in silence with me as I tried not to cry, holding me when I did; telling me it would be okay; him fighting to keep me in one piece.

Eight years ago: racing around my yard, switching between his house and mine; him doing backflips on his trampoline just to show off while I laughed and cheered; him letting me beat him in a race; him teaching me how to play video games and making stupid little posters together for each holiday that we eventually forgot about.

Five years ago: his face the day before it happened, when he grinned at me; his face the day I came home when he was sitting on my doorstep, eyebrows creased, and asked where I was; his relief when I told him I'd just gone away on vacation and hadn't known about the trip; the guilt I felt as we went back to our old ways, watching movies together and studying for tests we didn't have to study for.

Three years ago: first day of high school. Watching him make eye contact with me and then turn away. He didn't look back.

The past two years: every time he looked at me, smiled, and waved, and I walked past him as if he wasn't there.

He never stopped smiling.

He's not smiling now.

The years go by too fast. We make mistakes. We can't fix those mistakes. The years go by and the days go by even faster, until we don't know what just happened and what happened ten years ago. It's all a blur. And in that blur, we make mistakes.

But there are no mistakes. There are no mistakes in life, because we all say that if we could go back and change it, we would. But in that moment, that time frame, we did whatever we did for a reason, and if we went back we'd make the same mistakes for the same reasons.

There are no mistakes.

And the biggest ones, we can't fix.

My dad didn't make a mistake. He made a choice.

My sister didn't make a mistake. It was an accident.

I didn't make a mistake. It was my life.

There are no mistakes in life.

He started to turn away.

I grabbed his arm, "Wait a second."

"What?"

I kissed him.

After a second, he kissed me back. I felt his hands on the sides of my neck, and I let myself sink into it, without thinking, without caring.

When we broke apart, he looked down at me, "Why'd you do that?"

I shrugged, trying not to smile, "I don't know."

I don't. I don't know why I did it.

It was a mistake.

Chapter Nine

All the birds left.

It's quiet, now. The water makes soft noises along with the wind that rustles the trees. The air is colder, and I can almost see my breath suspended in time, suspended animation.

I spend too much time here. Time that would be better spent studying or spending time with the people I won't see again after I graduate.

My phone rang, breaking the quiet into ragged pieces. I didn't pick it up. It went silent, rang again, and then died. Whoever was calling gave up after that.

It's late. The stars have almost woken and the sun has almost gone to sleep. I should be tired, but I'm more awake than I've been in years.

I can't sleep anymore.

I haven't slept in a week. Maybe longer. I've forgotten to count the days as they pass, living in a continuous sequence, no starting and stopping, no days, no weeks, no anything. An automaton, one of the many. An automaton, believing to live their own life but living the same as everyone else.

A branch rustled behind me, and a bird flew over my head, going south.

It got left behind.

"It's okay," I whispered, watching it, "I did too."

*　　*　　*

"Hey," he placed a hand on my shoulder, sitting down next to me.

"Hey," I didn't look at him. The surface of the water glistened pink in the sunset.

"Are you okay?"

The sky shifted, the color becoming a darker violet, glowing violently against the dark landscape. "Yeah."

The wind formed ripples on the surface and with every ripple my heart beat faster.

The weight of a million worlds is resting on my shoulders.

I feel selfish sometimes. I feel so selfish that it makes me sick. There are some people who have it so much worse, but here I am, feeling as if my life is the worst of all, desperately wanting it all to end. I forget sometimes; I forget to think those things, or to feel those things.

But they always come back.

I want to run away to this world, to stay here and never leave.

But that would be selfish too. I would hurt everyone I left behind.

And I wouldn't even care.

The shadow next to me disappeared, pressure on my cheek, distant words, the sound of a car in the distance.

I looked up. The last stream of violet disappeared. It disappeared, and for a second, it's just me. Everything else is gone.

It's just me.

Me and all the glimpses of the things I have forgotten.

Me laughing when I was little.

Dad and Mom sitting together on the couch.

Rachel and I when we met in kindergarten and I yelled at her for taking my pencil.

Singing songs with Dad while he played guitar.

Reading stories with Mom.

My sixth birthday when Dad made me a horrific cake that was half burned and over sugared, that he'd covered in a hundred candles because the icing looked so bad.

Father's Day when I stayed up all night making a card, then fell asleep while he opened it, and he opened it again later so I could see his reaction.

When we all went to the zoo and Dad told me not to be scared of the spiders.

Days at the park, where Mom and Dad taught me to catch a baseball.

Sledding down the hill in the winter, Dad waiting to stop me at the bottom and laughing the time I hit a tree.

Ice skating on the lake, where I fell in and Dad yelled at me, then drove me home and made me sit in front of the fire.

Rachel sleeping over for the first time, when we told each other all our "secrets" and promised to be friends forever.

Dad teaching me the constellations from what he learned in college.

All the things that I thought I'd remember the most.

I reach for them.

They disintegrate in my fingers.

*   *   *

I stayed out all night, and I wouldn't have been surprised if Mom or Grandma had called the police. Then again, I wasn't surprised that they didn't.

Grandma isn't Mom's mom, she's Dad's. Mom's mom died a long time ago, before I was born. She doesn't talk to her dad much, or her sister. They didn't even come to the funerals. So Grandma moved in and helps as much as she can, mostly to make sure I'm doing okay. I don't make it easy.

She was watching from the window when I pulled into the driveway and opened the door before I'd even gotten out of the car. She watched me pile the textbooks and binders into my arms and didn't say anything as I walked up the steps and into the house. Her eyes didn't change, just the same wide, concerned look, her hair unkempt. On a normal day, if she's out of bed by now, her hair's in rollers and she has her bathrobe tied around her with a cup of coffee in her hands. Now, her hair's sticking up in random places and her bathrobe is loose and wrinkled and the cup of coffee is empty and cold. It's a Sunday, which is usually when she goes to church, but the clock hits nine and she's still there, watching me as I sit down at the table with a cup of coffee and open my chemistry textbook. Mom's car wasn't in the driveway, and I stopped at her doorway before going into my room. Her room is tidy, the bed made, a thin layer of dust on the nightstand, the curtains drawn and the room dark.

My room's not much different.

I heard Grandma's footsteps on the wood floor, pausing by my room, then they move on, and her bedroom door closes.

I plugged in my phone, the red light on the battery flashing. Two hundred and three missed calls and seven hundred and twenty four unread messages. I fished my earbuds out from my desk and turned on my music, turning up the volume until everything else faded away. I laid down on the bed, staring up at the ceiling. It's so easy for me to block out the world... why can't the world block out me?

Then the phone buzzed. Then it buzzed again. And again. I rolled over, checking it.

Rachel: Okay where the fucking hell are you?

Rachel: Like I get that you don't always answer your phone right away but you disappeared right after school and I've called you and texted you like two hundred times like what the fuck, come on

Rachel: I've texted everyone else and no one's heard from you since school Friday what's going on?

I turned off the screen again, listening to it buzz in the dead silence of the morning.

They all think they care.

They don't.

The day rolled by, and Grandma eventually left and went either to church or work, or both. Mom didn't come home.

At some point, I ended up on the floor, sitting against my mirror, back against the cool glass, ignoring the dark shape of a reflection on the other side.

I'm alone. I'm alone in a world where there is no one watching, no one to see that I'm alone, no one to comment on it, no one to ask why.

Too many people ask why.

They ask you and you tell them, and then they just keep asking.

Because they'll never understand.

They're lucky.

That is, the rest of the fucking world.

The people who aren't like me.

I pulled up my sleeve and looked down at my left arm. The first fifteen or so lines faded a long time ago.

But the rest are still there. They're all still there.

I run my fingers over them, watching as goosebumps rise under my cold touch. I used to be ashamed of them.

I still am.

Except for the fact that I don't care anymore.

On good days, I'm proud of them, in a weird, twisted way. Because on my good days, they're a sign that I'm strong. I'm stronger than what tried to kill me.

I'm stronger than myself.

* * *

The doorbell rang, voices yelling and pounding on the door.

"Cassandra! Come on, open the door!"

"We know you're in there!"

"We'll break down the door!"

"Wait, I know where the key is, here." The door clicked open and a stampede of footsteps made their way down the hall. I yanked my sleeve down as they pushed open the door. They stood there in the doorway, Rachel with her hands on her hips, Gabi with her arms crossed, and Maddy looking flustered, hair a mess and face red.

"Look at that, she's alive," Rachel said, irritated.

"Hey," I looked down at my hands.

"You seriously couldn't have answered *one* of our texts?" Gabi rolled her eyes.

"Dude, that was *not* okay," Maddy held back tears, "that was really, *really* not okay."

"Sorry," I muttered, pushing myself to my feet, "I had a lot of work, I wasn't on my phone at all."

"Bullshit," Rachel didn't take her eyes off me, "I call bullshit."

"Major fucking bullshit," Gabi nodded.

"Your *grandmother* called us," Rachel glared, "you weren't even home last night, you've barely been around, you disappeared right after school Friday, and nobody knows what the fuck is going on."

I shrugged, "It's nothing. Sorry to freak you out. It's really nothing. I fell asleep in my car last night, I was studying at the library and then drove around for a while."

Rachel's eyebrows shot up even further, "Right, because that's true."

I shrugged again.

"Well, fine, it doesn't matter, we're staying," Gabi picked up two bags of food and sat down on the rug next to the bed, "we're staying the night."

"But it's a school night-"

"Nope, doesn't matter, we all have clothes in the car. We're not going anywhere," Rachel sat down next to her and Maddy followed, leaving me standing there alone.

"You don't have to sit, but we're not going anywhere," Maddy leaned back, looking up at me.

I sat down next to her. Gabi passed around food, strewing out plates and dishes across the floor. No one said anything for a while. Rachel turned on the music, blasting 80s hits from her Bluetooth speaker.

Maddy spoke first, per usual. "I have a calc test tomorrow, I think I'm gonna fail."

Gabi rolled her eyes, "You won't fail."

"I might," Maddy shoved a whole piece of sushi into her mouth, "I really might." She chewed for three seconds and swallowed, "I don't know what's going on in that class."

"Does anyone?" Rachel leaned back on her forearms.

"Cass does, she has like a ninety eight in that class," Gabi glanced at me, apprehensive.

I shook my head, "I wish."

And just like that, everything went back to normal.

They chattered around me, oblivious when I didn't respond to questions or comments. I faded in and out of the conversation, adding a word or two here or there. All the while thinking how different I am from them. I'm not like any of these people. I act normal, I act like them, I can fit in with them, and I love them, they're my closest friends. But there'll always be a wall there, a glass wall, like the ones at the zoo, the ones you can see through but never break. Except I'm the one inside the cage acting like I'm the one watching them when really they're the ones outside watching me.

I'll always be the person on the other side of the glass.

For a while I got to sit there, contemplating the fact, free from having to do anything but watch them.

Then Rachel said, "Let's play a game."

"What kind of game?" Gabi grinned, making Maddy eye her nervously.

"A game," Rachel stood up, rummaging through her backpack, "come on," she pulled out her keys and left the room. Maddy, Gabi and I stared at each other. She reappeared in the doorway, jingling the keys, "Well, what are you waiting for? Come on!"

We did.

I locked the front door behind us and she got in the driver's seat of her car. "Cass, get in the passenger's side." I did, and Maddy and Gabi climbed in the back, looking as confused as I was.

"Rach, what-"

She slammed her foot on the gas.

And there we were, out of the driveway, flying down a narrow suburban road. She turned onto the highway and got off a side exit, turning onto a long, empty road bordered by miles and miles of empty fields. She didn't say anything, not a word, until about fifteen miles down the stretch, when she rolled down all the windows and opened the sunroof, and let out a yell. I watched her mouth moving, but you couldn't hear a word, just the wind.

She slowed the car down just enough for us to hear her and yelled, "Have some fun!"

Then she floored it.

There was no one around for miles.

Maddy screamed, tightening her seatbelt. Gabi undid hers and stood, bracing herself as she pushed her upper half up through the sunroof, lifting her arms and shouting. I turned in my seat to look at her, her long red hair streaming behind her. Rachel looked over at me, waiting for me to do something. I kept my eyes locked ahead, watching the countryside fly by. A blur. My heart beating so fast that it couldn't keep up with anything, not leaving space for anything. No space for the future and no space for the past. No space for anything but there and then, wondering if we'd live another second.

I stuck my hand out the window. The wind tore through my fingers. I let out a yell.

Rachel grinned.

*   *   *

She finally slowed down and pulled over next to an outlook. She didn't answer any of our questions, just bounded off down a small trail, forcing us to follow her blindly. When she stopped for good it was at a frail, rusted railing guarding anyone from stepping onto the rock ledge that jutted out over the lake below it. Next to it was a waterfall, ten times bigger and louder than the one in my secluded corner of the world. Like the wind, you could hardly hear anything over it. Rachel beckoned us closer to her.

"Wasn't that the game?" Maddy yelled.

Rachel shook her head, shoving a couple stones into her pocket and climbing out over the rail. "Grab three stones each," she shouted.

"Rach, that sign says not to climb over-" Maddy started.

Rachel grinned her mischievous, crooked grin, shaking her head and beaconing us to follow.

We did.

She held on to the rail on the other side, waiting for us. I could feel the spray from the waterfall against my skin.

"Rach, what are we doing?" I screamed over the rushing water.

"Playing the game," she yelled back, pushing her hair out of her face. She dug the rocks out of her pocket and held them up. "Each stone represents the thing you're most scared of, the thing you most regret, and the thing you wish most." She walked out to the edge of the rock, balancing carefully. "I'm scared of not being accepted!" and let the stone fly maybe twenty feet before hitting the lake surface. She held the next stone up to her face and whispered, then chucked it into the rushing water. I watched her mouth the final words and drop the stone at her feet, watching until it hit the surface and sunk beneath the water.

Gabi went next. Then Maddy. Their words got lost in the rushing water.

And then it was my turn.

I stepped closer to the edge, watching it get closer and closer. All it would take was one loose rock, one misstep, and I'd fall. All the way down.

I held up the first rock and rotated it in my fingers. I took a deep breath and shouted, "I'm scared of myself!"

I threw the stone as far as I could, watching it near the still surface, letting the words echo through the silent air. The stone hit the surface and a chorus of ripples expanded across it.

I held the second stone up to my face, noticing the way it sparkled in the light of the stars. "I regret all the minutes I've spent trying to change the past." I tossed it into the roaring water and watched it get sucked away, pushed down by the raging current, destroyed and buried so deep that it will be forgotten. I'll never see that stone again.

The last stone. I looked at it for a while, all the words I could say echoing through the air, drowned out by the water. "I wish I could have saved you."

Then I let it go.

I watched as it dropped, straight down, and entered the water below with a soundless splash. Sinking to the bottom like a stone. A stone weighted down by all the impossible hopes of a hopeless teenager.

I watched it sink into oblivion.

My foot slipped. A split second. And for that split second, I was falling.

In that split second, I didn't panic.

I thought, 'oh'.

Then Rachel's hand wrapped around my arm and steadied me. "Careful," she said, pulling me back to the fragile, rusted railing.

"Thanks," I stared at the edge, a couple small pieces of rock tumbling down, down, down...

Two seconds ago all I could think was, 'oh, thank god, now it's over'.

*　　*　　*

Dad is standing on the edge of the cliff, looking down at the water below him. He has his back to me, and I start, worried he's going to jump. But then I realize he's not going to. His stance is causal, his hands in his coat pocket, shoulders hunched as he takes off his army hat and drops it. The wind spins it on its way down to the water, and I watch as it hits the surface, causing an explosion of ripples.

Mom appears next to Dad and slips her hand into his. She puts her head on his shoulder and he wraps an arm around her. They don't turn around.

"Dad," I step forward, "Mom."

They don't turn around.

I say it again, louder.

They don't hear me.

I step up to them and look up into Dad's face. His eyes are sad, his expression hard. He pulls a flower out of his pocket.

A small, white flower.

He lets it go.

"What happened?" I ask, but I know they can't hear me. I don't know why.

"I miss her," Mom whispers.

"I miss her too," Dad says.

"Why? Why did she do it?"

"I don't know."

"I wish… I wish she was here."

"So do I. I wish I hadn't been gone for so long."

"She's- she grew up into an amazing young woman."

"I know, I know she has, because you raised her."

"She's- she was so smart."

"She always was."

"I know."

They stand in silence until Mom pulls a piece of paper out of her pocket.

"What's that?"

"Her- her goodbye."

"What does it say?"

Mom unfolds it and turns away as she hands it to him. I read it over his shoulder.

It looks like the piece of paper sitting on the desk in Dad's study. The same words I've written over thousands of pieces of paper ripped out of notebooks and pages and hidden under floorboards.

'I'm sorry.'

Turn it over, please let there be more than those two words. That can't be all. It can't be. How could it be? How could anyone just leave that?

"Is that it?"

Mom nods.

"I'm sorry you had to find it."

"We should have known. We should have done something."

"Don't blame yourself, we didn't know."

But I know Dad blames himself.

He blames himself for my death.

Because it's me they're mourning.

Because it's me who left that letter.

Because it's me who's dead.

Chapter Ten

"Do you want to run away?"

"What?" I rolled over in the grass to look at him. "Are you crazy?"

"Probably," he looked up at the sky, "but who isn't in this world."

"Someone who's sane."

"Funny."

"Mhmm."

"Seriously though," he ran his fingers through my hair, pulling me closer to him, "think about it."

"I did, I think it's crazy."

"I don't mean like *actually* running away, but we could take a road trip, we could camp out here over Thanksgiving break or something. Anything to just get away."

"Thanksgiving break isn't for almost a month."

"So, we still could."

"I still think it's crazy."

"Of course it's crazy."

"You're talking in circles."

"What better shape is there to talk it?"

"I don't know, how would you talk in triangles? Special right triangles, the 45-45-90 ones."

"You'd just keep saying the same things as always at the same times, the same angles, never changing. It'd get boring."

"As opposed to circles?"

"Well," his breath tickled my neck, "now with circles, you come back to the same point but always at different times and at different angles, different words, always the same point but always just different enough to confuse the living hell out of whoever you're talking to."

"Ah, yes, but you forget that *I* don't get confused."

"Of course you don't."

"No, I don't, and I'm always right, and I think you're crazy."

"Then I guess I'm crazy."

"Yup."

"What do you think about it, though? Other than it being crazy?"

"I don't know," I twisted my hair in my fingers.

"I don't know as in: I don't want to, or I don't know as in: that would be the best thing ever?"

"I don't know as in," I pulled away slightly, "I don't know."

He sighed sarcastically, rolling his eyes and chucking a fistful of grass at me. The blades fell in sporadic, gracefully spiraling loops until they finally collided with the ground.

"How did you find this place, anyway?"

He looked at me, shrugging, "I told you, my dad used to take me here."

"Used to?"

He looked away. "He's not around much anymore."

"Oh, sorry."

"Don't be."

I didn't say the words I wanted to. The insensitive words. The words that would shake the alignment of oblivion.

"How'd *you* find this place?" he said quickly.

"My car broke down."

"Yeah, but that's actually how you found it?"

I nodded.

"Nice."

"I guess."

"You know what we're going to do one day?"

"What?"

He nodded at the run down building and the cliff face, "We're going to climb up there."

I followed his line of sight, tracing the worn down path up the steps and over the ledge and the rusted railing up onto solid ground until the rock threatened to give way. "Why don't we just do it now?"

His eyebrows disappeared into his hair before he reached up and pushed it out of his eyes. "Now?"

"Yeah," I shrugged, pushing myself to my feet, "why not?"

"Why *now?*"

"Because," I took off toward the run down building, "why not now."

"We don't even know if the building is safe?"

"Guess we'll find out pretty quickly."

"But what if -"

"Live a little," I echoed Rachel's famous words. The philosophy of which she lived by.

I don't know how she lives like that. Planning, but altogether taking things as they come, learning as she goes, adjusting and replanning, no structure, no set definition or path to which her life belongs. She could do anything, and she'd be ready for it. She'd face it head on and never back down.

I wouldn't. I'd curl into a ball on the ground and wait for the storm to pass, wait for everything to go back to normal, and if it never went back to normal I'd never move. I need to a have a purpose, if there's no purpose, there's no reason. So what's the point?

"Live a little?"

"Live a little."

"Alright," he followed me, "fine."

I grinned, bounding off toward the run down building. It looked like it used to be a watermill or something, but with the rusted spires and rails, the miniature towers circling the top, it could have been a medieval castle. A castle now so run down and desolate that you'd never be able to see the magnificence it used to have, the magnificence hidden by years of neglect and despair.

No one realizes the magnitude of neglect and desolation until they look back at something like this, something so forgotten it could cease to exist, something so worn down that it is barely a relic of its time, the days when it was in its prime. The days before it could be so easily forgotten.

There are some things we remember.

But there are a lot of things we forget.

I glanced over my shoulder at Owen, and when I turned back to the building the castle was gone, and it returned to its place as an old, run down, forgotten mill.

I circled it until I spotted a railing guiding a steep, narrow staircase, and started up it. Owen hesitated a few feet behind me.

I just kept climbing.

Higher and higher and higher, until I couldn't look down and see the ground, just rotted boards and cracked, cobweb covered windows.

Relics of time. Relics of time lost in the ever turning relic of oblivion.

So many things confined to its consignment, circling in its loose, inescapable grasp, sucked in like the whirlpools we used to make in the pool as children. Growing stronger the more times you go around until you let go and get swept away, pulled with it.

When you finally allow yourself to be swept away into oblivion like all those who came before.

To become a relic of the past.

"Hey, wait up!" he called from somewhere below me.

"Move faster!" I called back. Then I kept going. My feet were a continuum of motion, unstoppable, chased forward by the whirlpool, fighting to keep ahead of the current, to keep from being lost in it.

The stairs beneath my feet threatened to give way, every second they creaked and protested, warning me to leave before I damaged the silent image of the past they have been frozen in.

"I'm moving faster! You're not slowing down!" his voice shocked the silence. The roof above me shook with the shockwaves of sound.

I flew past the dust covered objects of the past, my feet making no noise, my breathing light and inaudible.

I stumbled out into sunlight, and the relic was again that, a relic.

I stepped toward the small bridge creating an overpass above the water and ran my hands over the railing, rusted and creaking. My heart was pounding. I kicked off my shoes. I could hear his voice behind me, but I kept moving forward.

My toes made contact with the wood of the bridge, rotting and minutes from giving way under me. Then my heels were on it. And then I was on it. I stopped in the middle and turned out, facing the small world I left behind, the treetops becoming the horizon rather than the skyline, the water becoming a looking glass miles below me rather than an endless stretch of possibility, unexplored and unbroken. The waterfall under my feet roared, the spray jumping up to my face, my arms, my toes, my hair whipped backward by the wind.

I can't hear his voice over the water. I can't hear my breathing. I can't hear my thoughts.

I'm alone.

I'm completely alone.

The relics of the past lay behind me, hidden in dust and cobwebs and rotting away between rusted railings that could tear out of disintegrated walls at any moment.

The relics of the future lay behind doors hanging on their hinges, waterwheels that no longer follow their continuum; relics soon to be discovered and long to be disturbed.

A desolate wasteland of a world.

The faces reappeared, the ghosts returning from their hiding places. The thoughts creep back. I can hear my breathing over the wind and the water, steady and calm against my racing heartbeat.

With the deterioration of the wasteland, everything I fear most returns. With all of the thoughts, comes all of the sounds, comes all of the memories, comes all of the emotions, comes all of the pain.

But in that moment, that one moment, I had everything. And with everything, there was nothing.

Now, I have nothing, and with nothing I have everything.

I am standing. I am still standing. I have not fallen yet.

And in this moment, I'm on top of the world.

Everything the sun touches is mine. Everything the shadow touches is mine.

I'm king of the world.

*   *   *

Everyone has that fear. That one fear. The universal one. The one no one notices they have until they have to face it.

The fear of those relics. The fear of the headstones in a graveyard. The fear of those history books and images of the past.

The fear that they'll be one.

An unprecedented fear. A fear we should have gotten over by now. Everyone knows the truth. But everyone would rather be wrong than be right.

A lot of that fear centers around the unknown. The fact that we can't know what happens, if *anything* happens. We convince ourselves that something happens because no one wants to admit that they're living for nothing. That at the end of all those long, stressful years, there's nothing.

What would be the point of that?

Why should that just be the time you get?

There is no point. It shouldn't just be the time we get. But it is. All you have is your time now. There aren't any redo's. Just like there aren't any mistakes.

It's life.

What if there was a way to find out how your life would turn out? How would it affect your life? Would you spend your life trying to fix everything you screwed up in the past?

Some people call life fate. You can't mess with fate.

I would know.

I've tried too hard to change mine.

I've lost too many years trying to change mine, cursing the cards I was dealt.

Dad used to tell me stories of the Fates from Greek mythology, how they messed with hero's lives. They'd make them watch as they cut the string, make them wait for their life to end, to feel yourself leave your body, knowing that you couldn't do anything to stop it. Knowing that the last moment of your life would be spent thinking about what it would be like to die.

*   *   *

A dark cavern, dimly lit by candles lining the walls, casting a funereal, arcane glow around the room. The reek of eradication, heartache, desolation, apprehension, trepidation, fury, and iniquity filling every inch of the space. An imitation of hell. Where all the worst aspects of your life were released to reflect on each other as they passed through the gates of death, left to feel the worst of life before they left it behind.

Three young, beautiful women sit around the pool. Their skin glows, the color unidentifiable, always switching in the light. Their eyes are the only things that don't change color. They don't look at me.

But they know that I'm there.

Clotho, the one with violet eyes, sits spinning the thread, while Lachesis measures the length of each piece, her green eyes flickering around the room, glancing at the pool and the candles, picking and choosing life. The last, Atropos, holds the shears, switching them steadily between her hands. Her eyes are an unsettling gray, not light, but not black, just a cold, strong color. Her movements never falter, smooth and consistent, but never robotic. Never bordering on forced, but never becoming relaxed.

Creating life.

And destroying it.

"Cassandra James." Clotho whispers, never looking up from her work, never looking up at me. Her voice sends chills down my spine. "You wish to know your future."

I try to speak, but my voice doesn't work here.

"We can tell you your future," she continues, "but there is a price."

"Your price," she breathes, "is death, for knowing. But we can tell you, if you wish it."

I don't have an answer.

"First, you must know your past to know your future."

Lachesis speaks next, still watching the yarn spinning between her fingers. "You were born on the thirtieth of September," she says quietly, "you were the child of a man destined to die early in life. You were the child of a woman destined to meet despair and sorrow. You, child, were destined to both of your parents' destinies. I spun your life into being. I pitied you, because fate cannot be messed with once it has been dealt. So I gave you hope. I gave you light. And in that I gave you power."

The sharp snip from Atropos' scissors startles me as she begins to speak. "I cut your thread myself. Early sorrow and death lay ahead of you. You were too powerful. Power can't be contained forever.

"Power comes with a price too great to pay. I determined your end. Your mind will destroy you. Your soul will not survive your death. It will not exist. It will simply leave the existence it has known in this world and become nothing," whispers Atropos.

I'm choking on words, words that they don't let me speak. Words I will die without speaking.

"Your fate can be changed," she says in an even quieter voice. I can barely hear it, but it echoes through the cavern. "It can all end now, in our hands. You won't have to walk away knowing what will happen. You won't have to risk losing your soul. It will simply reside here with us, safe, away from you."

"Because, child," Clotho turns her head toward me, but doesn't look up, "the only demons that exist are the ones you have created in your head. The only monster, is you."

They look up. All three of them, their magnificent eyes shining, piercing me with creation, life, and destruction. The weaver of life, the determiner of life, and the ender of life. My heart stops. It no longer has a will to beat. It is too scared to dare move, to mess with the fate that has been decreed.

Atropos raises a single gold thread in her pale fingers. It glows bright as she slides it between the blades of her scissors.

She begins to close them.

I can't look away.

The thread drops into the black pool below them, and the water turns clear as it touches the surface, then black again as it disappears.

Chapter Eleven

"Any changes?"

"In what?" my eyebrows creased. Her hair was curled today, like she'd actually made an effort to look nice. Maybe she has a date later.

"Just in general, anything new?"

"So my grandmother hasn't been updating you recently?"

She shook her head, "No."

"And you haven't been updating her?"

"These sessions are confidential."

"Right. Unless I'm going to kill myself or something."

"Yes."

I studied her.

"Are you?"

"What, going to kill myself? Naw, not at the moment."

"Cassandra," she leaned forward. She has short hair, it stops right above her shoulders, and it's this really dark brown, not black, but almost. Her glasses were sitting on top of her head, and I could see her eyes more clearly. They're dark, like her hair, with this steady look, like she's trying to drill a hole through me to look at my mind, like she can see past all of my sarcastic comments and lies. It's a mask, but she wears it well.

"I'm *kidding*, you missed that moment by a couple years."

Her eyebrows shot upwards.

I shrugged, "Not relevant anymore."

"Do you remember why you wanted to?"

"To what, kill myself? No, not particularly, you know, it was just one of those random, sporadic times in my life, like when you get hungry in the middle of class. Not really a reason, just sort of happens."

She almost rolled her eyes, "*Cassandra.*"

"Look," I fixated on the ceiling, the hole from the bullet has stopped smoking and sits there, desolate and burned around the edges, "it's not relevant anymore. Doesn't matter. Doesn't exist. Barely even happened. How's your day been?"

She closed her notebook. "I'm going to ask you this again, why are you here?"

"I'm going to tell you what I told you last time, my mother wanted me to go."

"And I'm going to ask you this again, why?"

"Again, I don't know."

"I don't believe you," her dark eyes scanned my face, set in stone, cemented and unwavering.

I didn't say anything for a while, watching her watch me, waiting, calculating my next move. "You should."

She crossed her arms, not blinking, "And why's that?"

I didn't look away, "Because, I don't know."

"I still don't believe you."

"Why not? Aren't you supposed to listen to what I say and take my word?"

"Not exactly."

"Huh."

"Cassandra."

"Yes?"

She pulled the glasses off her head and held them in her right hand, swinging them back and forth, perfectly in time with the clock on the wall behind her.

I bit my lip.

She still didn't look away. Her face settled back into its cemented stature, eyebrows in their normal serious and calculating position.

I looked down.

"Cassandra?"

I bit down on the inside of my cheek. Hard.

"How has your day been so far?"

"Fine."

"What'd you do?"

"School."

"What did you do in school?"

"I had a couple tests, I hung out with a friend after school."

"Which friend?"

"Um... Owen."

"Owen?"

"Yeah," the corner of my mouth fluttered upwards for half a second. I glanced up at her, and her comportment changed, just barely, but just enough.

It shakes the comportment of oblivion.

*   *   *

School days couldn't go by slower. Sometimes it doesn't even look like the clock is moving, like it's stuck and time's stuck with it. Like today, when my English teacher decides to talk in shapes.

Well, she talks, and I add shapes to her words. Mostly 45-45-90 triangles. Her words go by unheard by the class, a jumble of useless information, most of which doesn't even correlate to the book we're discussing, or just points out obvious details that the ignorant kids don't notice.

"... This plays into your lives because it is important to remember that there is room to make mistakes in life, there's room to change your mind, life isn't a dress rehearsal..."

"Nope," a voice cut out over Ms. Hadley's. Everyone turned in their seats, scanning for the speaker. I found her, toward the back, her brown hair hanging down over her shoulders and her eyes shining. I don't remember seeing her before. "It's just the performance."

Even the kids who were asleep at their desks a minute ago are wide awake, staring back and forth between the girl and the teacher.

"Excuse me?" Ms. Hadley's eyes widened.

"In a dress rehearsal, you can make mistakes. You can redo the scene again and again and get it right the second time, even the third or fourth time, so you don't mess up in the performance. In the performance, you only get one shot to get it right. You can't make mistakes. You don't get to redo a scene or relive a second. If you screw up, you better hope you can improvise."

Ms. Hadley's eyes had narrowed into slits and she spoke through her teeth, "Class, meet our new student, Lily Peters."

I stared at her. She stood up and did a little bow, grinning. She had a sly smile, but not in a proud or stuck-up way, more so just a look that she knew what was going on in life, when no one else did.

A unique look, something no one else could ever pull off.

She caught me staring as she sat back down, and her smirk changed into a sort of sideways grin. I looked away quickly, shifting back to the front of the room. Ms. Hadley had returned to her monotone lecture, and I glanced over at Owen on the other side of the room. He looked between me and Lily, then shrugged at me, shaking his head.

I snuck a glance over my shoulder at the girl. She was looking back down at her book, but that sideways grin was still there, unchanged.

Her words made sense. More sense than anything Ms. Hadley had said all day. It's a concept that most people don't stop to think about, mostly because they don't want to, but also because it's just not something people stop to think about. No one wants to think that it takes so little to send them spiraling off the rails. It's like how even if we could go back and fix our mistakes, we wouldn't, because at the time they weren't mistakes, they were things we thought were right that we just got wrong.

"... Can anyone tell me about the character and her impact on the story?"

We are all our own heroine, our own main character. Our lives are written out for us, predetermined by a handful of factors that we don't have control over. The words defining us are written in pen, only able to be crossed out and never erased.

The bell rang, and Owen caught up to me before I left the room. "Well that was an interesting class," he said.

"Yeah," I scanned the crowd for the brown hair, but it was gone, "that's one way to put it."

"I thought Hadley was going to have a stroke," he grinned.

"Yeah, me too," I laughed, "I'll have to ask Rachel if she knows the girl or not."

"Why Rachel?"

"Because she literally knows *everyone*."

"Good point."

"Hey," he took one of my books, carrying it for me.

"Yeah?"

"What are you doing after school today."

"I- um, I- I don't know, why?"

"I was wondering if you wanted to run away with me."

"Um, I- I can't, sorry. I have to get home."

"Do you want to study together at least?"

"I can't, I really have to get home. Sorry."

"Okay, okay. Maybe tomorrow."

"Yeah, uh... maybe."

"Is everything okay?"

"Yeah, no, yeah of course."

"Okay, cool. I'll catch you after school for a minute?"

"Sure," I forced a smile, taking my book back, "bye."

"Bye! See you later."

"See you," I said quietly, turning away.

"Cass!" Rachel's voice cut its way over the crowds of people and she made her way toward me.

"Hey!"

"How's it going?"

I shrugged, "Pretty good."

"What are you doing after school?"

"I have to go home and study."

"Care if I come over?"

"Not at all, just don't bring a bunch of people," I grinned.

"I *won't*. That was literally once like, a year and a half ago."

"I'm aware, but you're *never* living that down."

She rolled her eyes, "Of course I'm not. Also, question."

"What?"

"How come you told Owen you couldn't hang out after school if you can hang out with me?"

"You *heard* that?"

"I hear *everything*, it's part of my gay powers."

"Of course."

"But anyway, answer the question."

"I don't know," I shifted the calc textbook in my arms, "I just didn't feel like spending time with him today."

"Everything okay with you two?"

"I mean, I guess, I don't know. Is anything ever *completely* okay with us?"

"Well, apparently you don't let anything ever be completely okay with you two."

"What's that supposed to mean?"

"Well, he seems to think everything's going well."

"Okay, I *hate* that he literally tells you *everything*, like what the hell, he needs to get his own best friend."

"We're friends and he knows both of us, so it's just easy for him to come to me. I'm sure he talks to his friends about it too, he just probably talks to them about stuff he'd like never talk to me about, thank god."

"Still."

She shrugged, "I guess it's a little weird, but we've been friends for a while. Just band-"

"Just band things, so I've heard."

"Cass, *come on.*"

"Sorry, I'm just still getting used to you knowing everything from him before I tell you."

"Well I clearly don't know *everything*, since you two have very different views on the goings on in your relationship."

"Okay, but it's not even a relationship right now."

"If you say so."

"It's *not.*"

"Mhmm."

"Can we like, not talk about this right now, it's *all* we ever talk about."

"Alright, sure. What do you want to talk about?"

"I have question," we headed down the hallway toward calc.

"Shoot."

"Do you know Lily Peters? The new girl?"

"Um," she thought for a second, "I think so, maybe. I have like one class with her. Why?"

"Just wondering. She almost gave Ms. Hadley a stroke in English today, it was kind of funny."

"Ooh, do tell."

I recounted the story and Rachel nodded, smirking. I stopped mid-sentence and gave her a look, "What's that for?"

"What's what for?"

"That look."

"I don't know what you're talking about."

"Sure you don't."

She grabbed my textbook and bounded off down the hallway, oblivious to the looks she got, making me run after her, muttering apologies and ducking through groups of people.

Rachel stopped outside of the classroom, and handed the book back to me.

"What was *that* for?"

"Fun, what else?"

"Um, humiliation?"

She shook her head at me, "You worry too much."

"I do not!"

"Yes, you do. You care too much about what other people think. It slows you down. It's senior year, you're never going to see any of those people *ever* again after this year, stop thinking about them."

"I'm not!"

She crossed her arms, tilting her head to the left to emphasize her skeptical expression, "I heard you apologizing to literally *everyone* you passed."

"I-" I stopped, making a face, "I *guess* you might be like seventy five percent right."

"More like one hundred percent."

"Eighty percent."

"Ninety nine percent."

"Ninety percent."

"Ninety eight."

"Ninety three."

"Ninety seven."

"Ninety five."

She paused for a second, "Fine, fine, yes, ninety five percent right, but regardless, I'm still more right than you are."

I rolled my eyes, "I was still five percent right."

"Yeah, and ninety five percent *wrong*."

"Wow, you can do *math*."

"Unfortunate that you can't."

"How so?"

"Ninety five is more than five, honey. Remember, greater than, the alligator sign, the alligator eats the ninety five over the five because it's *bigger*."

"Of course."

"But anyway, I'm right. Boils down to that."

"I suppose."

"It's *fact*."

"Uh, debatable, but why are you literally right like *all* of the time."

She held a finger to each side of her head, grinning maniacally. "It's my lesbian powers coming through. You should join my side of the pool, then you'll be right all the time, too."

"Sure, *that's* why."

"Hey, no one likes a homophobe."

"Um… and that makes me a homophobe, *how?*"

"You're questioning my lesbian powers, therefore you're questioning my abilities as a part of the LGBT community, and therefore you're suppressing me as a human being based on my sexual orientation, thus acting in a biased or judgmental way hence causing you to act in a homophobic manner and therefore making you a homophobe," she took a breath, "argument concluded."

"You," I said, "are the reason no one likes the gays."

Chapter Twelve

We never did run away.

I went back, by myself. I didn't tell anyone where I was going, I just sort of left. I wasn't planning to stay away long, just long enough to be somewhere where heavy footsteps wouldn't echo through the relics of oblivion.

It was colder. The air no longer tinted with the memory of warmth.

The first time I ran away, it was summer, so I figured I wouldn't have to deal with the cold for a while, and by the time I did, I figured I'd be dead. The second time, it was fall, during a school day. I just walked out of the building and didn't look back.

The first time it didn't take them long to find me, maybe a couple hours, three at best, because I turned around and went back to my backyard. They found me sitting on the swing, staring at the ground, kicking around the dirt pile beneath my feet. The second time took them a little longer, a week or so. I camped out in the woods near a gas station, but then the owner got suspicious and called the cops. I can't imagine what they must've thought, a dirty little teenager with scars running up and down her body, determined to escape the inescapable. Like every character in every cliché YA fiction book ever. To escape the inescapable, to deny the undeniable, to prove the unprovable, to imagine the unimaginable - all that shit. The little cliché plot holes I fell into, stumbled across, and eventually climbed out of.

That was a long time ago, now.

Back when I used to think everyone would be better off without me.

They still would be.

Some things never change. Some things like the paper shreds underneath floorboards. Some things like the paper clips and craft knives beneath paper shreds. Some things like the ghosts that sit around the room, the ones that I can still see when I let myself stop and look. They're hard to forget and easy to remember.

I sat down against a tree and scanned the horizon. It hasn't changed much, overall. The trees are the same trees, the run down structure is still the same run down structure, the sky is still the same sky.

The birds are gone.

But they all left a while ago.

A girl appears at the edge of the clearing, where the open grass melts into a tangle of trees. I watched her as she steps out into the open, looking around in awe, adjusting her backpack. She sees the water and drops the backpack, taking off across the grass. A boy steps out behind a tree after her, pushing aside branches. He watches her, grinning as she kicks off her shoes and runs across the sand, standing on the edge of the water. She makes her way around, and climbs out onto a rock, sitting with her toes skimming the surface. The boy makes his way toward her, sliding onto the rock next to her. I couldn't hear them. The water drowned out their voices, but I watched as she gave him a playful push, and he gave her a push, and then she shoved him off the rock and he grabbed her wrist, pulling her in after him.

Her head breaks the surface a couple seconds later, and they're both laughing, splashing each other.

They're so...

What's the word? The oh so simple, somehow forgotten word?

Happy.

They're so *happy.*

He floats on his back, and she sneaks up behind him, splashing water over his face and making him sputter and kick as he loses his balance and falls, tumbling, back into the depths of the water.

I watched them. From my tree, the one that sat alone in the middle of the clearing, maybe seven feet away from the others. I watched as they laughed, smiled, screamed, yelled.

So many realities. Realistic realities. Realities that, for some, are real, and for others, are not. Realities that remain a reality in a faded, blurry picture somewhere in the distance. Realities that remain falsities. Long forgotten fantasies, occasionally summoned by the mind to mull over the possible, and the impossible, the plausible, the implausible, the imaginable, and the unimaginable.

The points of which we hit on our way around the loop of oblivion. Loops that spiral into other loops, and twist into more loops, and double back to their original loop along their path. The predetermined line down which we all wander for the entirety of our predetermined lives.

Lives full of realities.

My reality stands in front of me, screaming, splashing, laughing, happy.

My blurred reality standing on the horizon, turned around to look at me, giving me a long, calculating look, beckoning for me to come, gesturing for me to follow, smiling, then frowning, raising an eyebrow, studying me, questioning me, and then shrugging, grinning, and turning away, toward the distance, walking forward into the blur that remains as a gray sky that leads to nothing.

Me, sitting there, against the tree, alone in a world in which so many are alone. Alone in a world in which everyone is alone.

Everyone is alone surrounded by a world of other people who are alone.

Everyone alone in a world of people.

Everyone alone with others who are alone.

People who are alone standing side by side with others who stand alone.

It's ironic. It really is.

Just like the fact that I have everything I want right in front of me, and I don't want any of it.

They sit together at the edge of the water. The boy keeps pushing his blond curls out of his face, the girl glancing over at him once in a while. Their lips move in conversation, but I can't hear the words they speak to each other. They get swept away into the current, traveling somewhere downstream where they will be reencountered by someone in another time or another life, traveling down a parallel path.

The girl looks down at her feet, and the boy leans back, watching her as she grins. She runs her hand through her hair, laughing at something he said.

Them, those two, with troubles so minuscule that no one would question the sanity of their unstable minds.

The boy stands, helping the girl to her feet. After a second, her face shifts, just barely, and she takes a step back, hands curling into fists that she steadies at her sides, concealing the slight quiver in her fingers.

The boy turns away from her, saying something quirky or witty, and she stares after him for a second, eyes lost in some distant reality. Then they readjust, set themselves on the water, following the ripples expanding into nothing, and then on him, and she follows him, tracing his footsteps that linger in the mixture of dirt and sand beneath their feet.

*   *   *

I fell asleep against the tree. When I opened my eyes in the morning, the clearing was quiet and undisturbed. The two kids are sitting down by the water, the girl with her head on his shoulder, still asleep. But he was awake, staring out across the water.

The few remaining birds sang in the quiet morning as the sunrise broke out against the horizon, splitting the world into a million different colors.

The boy looks down at the girl and smiles. He leans down and presses his lips gently to her forehead. She stirs, opening her eyes slowly.

"Hey," he says.

I can hear them, now.

"Hi," she grins.

"How'd you sleep?"

"Okay," she sits up, rubbing her eyes and pushing her hair out of her face. "How long have you been awake?"

He shrugs, "I don't know."

"You should have woken me up!"

"You looked too peaceful to wake," he laughs.

"Sure, whatever you say."

"Hey, I'm always right."

"No, *I'm* always right."

"We'll see."

"What's that supposed to mean?"

He stands up, and she scrambles to her feet after him. "We have things to do, today."

"Like what?"

"I, for one, am climbing to the top," he gestures to the cliff face.

"Are you crazy?" she asks, gaping at the top edge of the cliff.

"Yeah, aren't you?"

"Yeah, but not *that* crazy."

"There is no end to crazy. Crazy is infinite. You're as crazy as you let yourself be. There's no limit."

"If you say so."

He pulls a rope out of his bag and slings it over his shoulder. "You coming? Or are you going to watch?"

"I-" she hesitates, "I'll watch."

"Suit yourself," he shrugs and makes his way toward the cliff face. She sits down on a rock on the water's edge and watches him. She looks away as he begins to climb, but I watched. I watched every steady movement upward, I saw every loss of footing, every scare and unsteadiness in him until he finally climbed over the edge, onto the top, and stood up, yelling in triumph. He disappears for a second, then reappears, holding the rope. He tosses is down and calls, "Come on!"

The girl runs to the cliff, looking up at him. "Seriously?"

"Yeah, come on! It's safe!"

She wraps her hands around the rope, feeling the tension when she puts her weight on it. And slowly, she climbs it. The boy helps her climb over the top. She turns to face me, and the rest of the world, looking out over the treetops.

"Wow," she whispers.

*   *   *

The boy wanders away after a while, off on some other adventure while the girl stands by the edge of the cliff, staring off into oblivion.

Then her face changes, her expression shifting from one of deep contemplation to one of masked horror.

"*Jump,*" a voice told her. It echoed through my ears as though I were her, as though my thoughts were her thoughts, her demons my demons, my ghosts her ghosts.

I watched her as she whispers, "What?"

"*Jump. It's easy. It's right there. All you've ever wanted, it's there. It's right in front of you. All you have to do is jump.*"

"No."

"*Jump.*"

"*No.*"

"*Do it.*"

She closes her eyes.

She takes a small step forward.

"*Jump.*"

She takes another step.

"Don't do it," I whispered, the words barely audible over the voices.

"*Jump.*"

One foot leaves solid ground.

A hand wraps around her wrist and pulls her backward. He holds her tightly as she struggles, trying to take that one step that would send her tumbling down, down, down...

I saw him speaking, but I couldn't hear them anymore. Blood rushing in my ears, pounding in my skull. My vision went blurry.

I looked down, watching my hands twist.

When I looked back up, they were gone. Both of them. No where to be found. As if they both jumped in that brief window of time, and disappeared into the undisturbed water in front of me.

*   *   *

I went to Rachel's house Saturday night, because I didn't feel like going home. She looked surprised when she opened the door, "Cass?"

"Hey," I muttered, "can I come in?"

"Yeah! Of course, Gabi and Maddy are here. We couldn't get ahold of you so-"

"Yeah, I know, I've had my phone off."

I must've looked like shit.

"They're in the basement, if you want to go down too."

"Yeah, sure, I'll meet you down there. Can I use your bathroom real quick?"

"Yeah, of course."

"Thanks."

I ignored her questioning look and closed the bathroom door behind me. It took me a while to look in the mirror.

A dirt stained face. Unkempt, knotted hair.

I looked like I'd slept in the woods for days.

I did the best to make myself presentable, but I couldn't wash away the creases between my eyebrows, the hard, cold look, and the eyes that showed no emotion. My array of masks seemed to have disappeared. Usually there were many masks I could wear, different personas I could become, but they're all gone, now.

They must have fallen out of my back pocket. Maybe someone else will pick them up, or maybe I'll stumble across them sometime.

I made my way downstairs and sat down on the couch next to Rachel, who gave me a long look, but didn't say anything regarding my appearance.

"Where've you been all weekend?" she asked after a while, resting her head on my shoulder. Maddy and Gabi were playing *Just Dance*, which they both sucked at. It was actually pretty funny. Maddy kept hitting Gabi and Gabi kept screaming at her.

I shrugged, "Just out."

"Out where?"

"Driving."

"Anywhere specific?"

I shook my head, "Not really."

"Spontaneity, I like that."

"Haha, yeah."

"Alright, I'm going to go get some fresh air and leave these two kids alone, the screaming is giving me a headache."

"Sorry!" Maddy called over her shoulder.

"Not my fault!" said Gabi.

"You coming?" Rachel paused.

"Yeah, I'm coming," I followed her upstairs. "Where are we going?"

"The roof."

"Excuse me?"

"You haven't been up there before?"

"Um.... *no*."

"Huh, alright. Well, yeah. That's where we're going. And don't look at me like that, it's safe! I've been up there a ton of times."

"That doesn't mean it's *safe*," I muttered.

"I heard that!"

"Yeah, I *know*."

She closed her bedroom door behind us and opened the skylight, hoisting herself up through it. She helped me through. "See! Perfectly safe."

I sat down next to her, "I guess."

The night was cool, the stars staring back at us from their place in the dark sky. We didn't say anything for a while.

A streetlight flickered a couple houses down.

"You know what's crazy?" she turned to look at me.

"What?"

"We're seniors. I mean, we really aren't kids anymore. It's kind of weird when you stop to think about it. We always knew it was coming, but now that it came I think I want to go back to when it hadn't. I miss being able to just fool around."

"Yeah."

"Like, I don't think anyone really appreciates being a child until they have to deal with being an adult, and at that point, it's too late. It's just crazy how literally *everyone* tells you not to rush childhood, but everyone does anyway. And it sucks. It fucking sucks," she pushed her hair out of her face.

"Yeah, I know," I let out a deep breath, "it really fucking does."

The truth is, we stopped being children a long time ago. Once the world began to shape us into the monsters we've become. Each of us hiding evil in our different ways, hiding the monstrosity of a world destroyed by chaos and violence and hate.

A child who has not yet been shaped by the world will never know prejudice or judgement, will never look at another person with the same hatred that you see in adults.

A child is not born with hate. Or prejudice. Or evil. The world holds every child's future in its hands, and we continue to shape children with the same hatred that shaped us.

We all stopped being children a long time ago.

But it doesn't change the fact that we all wish we still were. That we all wish we were still those kids, the ones who played pretend on the playground, performed fake marriages with dresses made out of toilet paper stolen from the bathroom, the ones who made up stupid nicknames we wish they'd never made up, the ones who thought the world was made for them, that they could do anything.

The ones that watched the world become a war-zone and thought they would be the ones to escape the draft.

One of the great ironies of life.

It's funny how, when we're children, all we want to do is grow up, but once we grow up, all we want to do is be children.

One great irony, alright.

Chapter Thirteen

Time is just a construct.

Days slowly turned into weeks, and weeks into months, until the months melted back into weeks, and the weeks into days, and the days into hours, and the hours into minutes, and the minutes into seconds, and the seconds into milliseconds, until time no longer existed and there remained fragmented images, strung together in a succession called time. Until one image was all that could be seen, and time froze, still and immobile in the backdrop of eternity.

Time is just a construct.

A construct of the human mind that allows it to comprehend the ever-turning Earth and the continuous rise and fall of the sun. Something to give us something to live for in our short-lived lives.

Time is a just a construct.

A construct that we build up only to be knocked down. Our record of time grows every second in which we live, only to be set on some dust filled shelf the second in which we stop living. The last second in which the book is shut and signed, sealed, and never opened again.

CONSIGNED TO OBLIVION

There are billions of books on the shelf, all of which have never been reopened, never read. Minutes upon minutes that are now trivial, their derisory lives, the ones they suffered through, worked through, endured, are insignificant in the big picture, now resting on that shelf, dust creeping onto the pages that they thought they would never become a part of. The hardcover novels filled with words and memories and thoughts, every second of their respective lives. Ended, done, gone. Perhaps ended in the middle of a sentence, at the beginning of a thought, or with a period at the end, finished and complete. It's really just based on whether or not you are lucky enough to have an ending, or unlucky enough to die with your life unfinished.

Some of the stories overlap, the characters in the novels surrounding each other jumping between the pages to fulfill their short lived chapters of someone else's novel. The number of pages of each a different number, some shorter, only novellas, some longer, an imitation of *War and Peace* within a shorter construct of time. Some with so few pages simply because of the magnitude of insignificance, the lives filled with so few things that there were hardly any words and memories and thoughts to be recorded. Someone who lived a much shorter life could have a much longer story than someone who lived a much longer life, depending on how many words and memories and thoughts filled their pages, regardless of time.

The length of the novel is not measured by the number of minutes recorded, but the quality of the minutes recorded, the momentousness, the magnitude, the raw quality of the words and memories and thoughts.

Time is just a construct. A way to count the days that go by. A way to place a limit on the number of days that we live to see. A way to provide us with a sense of urgency. A way to stress that there is never enough time.

But time is just a construct. There is no way to run out of a construct because we are the ones that build them. We built time. We built the very essence that made time. We built the construct. And that construct was of time. And that construct is one we continue to build.

We built time.

There is no reason someone should not have enough time should they spend it in a way that satisfies them and makes their minutes worth while.

Time is just a construct.

We're all running out of time.

"Cassandra?"

I looked up the front of the classroom, "Yes?"

"Are you with us?"

My eyes adjusted to the light, "Yes."

"Alright," Ms. Hadley glanced down at the book in her hands, "would you, being that you are with us, be able to tell us a bit about the meaning behind the book? Take it to the next level. What did the author mean to express through the characters and their actions?"

I looked down at the book open on the desk in front of me. *Fahrenheit 451*. An easy read. Something we'd read in tenth grade. Something easy to keep us doing work until winter break.

"Well," I thought for a second, "it reflects our society, and I feel that it highlights overinflated intelligence. People thinking that they're smarter than they are. There is a difference between intelligence and knowledge. And knowledge is not intelligence. Someone who has a lot of knowledge is not necessarily more intelligent than someone of greater intellect. Bradbury-"

"But wouldn't you say that someone of greater intellect is not necessarily smarter than someone with more knowledge?" a voice cut across me.

I turned around. "Yes, well, that could be so. But someone with greater intellect, regardless of their knowledge, is able to better differentiate between those things that would confuse others, things that appear simple, however they understand to a greater extent. A person with greater intellect is better able to react well, as they can make more acute decisions regarding morals."

"Yes, true, however, a person with more knowledge is likely to be able to act correctly because they will know from the experience of others, rather than relying on their own experiences."

Ms. Hadley started, "I'd like it if Ms. James could finish her response-"

"Yes, I suppose that is so. But in this book, Bradbury uses Montag to show that unbridled determination, coupled with foolishness, results in irrational, impulsive actions."

"That, as well, is true," her eyes were alight, a fire burning in them, but not one of destruction, like the ones seen within the pages underneath our fingers. "Would you say that Beatty possessed intellect?"

"I think I would say that he did, in the way Bradbury wrote him, he would have to have. He knew what he was doing the entire time. By planting ideas in Montag's head, by quoting books at him, and then by dying, which Bradbury later said that he meant to do, he instilled rebellion within the characters, despite his position as an authority figure. His actions were always planned out, careful, and considerate, whereas Montag leaped at the chance to act without thinking through his actions."

"And why does Montag's overinflated intelligence hurt the world around him? Wouldn't an overinflated intelligence be better than no intelligence whatsoever?"

"No, because, as in Montag's case, when he believed himself more intelligent than those around him, he found himself in a power role, and believed that he should rightfully be there. Given authority, he let his actions run wild, believing them to be correct, regardless of anything Faber, who, clearly, was more intelligent than himself, said. This mimics our own society in the sense that everyone believes themselves to be smarter than everyone else, and in believing this they believe that they themselves are better. That they themselves can impact the world, and that their words and actions alone are undeniably correct. Anyone who questions them is wrong. When one thinks such things, they cannot scrutinize and correct their own actions because they cannot identify what is wrong with them."

"Agreed. But then, where does that leave us in terms of knowledge versus intellect?"

"I think," I said slowly, eyeing her carefully, "that we will have to come to a consensus as to the fact that knowledge and intellect vary, the way in which they vary is, at this point, unclear, however one that possessed both knowledge and intellect would be more adept than someone who possessed only one, no matter in which amount."

A small, sideways smile spread across her face as she watched me, never breaking eye contact, blue eyes ablaze. "I think that we have come to a consensus."

Ms. Hadley looked back and forth between us, eyebrows creased, while the rest of the class slowly faded back into the picture, a sea of faces with all eyes set on us. No one said anything. Not a word. Some appeared to be attempting to process the conversation. Most just stared, open mouthed, until Ms. Hadley cleared her throat and said, in a quiet voice, "Um... alright, class. Finish the book if you'd like too, and please start Jane Eyre for next class. Have a good break!"

The class returned to their notebooks and books, packing them up. They're never going to remember the conversation, or this class.

She looked down, still grinning, and pushed her brown hair out of her face. I tore my eyes away when she glanced back up and caught me staring.

I packed up my stuff as the bell rang.

The rest of the class may not remember.

But we will.

I smiled.

*   *   *

"Well, that was an interesting class," Owen raised an eyebrow at me, wrapping his arm around me as we walked down the hallway.

"Yes, I suppose it was," I shrugged.

"You *suppose*?"

"Yes," I smiled up at him, "I *suppose*."

"I didn't know you talked to Lily that much."

I shrugged again, "I don't. That was the first conversation we've ever had. If you could call it a conversation."

"You've never had a *conversation* before and you have a full out, mind boggling discussion about knowledge and intelligence?"

"Pretty much. Weird, I guess."

"Very weird."

"She's smart," I adjusted my backpack on my shoulders, "like *really* smart."

"Yeah, and so are you."

"I'm not that smart.

"Okay, but *are*."

"Eh."

"Hey, sorry to interrupt you two, but can I steal Cass for a second?" Rachel pushed between us.

"A second?" Owen asked.

"Well, no, more like an hour and a half, plus two minutes, but I'm going to steal her anyway."

"An hour and a half?"

"We have class together," I said.

"Right."

"I'm stealing her now," Rachel grabbed my arm, tugging me away.

"Alright," he laughed, "I'll see you after school?" he said to me.

"Yeah!" I waved as Rachel pulled me back into the sea of people. "Rach, what's this about?"

"Nothing, I didn't want to walk to class by myself, *again*."

"Hey, sorry, you're the one that *set us up* and then yelled at me for not spending enough time with him."

"Yes, yes, I know. I'm happy for you, but I need my best friend every now and then."

"Alright, *sorry*."

"Anyway, I heard about your English class."

"Already? From who?"

She shook her head, "Doesn't matter, anyway, is it true?"

"Is *what* true?"

"That you and Lily had a like ten minute conversation about the book?"

"Sort of."

"What do you mean, *sort* of?"

"It wasn't ten minutes, for starters, and it wasn't really a big deal!"

"Sure," she rolled her eyes, "*sure*."

"What's *that* supposed to mean?"

"Nothing, don't worry about it."

"Rach!"

"What are you doing tomorrow night?"

"Nothing, why?"

"Because," she turned the corner, "I'm having a little party at my house, just girls, not too many people. You in?"

"Just girls?"

"Oh, come on, it's not like that."

"Mhmm."

"It's not! Anyway, you in or not?"

"Yes, Rach," I laughed, "I'm in."

"Good."

"Rach, Cass!" Maddy jumped on me, energetic as usual.

"Maddy!"

"Sorry, Cass. It's last period! Last class for two weeks, I'm so happy!"

"Haha, me too, Maddy," Rach grabbed her shoulder and pulled her away from me, keeping her grounded. "I'm going to fail this test, though."

Maddy's face dropped like a penny off the Empire State Building. "We... we have a... we have a test?"

"Yeah, what, didn't you study? I heard it's awful," Rachel winked at me.

"Noooo, of course I didn't study, I didn't know it existed! Oh my god, I'm going to fail. I have such a good grade in this class. Oh my god, Rach, how could you not tell me we had a *test*? Usually you bring it up before hand, or we study together, or... oh my god. Oh my *god*. I'm going to fail. I'm going to fail, and then I'm not going to get into college, and then I'm not going to get a job, and then I'm going to work in some supermarket or trash dump for the rest of my life. What's the test on?"

"How much you've learned over the past, however many years, of knowing me," Rach grinned, "which, clearly, isn't much. So you might *actually* fail it."

"What?" Maddy looked back and forth between us, then a look of realization passed over her face. "Oh. My. God. Rachel. I'm going to *kill* you."

"Go ahead," Rachel walked backwards, facing her, "I *dare* you."

"I'm going to *kill* you!"

"It would be greatly appreciated if you would."

"Rachel!" Maddy groaned, "you just about gave me a panic attack."

"Serves you right, you worry about tests and stuff too much. *Live* a little."

"Okay, I get it, but that was cruel. I was up all night working on an English paper," she rubbed her eyes.

"Sucks for both of you, that we actually *do* have a test today," I pushed open the classroom door. They both gaped at me. I shrugged.

"Mr. Jordan!" Maddy said, "do we have a test today?"

He looked up at her over the edge of his glasses, "What, are you surprised?"

Maddy's face fell and Rachel hesitated behind her, "Are... are you serious?"

He stood up and tucked his glasses away in his shirt pocket, "No, I'm just kidding. There's no test."

"Oh my god," Maddy gasped, "thank god."

He chuckled, then looked over at me, "That was a cruel trick."

"They had it coming," I grinned as Rachel shoved me, glaring.

"Cass, I swear to *god*," Maddy took a seat in the back and massaged the sides of her head, taking deep breaths.

"I can play tricks, too," I laughed.

"Look at that, the cat has claws," Rachel studied me, her glare fading into a satisfied little grin.

"Grr," I curled my fingers at her.

"I'll be sure to tell Owen how intimidating his girlfriend is."

I choked on my laughter, "Um, *girlfriend*?"

"What, are you guys not 'official'?" she made quotations around the word 'official'.

"*No*, for your information, we are not 'official'," I mocked her.

She shrugged, "If you say so."

"Why, does *he* think we are?"

"Well, considering it's been a couple months, I'm going to let you answer that."

"Oh *god*," I buried my face in my hands, "lovely."

"Aren't you guys basically official?" Maddy asked.

"I don't know, man, I really don't."

"Think that's something you might want to figure out," Rachel made an 'I told you so' face.

'Fuck off,' I mouthed at her.

"Fine, fine," she held her hands up in surrender, "just saying."

*   *   *

There's a picture in the bottom of the middle left drawer of my desk. It's buried underneath notebooks and books and pencils and pens and other pictures. I haven't looked at it in a while. I remember all the details just the same as if I'd looked at it yesterday. It's from about six or seven years ago, I can't remember, now. In it, there's a girl and a boy. They're about ten or eleven, arms around each other. They're both smiling.

"Cassandra, you haven't been here in a while. You keep missing appointments. How have you been?"

They're both smiling, with their innocent little faces, messy hair, carefree shoulders.

"Okay."

It's the middle of summer, and her hair is still a little wet, while his has already dried. Their clothes are soaked, water guns lay forgotten behind them, along with all the games they used to make up and play, switching the rules, screaming, adding new devices, laughing.

"Why just okay?"

The sun's out, even though it's not as bright in the picture as it was in real life

"Because it would be a lie if I said great, because I'm never great. And I'm not terrible. And I always say fine, so I figured I'd switch it up a bit."

There's a pool in the corner of the picture, with a couple floaties in it.

"Why do you think you're never 'great'?"

The grass is green, dying in a couple patches, sure, but green, nonetheless.

"I mean, look at my life, does it look like any part of it was destined to be 'great'?"

The sky is blue. I mean a beautiful blue. Not pale blue, or too blue, but just right, so perfect that even the picture can't mar its image.

"But don't you think that everyone has a chance to have a 'great' life, or at least great parts of it? I don't think anyone is 'destined' to have a bad life."

They were so young, then.

"I don't know."

They were so innocent.

"Can you name five good things about your life, right now?"

They were so... carefree.

"I can name fifty bad things."

They were so... hopeful.

"Let's focus on the five good things, okay?"

They were so... so...

I blew a strand of hair out of my face.

I don't know.

"Five things, that's it, okay?"

There aren't really any words to describe what they were.

"Okay."

I mean, how can you describe something like that, something so pure and untouched that to add a description to it would be to tarnish its image?

"One. My friends."

You can't.

"Two. School. My grades."

I haven't looked at the picture in a long time. Years, even.

"Three. It's winter break, I guess. School's halfway done."

I remember every detail.

"Four. Hiking." *The world I run away to when I can't face reality.*

Every detail hidden in the faded polaroid.

"Five. My... my boyfriend." *Conversations in class.*

The faded polaroid hidden in the bottom of the middle left drawer of my desk.

"Good, see? You named five good things about or in your life!"

I dug it out when I got home. I picked it up, gingerly, and held it in my hands. It was so fragile that a single misstep could shatter it.

"*I guess.*"

I couldn't decide what to do with it. I just sort of rotated it in my fingers for a while, studying all the details.

How well did she really know him? How well do I know him now? What secrets is he hiding?

No one is devoid of secrets, as much as we like to think that we are.

"Five good things are better than fifty bad things. Remember that. The good always outweighs the bad. Five good things are better than fifty bad things."

Eventually, I tossed it back into the drawer and shut it. In a cliché book, or movie, the protagonist would have laid back on their bed and held the picture to their chest, mulling over all the memories that came with it.

It's stupid. Mulling over all the memories. They're memories for a reason. They don't need to be mulled over.

"Okay."

So back in the drawer they go.

Chapter Fourteen

"Hey," he whispered.

"Hey," I said.

"So," he kissed me, "we could go back to my place."

"Are your parents home?"

"No."

I kissed him back, "Okay," I said against his lips.

"Okay," I felt him smile.

I'm not sure what happened. If it's all the stress finally catching up to me and fogging up my decisions, or I actually have gotten comfortable with my predicament, or I might actually be sure about him. But whatever it is, whatever happened, this sure did.

Maybe it was guilt for neglecting him.

Maybe it was reassurance.

Maybe it was to take my mind off of her. To keep me from replaying our conversation over and over again in my head.

Maybe it was because I loved him.

No matter what was true and what was actually a maybe, *it* wasn't a maybe.

It happened.

He didn't even initiate any of it. It was me. All of it. I sort of attacked him when we got into his car, I jumped him, threw myself at him, and just starting kissing him.

I kissed him like there was no tomorrow.

Like all the cliché shit you see in books and movies.

So we went back to his house.

We pulled each other into his room.

I actually hadn't been in it for years. It changed, a lot. It changed like he did.

I guess that's to be expected. My room changed a lot. I cleaned out most of the things from my childhood and replaced them with books and pictures and college pennants. There's still a shelf, though, dedicated to my childhood. Only a couple things on it. Things from my favorite childhood books, including those favorite books, a stuffed animal I used to love, and a picture of my great grandfather holding me as a baby. A couple pictures of my friends and I from when I was little.

Other than that, most of it's gone.

His room is pretty much the same, but a little more of his childhood remained. He probably hadn't thought about it or just hadn't felt like finding other places for it.

We fell onto his bed. He kept kissing me.

"So, where were we?"

"I believe," I wrapped my arms around his neck, tangling my fingers in his hair, "somewhere around here."

He laughed against my lips.

If I were watching this in a book or movie, I would have gagged. But I kind of stopped thinking. I stopped caring.

Maybe it was guilt. Maybe it was reassurance. Maybe it was a distraction.

Maybe it was because I really did love him.

He unbuttoned my shirt, button by button.

I don't really know. I've never known what love is, but if it was love, I thought it would feel different.

I thought that, if it was love, it wouldn't have been a maybe. It wouldn't have been a question. I would just know.

What did I know? Of all things, what did I know of love?

For all I knew, it didn't even exist. Just another construct.

I think he said 'I love you', after. I didn't say it back, if he did. He probably just assumed I didn't hear him. Which, I didn't.

Anyone else would assume we were madly in love, high school sweethearts, etc.

I think I love him.

Shouldn't I love him?

I got up and pulled my top back on, re-buttoning it.

"Where are you going?" he asked.

"I'm going to go take a shower, I'll be right back."

"Okay. Hey, do you want me to order take out or something?"

"Yeah, that'd be great."

"Chinese okay?"

"Yeah," I nodded, then made my way to the bathroom.

I turned on the shower and stood outside it, staring at my reflection in the mirror. My blank, automaton face. Dead, unseeing eyes. I forced myself to smile. My features lit up, coming to life in the intake of a single breath, for a single moment until the breath was exhaled.

I love him.

Rachel's questioning look appears in front of me, eyebrows raised in an, 'I don't believe you, but if you say so,' look. I bit my lip and pulled my hair up into a loose bun, humming to drown out the thoughts that crowd my mind.

I leaned in closer to my reflection, staring into the eyes that stared back at me. I whispered "stop," and the girl whispers "stop" back at me.

"I'm trying," I said, "but I don't know what I'm running from. So how can I stop?" My feet move of their own accord, now. My heart beats in its own succinct rhythm of its own fashion.

"Figure it out," she whispers back.

I turned my back on her. I stepped into the shower, letting the warm water rain down on me. Then I turned it all the way down to freezing. I shivered, letting it wash away the demons, letting it drown out the thoughts, letting it do the work I've been trying to do. It's only a temporary fix, god don't I know it. If I could stay here forever, I would. But even then, it's only a temporary fix. Some things can go away in certain situations. But if it's still there when you step out of those situations, it's not fixed. I could stay under the water forever and forget that it's there, but it's not gone. It's temporary. Because as soon as I turn off the water and step out onto dry land, it'll all come back.

This is a temporary fix to something that was once a temporary problem.

It's funny how temporary problems eventually stop being temporary.

* * *

"Hey," he places a hand on her shoulder and sits down next to her.

"Hey," she looks over at him. The wind is making his hair stick up, and his green eyes are bright in the cold morning.

"Did you sleep at all?"

She shrugs.

His smile fades a little.

He's worried about her.

She wishes he wasn't.

She stands up and looks out across the water. The wind is forming ripples on the surface and every ripple makes her heart beat faster.

She doesn't know why.

She wants the demons to leave.

She wants them gone.

She hates being a shell of a person, never knowing why or how she feels that way, never feeling like she should be as sick of her life as she is.

There are people who have it so much worse.

She feels so selfish sometimes.

Running away was selfish. She hurt everyone she left behind.

And she doesn't even care.

"*Why should you, they didn't.*" The demons whisper.

But they did.

She knows they did.

They're gone.

The demons, they've fled.

She looks up. The last star has disappeared. For a second, it's just her. He isn't there. The demons aren't there. The angels aren't there.

It's just her.

I wish I could be her, running away to another world to escape the one she's in. I guess that's why she appears every now and then. She's a way to escape. A way to escape within an escapee. She's another world. She engulfs the world she's in and it becomes her. Running away to another world when yours becomes unlivable. Some of us just have to stay where we are and tough it out. We don't get to run away. We don't get to escape our reality. We aren't as lucky as she is.

I wish that could be me. It used to be, in a sordid, unequal way. I was almost her. But not quite. I never got my fairytale. My perfect escape into a perfect reality. A reality where I could learn how to just be me. A reality I still haven't found, anywhere.

A face that I look in the mirror and actually recognize? I haven't seen that yet. I just see her, when I look in the mirror. The face of a worn out seventeen year old doing her best to walk through a life that just keeps beating her down, over and over again, wondering when she's going to reach the top of the cliff and look down and realize that she's conquered it all. That her battles, her struggles, they're all over, and the land she's standing on was worth it, was worth it all, and she has no regrets, no 'what ifs', because she knows that she is standing where she was built to stand. The world is hers, spread out beneath her. She could do anything, because she has conquered everything. You can see it in her eyes, they shine, they sparkle, they're proud, they're brave. They've endured hardships and made it out the other side. She's made it to the other side, scarred, bruised, and broken, but still standing.

The face in the mirror that wishes to be all those things, but will never be any of them.

That's the face I see.

* * *

"How's your food?" Owen looked over at me.

"Good," I said, not taking my eyes off my fried rice. "How's yours?"

"Good," he eyed me timidly, "you haven't said much, is everything okay?"

"Yeah, yeah!" I looked up and smiled, "everything's great!"

"Alright, good," he grinned.

I picked up my phone, pretending to check a message, and texted Rachel.

Me: Get me out of here.

She responded a couple minutes later.

Rachel: Where are you?"

Me: *His* house

Rachel: Oh?

Me: Stoppp and get me out of here

Rachel: Cass, have *fun*, okay? You like him! What's the big deal. You don't have to do shit, just have fun

Me: Ugh, *Rach*

Rachel: Unless you already did shit...

Me: Rachel!

Rachel: Ooooooh, how was it?

Me: Rachhhhh

Rachel: You can't just disappear on him if you want to have any type of relationship after this

Me: I guess

Rachel: Try to make things less awkward by, um, I don't know, *talking* and *not* texting me.

Me: Ugh, *fine*, but I'm blaming you if shit goes down

Rachel: Oh hun, shit already went down, and that was *allll* on you

Me: Shut up

Rachel: Stop texting me!

Me: Fineee

Rachel: I'm going to stop responding now, okay? Okay. Love you, *byee*

Me: Oh my god Rach

Rachel:

Radio silence.

I turned my phone off and bit the inside of my lip. I looked back up at Owen and smiled, "Do you want to watch a movie or something?"

His face lit up, "Yeah, sure!"

I got up and picked a DVD from the pile next to the TV, "We're watching 'The Breakfast Club', and I don't care what you say."

"Hey, I like that movie!"

"Sure you do, who actually likes 'The Breakfast Club'?"

"Tons of people! It's a classic."

I sat back down on the couch next to him and pressed play, "Yeah, it's a classic, that's why everyone 'likes' it," I made air quotes at him.

"Umm, okay, whatever you say, I think it's a good movie," he put his arm around me.

"Of course you do," I shrugged, inching closer to him and pulling my knees up onto the couch.

"What's that supposed to mean?"

"Uhh nothing," I made a face at him.

"Hey, no, c'mon, what's that supposed to mean?"

"Nothing," I kissed him, "don't worry about it."

"Well," he kissed me back, "now I'm going to worry about it."

"Don't," I laughed, turning back to the movie.

"If you say so."

"I do!"

"Okay, guess I'll have to take your word for it."

"That would be smart."

"How come?"

"Because," I smirked at him, "I'm always right."

"Sure you are," he rolled his eyes, grinning.

"You know I'm right."

"Whatever you say."

"I am!"

"Haha," he kissed my forehead, laughing, "whatever you say."

My head found its way to his shoulder as his other hand found mine, "I'm right!" I watched as our fingers intertwined.

He didn't say anything, just smiled and shook his head.

I smiled, in spite of myself.

I smiled.

*   *   *

When she wakes up nothing is alive. The remaining world is dead and dark. Everything hidden from the waking demons.

Her demons have woken with fervor. Today, they are strong, and today, she is weak.

Angels don't exist today. Today is the day we are reminded that even though there are angels, there will always be demons.

"*Come join us in the fun, you're one of us,*" they whisper.

She's not.

"*You are.*"

She is.

It's going to rain. She can feel it.

She loves rain. But today it'll be raining cold, icy rain.

Maybe it'll thunder.

She wants to see her world shake on the verge of crumbling.

Maybe today it will crumble.

It starts raining. It rains harder and harder… and harder. Then all at once, she's surrounded by cold pellets of rain and demons.

She doesn't know where she is. The boy is gone. She doesn't know where anyone is.

She's alone.

The screams fill her head, echoing and echoing and echoing.

The chains, the chains that were breaking, they tighten. She can't leave. She has no way out.

She's trapped.

The thunder comes, and it shakes the ground beneath her and she falls to her knees. She covers her ears to block out the screams, but there's no way to block them out. They're a part of her.

"*Please, please leave me alone,*" she begs, "*don't do this to me. Leave me alone. Please.*"

They laugh.

She's shaking so badly that she can barely stand. She finds her way to a small alcove in the cliff face and pushes herself against the wall, rocking back and forth, back and forth.

The screams. They're so loud. There are so many voices screaming. No words. Just screams.

She's broken.

She's a monster.

The screams tear at her skin, ripping her apart, destroying the pieces that she had just started to find.

They'll leave her there.

They'll leave her there to die.

She can't do this.

She screams.

No one can hear her.

No one can hear her silent screams. The screams inside her head.

No one else is there.

She wants to die.

"*Let me die,*" she whispers.

The words echo through the cave, disappearing into the walls, where they will remain to forever haunt the world.

"*You die now, and we come too.*"

"*I know.*"

"*Do you still want to die?*"

"*Yes.*"

"*Then do it.*"

"*Okay.*"

But she can't move. She can't get up. She's paralyzed.

"*We knew you couldn't do it.*"

"*Please,*" she tangles her fingers in her hair, tugging at it in desperation, "*please.*" She sobs.

"*No.*"

"*Why.*"

"*You know why.*"

"*No.*"

"*Yes.*"

She can't cry.

She is still screaming with nowhere else to go to escape the sounds trapped inside her head, echoing around and around her mind, growing louder and louder and louder… like running and running and running toward a cliff and the faster you run the closer you come to plummeting off the edge.

But you're never going to actually reach the edge.

She feels insane.

The demons are crawling up and down her back, into her skin. They are all over her. The screaming continues. These silent screams shake her. They send vibrations down her spine and they send all of her angels spiraling away from their perch above her.

She is in hell.

There's no way out, not today.

She's trapped in a world of her own thoughts.

She has broken.

She is broken.

Everything inside her has shattered. All that's left is a body, hollow and breathing and screaming.

Lightning is flashing outside along with the thunder and the rain. It's the heart of the storm, the demons are at their height, and she can see the edge of the cliff. When she falls, there won't be any ropes to catch her, no hand to help her climb back into this world. She will be lost.

Screaming and screaming and screaming. And screaming.

It's all in her head. It's not real. It's too real.

Screaming.

She can't remember her name.

She doesn't know where she is. Where he is. She's alone.

The screaming.

"*Please*," she sobs.

They laugh.

And she's gone.

She's falling off the edge.

Down…

Down…

Down.

She screams, a piercing sound that becomes one with the scream inside her head. That last scream before you fall into the blackness. That last scream.

This is not a silent scream.

It tears at her throat as it leaves her and it rattles the rocks above her head. It shakes everything away from her, all the demons from her skin.

It leaves everything silent. Completely still.

There is nothing left.

She doesn't remove her hands from her ears. She lets the silence consume her, filling all the spaces the demons left bare. She lets the silence become her instead of the demons. She lets the silence be her rope.

The screaming is gone.

Everything is gone.

Is she dead?

This silence is deafening, but it soothes her. It calms her. She lets the silence reduce her walls to ashes.

She lets the silence be her angels.

She lets the silence set her free.

*   *   *

"Cass?" someone shook my shoulder gently, "Cass?"

"What?" I sat up, rubbing my eyes.

"The movie's over," Owen laughed.

"I fell asleep?"

"Yeah, just a little," he grinned.

"How far in?"

"The first like fifteen minutes."

"Wow, I think that's a record."

"Probably. I guess you really don't like this movie."

"Are you kidding? *I* love this movie. I'm not being sarcastic."

"I thought you said no one liked it."

"No one but *me*."

"Then how come you fell asleep?"

I yawned, "It's been a long week."

"If you say so."

"Sorry I fell asleep."

"Don't apologize! You needed it. Plus, you're cute when you sleep."

"I am *so* not, but okay."

"I know better than to argue with you," he stood up, "but you are."

"Shut up," I muttered, staring at the credits still rolling on the screen.

But I don't see them.

I see her.

The face reflected back at me in the mirror.

It's her. Of course it's her.

Why wouldn't it be her.

"Do you want me to drive you home?"

"Aren't your parents supposed to be home by now?" I looked up at him.

"Naw, they're gone for the weekend."

"Can I stay over? I don't really want to go home."

"Uh, yeah!"

"Sorry if I'm imposing. I can go if you need me to."

"No, no! It's fine, it's great! Stay as long as you need," he helped me up.

"Thanks," I gave him a pathetic 'I'm sorry' look.

"Of course! It's no big deal. I can make you breakfast in the morning, it'll be fun."

"*You* can cook?"

"Yes, *I* can cook."

I followed him into his bedroom. "You can sleep in the bed," he said, digging out a blanket, "I'll sleep on the couch."

I sat down on the edge of the mattress, and reached out a hand to him, "No, stay, please. I don't want to spend the night alone." Which was the honest response. I didn't. I couldn't. I escaped my house, but the ghosts, they follow you everywhere.

He paused for a second and looked at me, then he smiled and took my hand, sitting down on the bed. He held me close to him, and I could hear his heartbeat through his shirt.

For the first time in a long time, I felt safe.

"Okay," he whispered.

"Thank you," I whispered back.

Chapter Fifteen

It's damp outside when she stumbles out in the morning. She didn't sleep at all. She stayed in her spot on the ground, curled up in a ball, too scared to move, and watched the water trickle down in the silence. She's too tired to care that today the angels come back.

"*Good,*" she thinks, "*let them clean up the mess the demons made of the world.*"

They'll never be able to clean up the mess the demons made of her.

It's still drizzling, but in a calm, quiet way, and she turns her face upward to the sky and lets the rain wash away the remains of the demons.

She's still broken.

She's alone again. She's alone with the silence. There are no demons, and with no demons there are no angels.

For once she's not stuck in the middle of a war.

She hasn't spoken in a while. She doesn't know where the boy is, and she doesn't care all that much. She doesn't want to be around people today.

Not even him.

It's quiet here. It's silent, and the silence is a blessing. Silence means that nothing will haunt her, nothing will hurt her.

She's tempted to run away again, but it's a stupid idea. She's not going to escape anything by running away.

She's not going to escape herself.

She needs a promise. She needs to make herself a promise. The promise that if she goes, *when* she goes, when she *dies*, she will be free. The promise that if she dies today or tomorrow she will not take the demons with her, that she will leave the chains here on Earth and await whatever is to be awaited.

She can't go through that again.

She doesn't understand why she's still here.

She should be dead.

No one helped her. No one threw her down a rope.

No one wanted her to stay.

*   *   *

I woke up to the smell of pancakes, as promised. I smiled and stretched, letting myself take in the morning. It seemed too perfect to do anything more than lie there and take it in, to capture the moment, to pretend that it could stay that way forever, just that one moment for the rest of eternity.

I got up, eventually, checked my reflection in the mirror, and followed the smell of pancakes down to the kitchen. He looked cute, standing there with his blond hair sticking up in random places, leaning over the stove to check his handiwork.

He glanced over at me standing in the doorway, watching him. "Good morning, beautiful."

"Oh, shut up," I blushed, pushing my hair back out of my face.

"The pancakes are almost done, if you want to get plates out."

"Okay," I walked over to the cabinet and reached up, taking down two plates. "What drawer are your forks in?"

"Middle," he set a plate of pancakes down on the table, "syrup is in the right cabinet."

"Got it," I stood on my tiptoes to reach it, and he wrapped his arms around me from behind, "hey!"

"Did you sleep okay?"

"*Yes*, I did, thank you very much."

"Good."

I started making coffee, "Hey, thanks again for letting me stay here. I really appreciate it. I didn't want to bother Rachel again."

"You haven't been home much?"

"Not really," I shrugged, pouring the coffee into a mug and sitting down, "I just haven't felt like hanging around Mom. The more worked up Mom gets the more senile Grandma gets, and at least I know *she* cares, but it's just frustrating. Of course, I can't blame *either* of them, but it's just... it's not fun," I poured syrup over my pancakes, letting my words get ahead of me. "Sorry," I looked up at him, "I just like completely dumped a bunch of random shit on you."

"Don't apologize, you don't usually talk about your personal life, I don't mind it."

"You're too nice to me, you know that?"

"Isn't that my job, as your boyfriend?"

I choked on my coffee, and tried to hide it with a laugh, "Yeah, I guess."

"You good?"

"Yeah, yeah! The pancakes are great!"

"And *you* didn't think I could make them."

"Well, you certainly proved me wrong."

"I thought you were always right?"

"Don't quote me on that."

*   *   *

"Cassandra!" the boy stands and runs toward her. He was sitting by the edge of the lake, waiting for her.

She looks down. She can't do this right now. She doesn't try to run. She stands there and lets him wrap his arms around her and hold her, but she doesn't move. His voice pains her.

It breaks the silence.

It breaks her refuge.

And she breaks all over again.

He lets go of her and tries to meet her eye, but she avoids him.

"What's wrong? Where've you been?"

She walks away.

"Cassandra," he grabs her arm. She pulls away. She keeps walking. He follows her.

She sits down on a log and hides her face in her hands again. She needs him to go away. He needs to leave her alone.

But he won't.

Because he's him.

She doesn't know him.

She did once.

She's not a person anymore.

She's a shell, made of human skin and bone but devoid of feelings.

She's nothing.

At least with the demons there are angels, and with them she's a *thing*.

She's just a *nothing*, now.

He sits down next to her, "Are you okay?"

She looks at him.

Her walls are in place again.

They got weak last time she started letting people in, when she started letting *him* in. She let her defenses down and she came out into the open.

She's never making that mistake again.

To survive in this world she has to follow the rules.

It's not safe out in the open.

He isn't talking to her anymore. In her place is a shell. The body of the girl she used to be. The body, breathing and moving but not living, because she left all her life somewhere else. She left her life in the pieces that have been destroyed.

She should have died, but she lost herself instead.

It, the shell, *her* shell, It won't talk to him. It won't talk. It has no emotions, It has no thoughts, and It has no words.

It's not her, It's just the body she lived in.

She's not separate from her shell. She's still there, watching from Its eyes as she watches the boy speak to her, and touch her, and worry about her. But she can also watch from the trees as It gives him a smile to quiet his anxious words.

She can still be It. She can watch from Its eyes and hear from Its ears.

But It has little to nothing living inside It.

Because she's not really the girl sitting there.

She can't move for It. She can't speak for It. She can't feel for It.

She's not It.

* * *

"I think I'm going to get going," I said.

"Are you sure? You can stay as long as you like."

"I should probably get home, at least for a little bit."

"Okay. Do you want me to drive you?"

I shook my head, "No, I can walk. Thank you for everything, really," I gave him a kiss on the cheek.

"It was no problem."

"Bye, Owen."

"Bye, Cassandra."

I walked away before he could say the three words I don't think I'm ready to hear.

* * *

"Cassandra, are you okay?" he asks again for what must be the hundredth time.

No. No she is not okay, isn't it obvious? Use your brain, you idiot. She's not talking. She's not feeling. She's doing nothing but thinking thoughts that she can't speak and she can't express and thoughts that will only ever stay in her head because they can't leave it. She can't move unless her body moves. She can't control how her body moves. She can't even make her shake or nod her head.

She can't deal with this anymore, this *thing* that she is. This monster.

Does it look like she's okay?

She's trapped somewhere between living and dying.

There's no escape now.

She can't. She can't do it.

She watches from Its eyes as the day turns to night, leaving them in the dark. It hasn't moved since she sat down on the log, before she lost control. She can hear from Its ears the sound of the wind rustling the trees. She can feel his warm hand through Its cold fingers as he holds it gently, waiting for the life to come back to it.

He'll have to wait a long time.

* * *

"Cassandra!" Grandma looked surprised when I opened the side door and stepped into the kitchen.

"Hey," I gave her a little wave.

"Where've you been?"

"I spent the night at a friends."

"And the night before?"

"I was out late, and then I left early, you must not have heard me come home."

"I was up the whole night, you never came back."

I bit my lip. "I slept over at Rachel's."

"Is everything okay?"

"Yeah," I threw my bag down on the table, "everything's been great."

She eyed me wearily, "Your mother's in Claire's bedroom."

"She's- she's *where*?"

"Claire's bedroom."

"Why is she in there?" She hasn't been in there since...

Eleven years ago.

"I don't know, but she won't come out."

"Oh my god," I ran my hands through my hair, sighing, "alright, I'll go talk to her."

Grandma raised her eyebrows at me over the dish she was washing in the sink, but didn't say anything.

I braced myself as I walked down the hall and knocked on the door. "Mom?"

She didn't respond. My heart began to pound.

"Mom!" I pushed open the door and sighed in relief when I saw her sitting on the bed, staring down at her hands. I rubbed the sides of my head; my skull felt like it was splitting in two. "Mom, what are you doing?"

Her bottom lip quivered, but she didn't blink, and she didn't say anything. She didn't move.

"Mom, come on, why are you in here?"

Her mouth formed words, but no sound accompanied them to allow them to be heard.

I kneeled down next to her, putting my hand over hers, "Mom?"

"I- I..." she started. Then she stopped.

"Mom, what's going on?"

"I..." she took a deep breath, "him."

"What?"

"Him." She doesn't raise her eyes. "He's gone."

"Mom, are you okay?"

Her head turned toward me, and her hollow eyes met mine, but she didn't see me. She couldn't.

"Her," her voice was quiet, and it shook. "Them."

"What about them, Mom?"

"Where are they?"

"They're gone, Mom, they're gone."

"Where are they?" she repeated. She looked so helpless, so pathetic. I almost felt sorry for her. She's never gone into Claire's bedroom during an episode before, but this happens a couple times a month. She forgets. Something happens, and she forgets that they aren't there, and then when she can't find them, she goes into a sort of haze. Denial, I guess.

"Mom, they're gone. They died ten and eleven years ago."

"What?" she sounded so heartbroken. "No, they're here. He was here this morning. She was there. They were both here." She looked through me. Looking at ghosts that only she could see.

"I'm sorry, Mom."

"They're gone?"

"They're gone."

"I've lost them."

"No, you didn't lose them."

"Who's fault?"

"It wasn't anyone's fault."

"I'm alone?" she looked at me, actually looked at me. I'm not sure who's face she saw, but she saw someone.

"No," I said, "you're not alone."

"Everyone's gone."

"I'm here, Mom, *I'm* here."

"Gone." She turned back to the table, staring at her hands.

"Mom, I'm here, I love you and I'm *here*."

She pulled her hands away from mine. She didn't speak again.

She saw someone. And that someone wasn't me.

*   *   *

She's outside her body again, watching from the water as he continues to talk to her. It hurts. It hurts her numb mind that she can't reach him, that she can't tell him to stop or reassure him.

She takes so much for granted. She used to think that thinking was the only thing she could really do, but now she understands that while thinking was the one thing she paid attention to doing, there was still the action of moving her arms and legs and blinking and listening and talking.

She misses it all.

She looks up at the sky again, which is now alight with stars. When she looks back at the shell and him, she sees him lean in. In one last attempt to bring her back to life, he kisses Its lips. *Her* lips.

She wants that to be her.

She's in her body again, but this time, it's hers. It's her.

She's been given the chance to start over.

She kisses him back and wraps her arms around his neck. She needs him to know. She needs him to know that it's her. She pulls away and whispers in a hoarse, unused voice, "I'm sorry." She's crying. "I'm so sorry."

The angels have come back to her.

But so have the demons.

She doesn't care. It's okay. She's back. The world is quiet again, and she uses the silence one more time. She lets it reattach her missing, broken pieces.

She lets it bring her back to life.

*   *   *

I mingled for a little at Rachel's 'all girls' party, talking and laughing like usual. After a while I got tired of it. All the fake smiles, the fake laughs, the fake people. Everything. So I snuck up to Rachel's room and climbed up onto her roof. It was dark, the stars starting to make their short lived appearance in the sky billions of light years away. The only part of the past we get to see in our present.

I could fall at any moment.

*   *   *

"*You almost died last night,*" they whisper.

"I know," she says aloud, laying in the grass under the stars. She pulls her blanket closer around her as the night gets colder.

"*Don't you wish you had?*"

"No."

"*Why?*"

"Because."

"*Because you haven't given up?*"

"Something like that."

"*You should give up.*"

"Why?"

"*Because you've already lost.*"

"And how's that?"

"*We've already won.*"

"That doesn't mean I've lost."

"*It means you haven't won. It means you won't win.*"

"I'm going to keep fighting."

"*Your choice.*"

And they're gone again. Silenced. Waiting for their next turn to come back and whisper in her ear.

She closes her eyes and rest her head on his chest. His heartbeat is steady.

"You okay?" he mumbles.

"Yeah," she whispers.

*   *   *

Someone climbed up onto the roof next to me. "Oh, sorry," she said, glancing at me, "I didn't know anyone else was up here. Rachel said I could come here to get away from the party."

"It's okay, I was just leaving," I started to get down, when I realized who it was. Dark hair, blue eyes. *Those* blue eyes.

"No, it's okay! There's enough room for both of us," she laughed.

"Okay," I grinned.

"I don't think I've ever formerly introduced myself," she used one hand to balance herself and offered me the other, "Lily Peters, nice to meet you."

I shook it, "Cassandra James, it's a pleasure."

"So what brings you up here tonight?"

"I got tired of talking to people. How about you?"

"Pretty much the same," she leaned back, looking up at the sky. "Gets boring talking to the same types of people about the same things over and over again."

"Yeah," I laughed. She caught me looking at her and I glanced away quickly.

"Rachel's nice," she said, "she's been very welcoming, I don't know very many people here."

"She's the best," I agreed, "I've been friends with her for forever."

"Long time," she grinned.

"Yeah," I bit my lip. "So where are you from?"

She shrugged, "Just somewhere."

"Just somewhere?"

"It doesn't really matter. I'm here now, so, that's that."

"Yeah, that's that."

We sat in silence for a while. But it was a good silence. A silence that was filled with words. Things we've said, and things we are yet to say.

There are a lot of kinds of silences.

This was one of the good kinds.

× * *

A branch snaps.

She freezes.

She looks up and sees a figure dart behind a tree.

"Hey!" she calls. No response. She steps forward and shouts again.

They step out from behind the tree. It's a girl, maybe her age or a little older. The girl's blue eyes meet her brown ones and the girl glares at her.

"What are you doing here?" she asks, stepping toward the girl.

The girl takes a step back. "Who are you?" she says in a cold voice. Her chestnut hair is messy and her face is covered in dirt.

"I'm... Cassandra. Are you a runaway?"

"Why do you care?"

"Because I'm one too."

The girl's glare falters and her composure relaxes for a second. "Maybe I am."

"Where are you from?"

The girl shrugs, "Doesn't matter. You alone?"

"No, he's just off somewhere else right now."

"He?"

"Yeah, he."

"There some sort of romantic thing with you two?"

She blushes.

"Ah, I see."

"Is there anywhere in particular you're going?"

The girl shakes her head.

"Do you need somewhere to stay?"

"No. I'm just passing through."

"Okay."

"Okay," the girl turns on her heel and hikes off, but she catches the glance the girl throws at her when the girl thinks she's not looking.

This world is a very strange place.

This place is a very strange world.

Chapter Sixteen

"Hey," Lily dropped her backpack down next to my table in the library, "do you mind if I sit here?"

I looked up at her, a little startled, "Sure!"

"Ugh, thank you, all the other tables are either full or have people I hate."

"Wow, so I'm one of the ones you don't hate."

"Yup."

"I'm flattered."

She rolled her eyes, pulling her hair up into a messy bun, "You come here to study a lot, don't you?"

"Yeah, how'd you know?"

She shrugged, "I've seen you here a couple times, that's all."

"What classes do you have to study for?"

"Are you kidding?" she pulled a pile of books out of her backpack, "fucking *all* of them."

"Nice."

"What about you?"

"Pretty much the same."

"Ugh," she pulled a pair of glasses out of her bag and put them on, "I was stupid and figured I'd have fun over break and not study for any of my midterms. Great move on my part. Really top notch."

"Felt that, I did that too."

"How was your break, other than procrastinating studying?"

I leaned back in my chair, thinking. "Pretty uninteresting, actually. We didn't go anywhere."

"We?"

"My mom, my grandma and I."

"Oh."

"How about you, anything special?"

"Nope, my aunt and I just played a lot of board games, watched a bunch of movies, and got each other stupid gifts because I can't afford anything and I could never ask her for anything."

"You live with your aunt?"

She fidgeted a little in her chair. "Yeah, but it's just temporary, I'm finishing up the year here, so it was just easier to live with her."

"Cool."

"Yeah."

She became immersed in her many books, pouring over pages, and I went back to my math.

*   *   *

"Hey."

He looks up, startled, "Who are you?"

She's surprised too, it's been a couple days, maybe a couple weeks, since she first saw the girl. She'd assumed she'd never see her again.

He doesn't know about the girl.

"Hey," she stands so they're at a more even height.

"Do you know her?" he says, confused. He drops the box of matches, intending to get up, but doesn't.

She hesitates, "yeah. Kind of."

"You didn't tell him?" the girl raises an eyebrow at her.

"I didn't think you were coming back."

"Neither did I."

"Why did you?"

The girl shrugs.

"Cassandra, who-" he's looking from her to the girl.

"I'm Lily. Lily Peters," the girl shoves her hands into her pockets. "And I want in."

"In?"

"This thing you have here. This place, this... world. You asked if I needed a place to stay, Cassandra."

"And you said no."

"And now," the girl takes a deep breath, "I'm saying yes."

She catches his eye, and he nods.

She holds out her hand, "Welcome to the runaway club."

The girl shakes it and grins, "Welcome to the runaways."

*   *   *

"Do you want to go get a coffee or something? My brain's just about fried," she looked up and said after about an hour.

I glanced at the clock, "Sure."

"Great!" she picked up her bag and gathered her books in her arms. "There's a little place down the street, I don't know if you know it."

"Not really, I don't usually hang out anywhere in this area, besides the library."

"It's a nice little place, I think you'll like it!"

I followed her out the door, making small talk on the way there. It was only about a five minute walk, and she smiled as she pushed open the door, letting me go in first. We ordered our coffees and sat down at a table by the window. She was right, it was a nice little place, small, but not too small, with round tables and comfortable chairs. It wasn't overdone, just done enough, not too fancy, and not too messy. Organized. Cozy.

"This *is* a nice place," I said, looking around.

"I told you." She took a deep breath, sighing, "I love the smell of coffee."

"Me too," I grinned, "it always calms me down."

"Me too."

*   *   *

The girl doesn't talk much, and tends to keep to herself, only coming close when it gets cold at night to huddle around the fire. She doesn't know anything about her.

She knows the girl's name.

And for now, that'll have to be enough.

It's different now, with three of them. She hasn't decided if it's a good different or not. It's just a different, different.

"Hey," he says, joining her to help start a fire.

"Hey."

"How are you doing?"

"I'm okay," she nods. She's stopped saying she's fine. 'Okay' is a little closer to the truth. "You?"

"I'm cold," he shivers.

"Yeah, me too."

"Cassandra?"

"Yeah?"

"What do you think of her," he nods over at the water, where the girl is sitting alone, staring into space.

"What do you mean?"

"It's just – we don't know anything about her."

"I didn't know anything about you."

"That's a good point. But- I don't know. It's just… so random. Her showing up. Where did she come from? Why is she here?"

"Those are things she'll have to tell us in her own time. But she's here because, like us, she didn't fit in where she was. Sometimes society has to spit you out for a while, I guess."

"Cassandra?"

"What?"

"Why didn't you tell me."

"Tell you?"

"About her?"

She shrugs, "I don't know, I guess- I guess I didn't think it was important? I don't know, it all happened so fast, she was there one minute and the next she was gone."

He looks at her, still questioning her.

She can't tell him that she didn't tell him because she's still used to not telling people things. She's the type of person who would rather keep things to herself than have deep, emotional, or even slightly questionable conversations. And for some reason, she thought that the girl would be a questionable conversation.

The fire springs to life, and the girl makes her way over, sitting down on the grass across from them. Besides a short "hey", the girl doesn't say anything.

*   *   *

I watched her across the table. I didn't mean too. But I was curious, I mean, I didn't know anything about her. Just her name. Age, too, I guess. I didn't know where she was from, or why she moved here, or why she lived with her aunt, or why she liked *this* coffee shop of all places.

She's hidden well, like me. But even she has to have a fracture that exposes everything that she tries to hide.

Sometimes it doesn't take much for that crack to break.

Lily Peters. She's my age, give or take a couple months. Seventeen. She's about my height. 5' 5" or so. Short hair that comes to about three inches below her ears, which are small and elfish. Dark hair. Chestnut brown. Eyebrows permanently shaped in a brave, defiant way. Prominent cheek bones. A navy Yale college sweatshirt. Jeans. Hiking boots that she tucked the jeans into. Thin lips that don't curve downward, but never upward. Blue eyes. Ice blue. Dangerously blue. Perceptive, unwavering.

Lily Peters.

*   *   *

"You know, I haven't met your boyfriend, yet," Lily raised an eyebrow at me. It's been a couple weeks since the day in the coffee house, and now we're at the little spot Rachel brought me, Maddy, and Gabi that one day. The little spot with the cliff, the railing, and the waterfall. And the secrets.

I shrugged, "You've seen him, he's in our English class."

"I know, I mean I know who he is, but I haven't *met* him."

"Why do you want to meet him?"

"Uh... I don't know, because you're my friend and he's sort of your *significant other*."

I shrugged again, wrapping my arms around me as a cold wind blew across the landscape. The grass crunched under our feet, the frost breaking at our touch. The waterfall is dead and gone for the winter.

"He knows we're friends, right?"

"It didn't really come up, but I'm pretty sure he knows. Why?"

"Nothing," she shook her head, "he just seems like a nice guy."

"Yeah," I sat down at the railing, resting my arms on it, "he's a pretty nice guy."

She sat down next to me. "You guys are cute."

"Do you have a guy? Or, did you?"

She laughed, shaking her head, "Nope, not particularly interested."

"Okay."

She fidgeted with her fingers, always moving. She always looked like she'd just downed a pot of espresso, always fidgeting, never staying still for too long. "I know you're wondering why."

"Why what?"

"Why I left- why I'm here. I know I haven't told you anything"

I don't say anything.

"It's just- I didn't do anything bad, okay? I just needed to get away," the girl says.

"Why do you think he and I are here?" she asks.

"Really?"

"Yeah," she nods.

"Did you guys run away together?"

"Kind of."

"Kind of?"

"It's a long story."

The girl doesn't say anything else.

"I figured it was something you'd tell me when you were ready," I said.

"Okay." There's silence for a couple minutes. "How come you never talk about it?"

"Talk about what?"

"Your past."

"Oh," I looked down, twisting my fingers, "I don't know. It's not the most pleasant thing. Why don't you talk about yours?"

She bit her lip, "Mine's not the most pleasant thing, either."

"I'm sorry."

"For what?" the girl asks.

"I'm sorry that you ran away. That you had to."

"For what?" she asked.

213

"I'm sorry that whatever happened that made you come here was so bad."

"Don't be," she shrugged, "it is what it is. It would've happened eventually."

"That bad?"

"I mean, I would've left voluntarily or they would've made me," she picked up a stone and flipped in her hand. "I hate them," she chucked it across the open sky, until it fell down to the surface of the water, "every fucking one of them."

"Your family?"

She nodded.

"Why would they *have* made you leave?"

"Oh, they *did* make me leave. They practically disowned me."

"Oh my god, why?"

"They had their reasons," she picked up another stone and chucked it.

"My dad died when I was seven."

"Yeah?"

"Yeah."

"I'm sorry."

"There's no reason for you to be."

"I think from here on out we should agree not to say sorry to each other anymore," she looked out across the water, stone in one hand, eyes distant, thinking, then she dropped the stone and looked at me. "We don't have anything to be sorry for. We're both sorry we've each had shitty lives, we're both sorry we can't change the past or the shitty set of cards we were dealt. We're both sorry for being sorry."

"Fuck being sorry."

"Fuck being sorry," she nodded.

There was a long silence before she said, quietly, "How- how did it happen?"

"I don't remember."

"Okay."

"I had a sister."

"Had?"

"She- she drowned when she was three."

"That's terrible," she looked horrified.

"That kind of tore apart my family. Dad got really distant, Mom cried all the time and barely left the house. But it was just... it was one of those things you expect a family to get through."

"What happened?"

"Dad died, a year later."

"Oh my god."

I couldn't look up from the water. I didn't even tell Owen all of that. He knows, sure, everyone knows. But he doesn't know that after that, I didn't eat for months, I didn't speak for months, I didn't sleep for months. Mom got so distraught that she wasn't around for days and weeks on end. She tried, but she couldn't. Grandma took care of me most of the time. He doesn't know that when Mom was finally able to be around all the time, she yelled at lot. She was so mad. Not at me, just at the world. For taking away her child, and for taking away her husband. She was scared it was going to take me too.

She wrapped her arms around me. I didn't flinch away.

"Thank you," I said.

"For what?" she sounded surprised.

"Thank you for being here."

"Thank you for letting me," she let go of me, and smiled. There were tears in her eyes and she wiped them away. I smiled, too, and this time, I didn't look away.

I didn't want to look away.

*   *   *

When I finally did introduce Lily to Owen, they hit it off right away, making conversation and talking about the different activities they do. Owen showed Lily how to make pancakes, the 'right way', as he called it. She and I went to the coffee place to study and talk, and sometimes Owen would come, sometimes Rachel would, sometimes it would be a big group of us, but I liked it best when it was just the two of us, just Lily Peters and I. Her laughing, telling me things about her life, people and things she misses, things she has no want to see ever again. Her favorite things. Things she hates. Casual conversation.

I started making a list in my head.

Lily Peters:

Favorite color: periwinkle

"Not purple, not blue, not gray, periwinkle."

Least favorite color: orange

"Sunset orange, okay, but like, anything but that, just no."

Her home town: a little place just on the border of New Hampshire and Vermont

"It was nothing, really. I went to school in another town, we had one small church, two grocery stores, a gas station, and maybe two or three traffic lights. I mean, it was a cute town, it had a little country store and a square, a couple stores. My favorite was the book store. We didn't have a library, so I'd spend hours in there. That and the coffee shop, my best friend's parents owned it."

Siblings: Three, one sister and two brothers

"I'm the oldest, they were great. They're wild, all three of them."

First kiss: Michael Wild

"One word. Disgusting. Kissed like a god damn frog with overinflated lips."

Just the little things like that.

In group settings she laughed, told stories and jokes. She was completely normal.

But I noticed the times when she wasn't. The little slips in her composure. The moments when her smile faltered or her eyes glazed over and she looked away. The times when her voice broke during a laugh. The way her hands twitched when she was nervous or unsure. How she disappeared into herself when she couldn't hide. How she texted me when she couldn't sleep and stayed up and watched the stars, counting them or naming off planets and constellations.

She and Owen got closer. She spent a lot of time with him, I think because she found it easier to hide around him. I mean, he noticed things, but he didn't notice them the way Rachel did, or the way I did, with the amount of detail that I did. I didn't always ask her what was going on in her head when I noticed, but she knew that I noticed.

It's easier to be a different person around Owen. It's just who he is. He's a lot easier to be around than I am. He's more easy going, he's more honest, more open, more free. He's not so… tied down. He isn't grounded. Maybe that's why I feel safe with him, why I let him back into my life. Maybe that's why I haven't become a me-shaped hole in the nearest wall just yet.

"What are you up to?" he asks, sneaking up behind her.

"Nothing," she shuts her sketch book and tucks the pencil behind her ear.

"Aw, c'mon, show us," he says playfully, trying to take the book, "I didn't know you draw."

"No!" she yanks it away and Lily grabs it from behind her.

"Hm… let's see," Lily flips through it, stopping at the page she was just working on.

"What is it?" he circles her to look over Lily's shoulder, pulling her close to him. He hasn't done that in a while. She's missed it. Him wrapping his arms around her waist, pulling her so close that she can feel his breath on her skin, feel him speak, breath, laugh.

Something inside her twists.

Lily glances at them, and something in her face changes for a second.

The something tightens, wrapping around her lungs.

"Cassandra, that's amazing," he says.

"Yeah, Cassie, it really is."

"Wait, Cassie?" he laughs.

She shrugs, "she calls me Cassie."

"Can I call you Cassie?"

"No," she grins.

"Why not?"

"She's special."

"You're mean."

She shrugs again. "Lily, can I have it back now?"

Lily does that sideways grin, "I don't think so."

"Why not?"

"Because," Lily holds the picture out toward her, "this is amazing, and I want to look at it."

"It's nothing." It's just a sketch of the cliff, the wall devoid of water, the lake surface, the small crack that is the cave entrance, and the roughly drawn figures of him and Lily at the bottom.

"Hey, why's Lily drawn more than me?" he pouts.

"Because someone *interrupted me before I could finish," her laugh catches in her throat. He doesn't notice.*

But Lily does.

Chapter Seventeen

"Cass!" Maddy caught up to me after class, waving around a book to get my attention.

"What?" I asked. She kept pace with me, panting after her race down the hallway even though I'd stopped to wait for her.

"What are you doing today?"

I shrugged, "I'm not doing anything besides studying. Why?"

"We need to hang out sometime, we haven't hung out in forever, and I was going to see if you and the girls wanted to do something for dinner or something. I mean, it's Friday. I'm busy the rest of the weekend."

"Why, what do you have going on?"

She blushed, "I, uh, may or may not have a date Saturday night."

"Maddy! What? Okay, start explaining, *now*."

She giggled, "It's really nothing, it's a double date with Gabi and John. Gabi set me up with one of John's friends, Alex. He's really nice, though. Like *really* nice. We've been talking for the past couple weeks."

"And you didn't mention this to me because…"

"Well, you've just seemed so busy, with all the time you spend with Lily and then Owen, I didn't want to bother you."

"Oh, Maddy, stop, you never bother me."

"That's *funny*, but thanks, Cass."

"Are Gabi and John official yet?"

"Haha, *no*, of course not. You know Gabi."

"*Yes*, yes I do."

"But anyway, so tonight's good? Around five?"

"Yeah! Sounds great! Let me know if you need a ride."

"You read my mind!"

I rolled my eyes, "Of course I did."

"Alright, well, see you later!" she turned a corner, waving.

"See you," I waved back, laughing. I caught sight of Owen coming around the corner and smiled at him. He didn't see me right away, and I waved to get his attention. He smiled and waved back, making his way over to me.

"Hey," I said, slipping my hand into his.

"Hey," he gave me a quick kiss on the cheek, "how's your day been?"

"Good," I nodded, "not too much homework, which is nice. What about you?"

"Pretty much the same, what are you doing tonight?"

"Hanging out with Maddy and some of the girls, I guess."

"Aw, I was hoping we could do something."

"We do have *all* weekend."

"Okay, how about Saturday?"

"I can until two, I have plans with Lily after that."

"Okay, and Sunday?"

"I have plans."

"All day?"

"Potentially."

"With who?"

"Lily."

"*More* time with Lily?"

"Yeah," I shrugged, "why?"

"I don't know, you've just been spending a lot of time with her."

"Jealous?" I teased.

"I mean, I have a right to be, because she's stealing all my time with *my* girlfriend. I don't care that you're friends with her!" he said quickly, "but hey, she could *share*."

"Sucks for you," I stuck out my tongue, making a face.

He rolled his eyes, "You're so difficult."

"And this," I said, "we already knew."

"What are you doing now?"

"Going home, I guess."

"Do you have time before the 'girls' night'?"

"Yeah," I nodded.

"Can I pick you up at your house in ten minutes?"

"Where are we going?"

He shrugged, grinning as he let go of my hand, "Somewhere."

I stood there, watching him get in his car, "Where?" I shouted after him.

"Somewhere!" he called back, pulling out of the parking lot.

I shook my head, smiling at the ground, turning away from the school. I shoved my hands into my coat pocket and shivered. I didn't drive today. Grandma got up early and took the car before I could leave. I haven't really noticed how much colder it's gotten. The world has become a frozen snapshot of the world it used to be, a wasteland more desolate now with the bare, frost covered trees.

It took me about seven minutes to walk home, and by the time I could dig gloves out of a drawer and pull on boots, Owen had pulled up in front of the house. He didn't get out of his car, just honked the horn to let me know he was there.

I looked in the mirror before I left. Just a quick glance, but long enough to remind myself of everything I hadn't forgotten.

I closed my eyes.

When they opened, the same face was there. The girl with the hollow face, pale skin, dark eyes. The ghost. A living ghost, this time.

A mirror reflects light.

It's a miracle I can still see any of myself reflected back at me.

My phone buzzed, and I grabbed it, shaking myself out of the world I crossed into when I looked at the girl's face. The world I stepped into when I let myself close to her dark, terrified eyes. The world I let myself acknowledge by looking at it for longer than I was supposed to.

The world I turned my back on.

Grandma pulled into the driveway as I was leaving, and I waved, pointing at Owen's car as I crossed the front lawn. She nodded and waved back, opening the back door of the car and trying to get Mom to step out.

"Hey," he grinned.

"Hey," I climbed in the passenger seat, giving him a quick kiss.

"Is your mom okay?" he asked, nodding in the direction of Grandma's car.

"Yeah," I said, watching her stare blindly at the seat in front of her, not hearing Grandma's words or taking notice of her surroundings. She looked thin, worn out, "she just hasn't been feeling well the past couple days."

"Oh, that's too bad. Tell her I hope she feels better."

"I will." Grandma took Mom's hands in her own and tried to gently pull her out of the car. I looked away. "So, where's this *somewhere* we're going?"

He shrugged, switching the car into drive, "Guess we'll just have to see."

I rolled my eyes, "You're so annoying, you know that?"

He shrugged again.

*   *   *

"How have things been going, Cassandra?" she asked, looking at me over the rim of her glasses like she did all the other days.

I shrugged, not making eye contact.

Her eyebrows creased slightly, but for once, she didn't comment on my silence. She leaned back in her seat and watched me trace the bullet holes scattered around the room like one of the connect-the-dots puzzles.

My fingers twisted in my lap, trying to make their way to my palm. It was taking all of my self restraint to not let them.

"Things," I said slowly, "things have been okay."

"What's been going on in your life?"

I shrugged again, "I met someone new, I guess, I don't know. She's cool. We spend a lot of time together."

"What's her name?"

"Li-" I saw her start to scribble something on her clipboard, "Laila Parker."

"Laila Parker?"

I nodded.

"How did you two meet?"

"She's in my English class."

"Did you two get paired for a project or something?"

"No," I shook my head, "we just sort of started talking."

"Alright," she paused, looking back down at her clipboard, "and how's your grandmother?"

"She okay."

"Why just okay?"

"Because," I made eye contact with her, only for a brief second, but I made eye contact, "no one is ever more than okay, for one reason or another."

"Okay," she nodded, hesitating, and jotted down a quick note, "and your mother?"

I bit my lip. "She's... she's okay."

"Are you sure?"

"Well, I mean," I shifted in my seat, "she's going through one of her shock phases."

"Shock phases?"

"Sometimes, for one reason or another, most of the time something triggers it, she goes into this like trance, and she can't remember who some people are, and she doesn't know that Dad and Claire aren't here anymore. Sometimes she thinks they're standing next to her, or that she can watch them play in the yard. Most of the time she asks where they are, and doesn't understand when I say they aren't there. We call it her shock phase."

"And who talks to her while she's in these phases, you or your grandmother?"

"Grandma kind of helps her out around the house, takes her to therapy and stuff like that. I'm usually the one who actually talks to her."

"And does she listen to you?"

I hesitated, "Yes."

"Cassandra?"

"What?"

"You can tell me the truth, you know. I'm not here to judge you or anything like that, I'm here to help."

My nails found their way to my palm. I looked away from her, fixating on a spot on the floor.

"Does she listen to you?" she repeated.

Slowly, I shook my head. "No," I said quietly, "she doesn't even know that I exist."

* * *

"Alright," he pulled the car onto the shoulder of the road, "we've reached somewhere."

"And somewhere is?"

"Here," he got out of the car and opened my door. I climbed out, looking around. Ironically, it was the same place Rachel had taken us, and the same place I'd returned to with Lily.

It wasn't 'somewhere', so much as it was *my* somewhere. Not so much just a random place of Owen's choosing, but a place specific to a point in time in my life. A point he was not part of.

The railing is still the rusted railing it was last time, threatening to fall over into the abyss should someone put all their weight on it. The rusted railing that, despite its looks, doesn't fail to protect those that lean over its side to look down into the water below, to feel the spray from the waterfall, to take a chance with the unknown in the hopes of finding something that is still lost.

It's not so much *his* somewhere as it is *my* somewhere.

"Do you like it?" he wrapped his arms around my waist, his face next to mine.

"Yeah!" I decorated my face in a plastic smile, an illuminated plasticity of excitement and happiness.

There's something about plasticity that makes us not notice that it's plastic. Like the way everything in the world is made out of plastic, but we pretend it's all made out of the same material that made metal. The same sturdy, dependable material that we can rely on. But the thing about plastic, is that it has a plasticity that we cling to, it is something we can change just by holding in our hands. It gives us an illusion of power, the plasticity that turns plastic to aluminum and limestone to gold.

Everything in this world is plastic. Everything and everyone can be and is molded by its maker, but with people, the maker continuously changes, and with the change of the maker, comes a change in the mold. Sometimes things are learned from the previous maker, knowledge is gained, and the mold is strengthened. But sometimes, the previous maker breaks us a little more than they were supposed to. They chip off a little more than we meant them to, and leave us broken. Sometimes we break so much that we do actually stop being plastic. And because we stop being plastic, we lose our plasticity. And because we lose our plasticity, we can't be remolded.

"Are you sure?" his face is alight with pride, "I found it the other day, I was hoping you hadn't been here already."

"No, no, I haven't! It's beautiful, Owen."

"It's not as beautiful as you."

I rolled my eyes, grinning, "That was very, *very* cliché."

"I am very, *very* aware of that," he laughed.

His laugh faded against the wind, and I looked out across the water, half hidden by the rail. There were ripples in the surface as the wind tossed it back and forth.

A stone falling down toward the surface.

My foot slipped.

The water grew closer, and closer, and closer.

All the feet you'd have to fall to hit the surface.

My eyes closed.

All I could think, was "oh".

Then a hand grabbed me by the shoulder and pulled me back.

"Oh... thank god, now it's over."

The stone hit, and the glass-like surface shattered.

*   *   *

"Alright, who else am I picking up, Maddy?" I raised my eyebrows as she climbed in the passenger seat.

"Uh..." she said, looking guilty, "Gabi and Rachel."

"So... everyone."

"Yeah!"

"You know, one of these days I'm just not going to say yes to picking you guys up, and then what'll you do?"

She shrugged, "Guess you'll have to actually say no first."

"Are you calling me a pushover?"

"No! Well... maybe sometimes."

"Really? Is that so?"

She shrugged again, smirking.

Rachel opened the back door and climbed in, "How come Maddy's in the passenger seat?"

"Rachel!" Maddy turned around to look at her, "do you think Cass is a pushover?"

"Depends who you're talking to and what the situation is."

"Well, talking to you, in a situation such as driving everyone."

"In that case, yes, she's a pushover."

"Hey!" I glanced at her in the rearview mirror

"Sorry," she leaned back and put her feet up on the back of Maddy's seat, "I speak the truth, and nothing but the truth."

"Like hell you do," I muttered.

"What was that?"

"Nothing," I gave her a fake smile.

"Fine, well, ask Gabi and see what she says!"

Gabi stopped to check her makeup in her front door, and Rachel rolled down the window to yell at her. "Gabi, do you think Cass is a pushover?"

Gabi made her way to the car and shoed Rachel to the other side, "Uh, yeah, why, who's asking?"

"Cass thinks she's not a pushover," said Maddy.

"I'm not!"

"Yes, you are," they said together, then laughed.

I rolled my eyes, "Maddy, where are we going anyway?"

"Uh..." she pulled up a page on her phone, "it's like a town or two over, it's this little like cafe I found."

"What's it near?" Rachel asked.

"I don't know specifically, but it looks like a cute area, so we can walk around and stuff after. There's an ice cream place near it."

"Alright, it actually doesn't sound terrible," she nodded, "nice job, Maddy."

"Thank you!" her face lit up.

"And how do I get to this place exactly?" I glanced over at her.

"Uh, take a right here, and then... left here, follow this road for about a mile, then take this left..." and so on.

We finally pulled over on a main road. It was a small town, like a typical old town in a movie or book.

"It's very *aesthetic*," Gabi said, getting out the car after Rachel.

"It *is*," Rach nodded.

"So the cafe is there," Maddy pointed across the street.

"Is that a pub next to it?" Rachel raised an eyebrow, grinning slyly.

"Uh... I think so. Why?"

"Who wants to go there instead?" she raised a hand, looking around.

Two more pairs of hands went up, leaving Maddy with her arms crossed, pouting.

"Aw, c'mon, we'll go to your cafe another day," Rachel tugged at her arm, "but it's Friday night, it'll be fun."

"We don't have ID's or anything!"

"Who said we're going to be drinking?"

"Oh, I don't know, but-"

"Well, I say we'll be drinking," said Gabi, crossing the street.

"What about ID?"

"Worst comes to worst, they ask, we apologize, and don't get drinks. Sound good?"

Maddy nodded, still pouting.

Rachel pushed open the door, and the four of us stepped into the pub. It was a small place, dimly lit, but clean and tidy. A waitress passed us with a tray of beers and told us to pick a table, so we sat in a booth against the far right wall. The tables were only about ten feet from the bar, and it was loud, but the fairy lights scattered across the ceiling gave it a more peaceful air. The tables were covered in white paper with a glass of crayons next to the salt and pepper shakers.

"How are we doing today, folks?" the waitress asked, pocketing a tip from the previous table.

"Good, thank you," said Rachel, shooting Maddy a look as she picked up a blue crayon.

"And are we drinking or eating today?"

"Both."

"Alright, and are you ready to order drinks, or do you need a minute?"

"A minute, thank you."

"Alright, I'll be back in a few."

"Rachel!" Maddy hissed across the table.

"What! Don't order a drink if you don't want one, but I," she picked up a menu, "am ordering a Manhattan."

"I think I'll try a Long Island Iced Tea," Gabi grinned.

"I'm going to get an Old Fashioned," I put down my menu, "come on, Maddy."

"Live a little," said Rachel.

Maddy huffed and grabbed a menu, "*Fine*. But one of us has to be able to drive home."

"We'll get coffee and walk around for a while before we leave, and we're not getting drunk, chill out," said Rachel, taking the menu out of Maddy's hands as the waitress came back over.

"Well, what'll it be, girls?"

"A margarita for her," Rachel nodded at Maddy, "and I'll have a Manhattan."

"I'll have a Long Island Iced Tea."

"And I'll have an Old Fashioned."

"Alright," she wrote down the orders, "I'll have those right out for you. And are you ready to order food?"

"Not yet," Gabi said.

"Alright, I'll be back with your drinks in a few."

"Thank you!"

"Yeah, thanks," Maddy muttered weakly, sinking down in her seat a little.

Gabi pulled her back up, handing her the blue crayon. "Here, knock yourself out."

Maddy eyed her wearily, taking it. Gabi grabbed a purple crayon, tossing it to me, and then a green one to Rachel, taking a red one for herself.

The waitress came back with our drinks, and we ordered our food. After she'd disappeared again, we each took a sip of our drinks. Maddy made a face, and then nodded grinning, and we laughed.

"So, how's everybody been?" Gabi asked, stirring her drink, "I feel like I haven't seen you guys in years."

"I know! We need to start hanging out more," Maddy added.

"We really do," I said.

"Yeah," Rachel gave me a playful shove, shooting the paper straw wrapper at Maddy. "I've been good, though. I've sent in a few applications, and now I'm just waiting to hear."

"Early decision?" I asked.

She shook her head, "No, regular. I'm going to send in a few more soon, I'm just working on finishing them."

"Congrats!"

She shrugged, "It's nothing to be excited about, I haven't gotten in yet. Didn't some of the early decision people hear back?"

"I think so," Gabi took a sip from her drink, trying to hide a shudder, "I wouldn't know, I didn't do early app."

"Maddy, didn't you do early app?" I looked at her.

Her face turned red, and she nodded.

"Did you hear?"

"Well," she moved her glass in little circles, leaving ringlets of water, "actually, that's part of the reason I wanted to get you all together tonight."

"And?" Rachel leaned toward her.

"And," she tried to hide her grin, "I got into Brown."

"Oh my god!" we shrieked, making a couple people look up from their conversations.

"Oh my god!" we lowered our voices to a whisper, "you did?"

"Yeah," she bit her lip, smiling, "I did."

"Maddy! That's amazing!"

"I'm so proud of you, oh my god, I knew you could do it."

She buried her face in her hands.

"Maddy that's incredible."

"Thank you guys," she lifted her head, her eyes teary, "I love you so much."

"I love you too," we echoed.

"Anyway," she wiped her eyes, "what about the rest of you?"

Gabi shrugged, "I'm going to send in a couple applications soon."

"And what about you and a certain someone?" said Rachel.

Gabi rolled her eyes, "he's *fine*."

"Oh, I'm sure," Rachel winked.

"And what about you and whoever you're dating now?"

"*Julie* is fine as well."

"Oh, so it's still Julie then?"

Rachel chucked her crayon at Gabi, who ducked. "*Yes*, it's still Julie."

"Cass, how about you?"

"Things are good," I shrugged.

"*Good* as in..." Gabi said.

"*Good* as in good."

"Have you guys... you know," Maddy made a teasing face.

I shrugged again, smirking in a 'you'll never know' way.

"Cass!" Rachel punched me.

"What?" I rubbed my arm.

"What do you mean, *what?* You know exactly what."

I shrugged again.

"Oh my god, you're impossible."

"I am aware of that."

"Good," Gabi threw Rachel's crayon back at me. I caught it and flung it toward Maddy, who ducked, shrieking. Soon it was a crayon war, coupled with various insults, and incessant laughter and screaming, until none of us could breathe and we just sat there, giggling and finishing our drinks, fully aware that the entire pub was watching us.

I looked around the table, Maddy inhaling her drink, Gabi scribbling the 867 - 5309 number on the table, and Rachel with a toothpick between her teeth, fiddling with her straw and staring into space.

These are the people that made me. These are my makers. And so far, they've done a pretty good job. They haven't chipped away too much, but just enough, and they added more than they took. They haven't broken the mold, but rather added their own designs to it.

These are the people that made me, and I wouldn't ask for any other makers.

Chapter Eighteen

I pulled on my skates and she helped me up. "You sure about this?" she asked.

"Yeah," I put one foot on the icy pond surface, then another, waiting for it to give way. When it didn't I took a couple cautious steps, making my way toward the middle. "Come on!" I called over my shoulder.

"Is it safe?"

"Yeah, I used to come here with my dad, and he showed me how to tell where it's safe to skate. This looks pretty frozen over, and it's not melting, so it's okay."

"But it's safe?"

"I think so."

"Good enough for me," she wobbled a little as she made her way over to me. "Help!" she reached out a hand and I took it, helping her steady herself, "why do you have such good balance?"

I shrugged, "I have absolutely no idea."

"You know what's sad?"

"What?"

"I've never ice-skated before."

"Are you serious?"

"Yeah," she tucked her hair behind her ear, pulling her hat farther down over her head.

"Wow, alright then. It's not that bad, you'll get used to it."

"If I don't fall in!"

"You won't, trust me."

"Are you sure?"

"Nope."

"Exactly the reassurance I needed."

"What's the fun in being reassured, wouldn't you rather live in fear?" I took her other hand in mine and started to move backward, pulling her with me. She smiled, watching the ice below her. "Lily, you've got to move your feet!"

"I'm trying!" she looked up at me, almost losing her balance, "it's not that easy!"

"I'm doing it just fine," I gave her another pull.

"Well, good for you," she rolled her eyes at me, screaming as she slipped again.

"Oh my god, Lily," I shook my head at her.

"What!" she said indignantly.

"Nothing," I grinned.

It took at least ten minutes to get her to start moving her feet properly, and then another twenty to get her to let go of my hands.

"See, you're a natural!" I clapped as she slid a few feet, starting to move around me on her own.

"Pft, please, you're funny."

"I'm serious!"

"*No*, you're not!"

"Well, maybe I'm not completely serious."

"I told you!"

"But you are doing a good job, considering you've never skated before."

She slipped, falling backwards. I skated over to her and helped her up. "You jinxed me!" she said, brushing off her pants.

"Are you okay?"

"Yeah, I'm fine," she looked up at me. Our eyes met.

I let go of her hands and looked down at the ice, skating away from her.

"Cassandra?"

"What?"

"I- nothing. Are you okay?"

I didn't look at her. "Yeah. I think I heard the ice crack or something, it's probably not safe. We should go."

She caught up to me, wobbling a little, and grabbed my shoulder for balance.

Something inside me twists.

*   *   *

Dad and I woke up at five in the morning, while Mom woke up at nine. It killed me to wait that long to pull on my mittens and rush out into the snow, and when she did finally meet us in the kitchen I'd drag Dad outside to build a snowman. We had little success as the snowflakes were no more sticking to each other than they were to the road. It had begun to pile up though, and by the time I had finished breakfast by the fire, thawing my frozen toes, it had accumulated into a pile about three inches high. I wanted to go back out again, but Dad told me to wait until tomorrow, because then I would really be able to build a snowman. We spent the day drinking hot chocolate and watching winter movies until Mom said it was time for the both of us to get some sleep. Dad told her she was spoiling the fun of the first snowfall of the year, but he was laughing, and when she began to protest he turned on another movie and the three of us huddled under a big blanket. That was one of the good days.

I've always loved the first snow fall.

I love watching the world transform. Coated in white, innocent and new, drenching the evil and washing it away with the spring.

It's one of the few wonders of the world that I understand in its entirety.

I got up early again today and walked down to the park. I sat down on a bench and watched as the sky began to darken with the sunrise. Then, the first speck of white fell, spiraling in the light breeze.

And with that, it started to snow.

*   *   *

"Do you sleep anymore?" I felt his hand on my shoulder as someone sat down on the bench next to me.

"As much as the world does," I turned to smile at him. He kissed me. "How'd you know I was here?"

"I didn't."

"You just decided to get up early and come to the park?"

"Yeah, pretty much. I come here a lot, actually."

"It's snowing."

"So it is."

"I like it when it snows."

"Yeah, me too."

It was nice, just the two of us sitting there together, watching the world transform. It was so peaceful.

"Cassandra?"

"Yeah?" I looked over at him.

He leaned in and kissed me gently. When he pulled away he whispered three words.

"I love you."

And everything shattered.

It all happened so fast.

I stood up from the bench, stumbling a little as I stepped back. He followed me.

"Are you okay?"

I shook my head. I could feel myself collapsing, the foundation I'd built over the years crumbled beneath my feet as the world fell away. The world fell away, and it was just me. I had a choice. I could say it back. Because I did. I did love him.

I *did*.

And who am I kidding? It's *me*. Poor fucked up me, poor fucked up Cassandra with such a shitty life that she can't love anyone. With a shitty life and a mother who's taught her to be scared of love, because when you love people you lose them. You lose them and you get hurt.

So many voices. Conflicting screams. Thoughts racing to catch up to one another. Emotions fighting one another to be felt.

And then there's me standing in the middle, watching the storm break around me.

And then he's there, standing in front of me, looking hurt and confused and scared.

And it kills me.

"I- I- please, I- I can't."

Dead silence.

A silence in which a part of me dies.

I watched a tear fall and dissipate when it hit the frozen ground.

"Why?" he asked. He didn't even sound mad, he didn't even sound upset. His voice didn't break, it didn't crack. He didn't sound hurt.

He sounded broken.

And it's me that broke him.

"I don't know what love is."

He looked at me, meeting my eyes and holding me locked in his strong, steady stare. "That's *bullshit*."

"What?" I took a step back.

"You heard me. That's bullshit. I know it, and you know it." He was raising his voice. "Don't use all that 'I'm too damaged to love' shit on me, Cassandra. Because you know what? I'm damaged too. And I still know what love is. I know how to let yourself accept someone else, instead of push them away. And I know you do too. You're lying to yourself if you say you don't know what love is. Because what *we* have *isn't* bullshit."

"You're wrong."

"Am I? I don't think I am. You can tell me that you don't love me, but don't give me that shit. You want to know something? Everyone in this world is damaged. In some way, in some form. We've all got baggage. We've all got shit. Emotionally, physically, mentally, and it doesn't fucking matter. Because you know one thing that everyone, no matter how damaged they are, knows how to feel? Love. It's ingrained in us. We might not feel it with everyone, we might not know what it's like, but when you love someone, you know it. You know who I loved before you? Huh? No one. Not my mother, not my father, no one. I loved them in an 'I have to love you because you're family' way, but I didn't love them. They didn't and they don't love me. So don't tell me that you don't know how to love. Because that's bullshit."

"Stop, please. Stop." I felt tears start to cascade down my face.

"Don't cry, god dammit don't fucking cry. *I'm* not crying. And I'm the one who just said 'I love you' for the first time in his *life*. God *dammit* Cassandra."

"I'm sorry," I whispered, my voice breaking.

He looked like someone just cut out his heart and was squeezing the life out of it while he watched. He looked away from me. "Don't say that. Don't say you're sorry. Don't be sorry for me. Be sorry for yourself, because I'm sorry that you're too scared to be honest with yourself. You're too scared to be open." He was shaking his head back and forth, biting his lip. He looked up at me one more time. "Maybe someday, with someone, you'll let yourself feel something besides fear and hatred and pity. Besides feeling sorry for yourself. For being sorry for the shitty cards you were dealt. I'm sorry your life wasn't perfect, but neither was mine."

"I didn't... Owen-"

"Please, don't." And finally, finally his voice cracked. And then it shattered.

"Please, don't go," she sobs, sinking to the ground as her legs refuse to support her weight.

"What am I supposed to do then? Stick around here and act like everything's normal?"

"I don't know... just please, I don't know..." her voice fades into nothing.

"Cassandra," he took a deep breath. "If you were just going to tell me this, if this is all that you could say, then what the hell was all that, everything for the past couple of months. Was that just for fun? Some kind of twisted game?" his voice echoed across the empty landscape

I looked up at him, horrified at his accusation. "No."

"Then what the hell was it."

I didn't answer. I didn't have anything to say. I didn't know what I could have possibly said.

"I'm leaving," his voice is numb, devoid of any emotion, "tell Lily that I said goodbye, and I'm sorry to leave like this."

"I'm going to leave now. I'm sorry, I can't."

And then he walked away.

And he was gone.

I buried my face in my hands. I just sat there, crying and shaking.

And then I scream.

A heartbroken, pained scream.

It's my fault.

I broke my own heart.

Just like I broke his.

He was my best friend.

And now, because of me, he's gone.

"Come back!" I scream. Over and over again. Over and over and over again.

What is Lily going to say?

Before she can find me, I manage to push myself to my feet and stumble away from the clearing. I don't care where I go, or how far I go, I just go. And then I start to run. Adrenaline courses through me, and I don't care how many branches scratch me, or how many times I stumble, I just run. I run until my lungs give out and I trip and land in the cold dirt. I don't move. I can't move.

I want to die.

I roll over onto my back, staring up at the trees and the snow that keeps going in and out of focus.

The voices that faded in the cold of the winter return with the cold of my heart.

Then everything goes black.

Everything that just happened was a blur. I don't remember what I said.

But I knew one thing.

He was gone.

And he wasn't coming back.

When they fight their way back, you let them. You let them because they've made the decision for you, and it doesn't happen often. Those people are rare. Those are the people you won't have to fight to hold on to.

They're the people you'll have to fight to lose.

Chapter Nineteen

I went back. To the little world I'd abandoned. The one with the lake, and the waterfall, and the relics.

I went back.

But once I was there, I couldn't remember why I was. And then it hit me all over again. Over and over again. I closed my eyes.

I can't face the world right now.

His words echo through my head. He was right. He was right about everything. I don't know why I couldn't just say it.

I opened my eyes. The snow was still falling, quiet and innocent. I tried to count the snowflakes, but there were too many. There must have been over a billion.

All of those snowflakes, they're different.

Just like people.

I sat there for what felt like hours, not moving, not speaking, barely breathing.

I'm so sick of my life. Every good thing that's ever in it I find some way to ruin. I self-sabotage. That's what I do best. Forget self-preservation.

I self-sabotage.

His words cut me. They'll bleed for weeks. Then they'll leave scars. Scars that, like the ones covering my body, will never fade.

Scars that you make yourself don't fade. It doesn't matter what you used, it doesn't matter why you did it, it doesn't matter how deep it was, it doesn't matter if you took care of it, it doesn't matter if you wanted it to leave a mark or prayed that it didn't.

Those cuts heal, but they never fade.

They're permanent. They're permanent for a reason. They're permanent so you remember. You remember why you did it, you remember how you felt, the emotions that made you do it, the exhilaration, the adrenaline, the fear, the relief, the power, the control. The guilt. The horror. You remember how you wore long sleeves all through the spring and all through the summer just to hide the hideous marks you left, how you avoided wearing bathing suits to hide the ones on your stomach, hips, thighs. You remember all the places the scars are visible and all the places they aren't. You remember the way you jumped when anyone touched you, or when your sleeve slipped. You remember all the stupid excuses you made. You remember the way you cried at three in the morning, wanting to know that you were alive, that you were there. Wanting confirmation. Because if you're real, you matter, right? You remember the way your friends looked at you when they saw them, even the ones who pretended they didn't. You remember how you never looked at yourself the same way again.

You remember all of that.

No matter when, no matter why, when you see them, you remember. It's haunting, like a ghost. Except it's not "like" a ghost. It is a ghost.

It's your ghost.

The ghost of the person you used to be.

* * *

My phone was almost dead, but it had enough battery left for me to text Lily, asking her to come. My phone died before she could respond, but she showed up within the next half hour.

I was sitting by the water, and she sat down next to me, wrapping an arm around me.

"Have you been here all day?" she asked in a quiet voice.

I nodded.

She let go of me and held me at arm's length, taking in my dirty, matted hair, the tear streaks frozen on my pale face, shaking body, blue lips, broken expression. "What happened?"

I couldn't find words, and turned back to the frozen water, staring across the glass surface.

She didn't ask me again.

I didn't want to say the words, because saying them aloud would make them true, more true than they already were.

"I..." I started. She looked at me. "I, I broke up with him."

"Owen?"

I nodded, "Yeah."

"Why?"

"I don't know. He said I love you and I... I couldn't say it back."

"Did you love him?"

"I did."

"Then why didn't you say it back?"

"Because," I looked at her, at her eyes shining in the darkness, "because that's the thing. I *did*."

"You don't now?"

"I don't think so. I don't even know *when* I loved him. I just know that I did, at one point."

"How'd he take it?"

"Well, I didn't really say it all that well. I told him I couldn't love or something... it's all a blur. I don't remember."

"And he said?"

"He got mad. Well, not really mad, just hurt. Upset. He kept telling me it was bullshit, and that he was broken too, and that he'd never loved anyone before and just because I didn't want to say it didn't mean it wasn't true."

"He said that?"

"He said a lot of things. And they were all true."

"No," she put her arm around me again, "no, they weren't."

I pulled away, "They were."

He was right, about everything.

I need to stop feeling sorry for myself. But I'm *not* feeling sorry for myself. I'm just lost. The life I spent years building shattered, and I watched all the pieces disintegrate.

And I'm the one that broke it.

*   *   *

I visited Dad again later that week. Him and Claire. I brought flowers to replace the ones the snow and frost had killed.

I didn't say anything for a while. I just sat at the foot of their graves, pouring over memories and words and pictures and things that I'd forgotten.

The sky is dark. The snow is starting to fall again.

"Hi, Dad," I whispered, my voice hoarse from lack of use.

"Hi, Cassie," his voice echoed in my head. A sentence from some time so many years ago.

"How have you been? How's Claire?"

"I'm better now that you're here. Claire's doing just fine, sweetie. We miss you! I can't wait until you come home." I think that's from when I went away with Grandma for the weekend.

"Dad?"

"Yeah?"

"I'm scared."

"There's nothing to be scared of, Cassie."

"I know."

"What are you scared of?"

"The dark."

The same dark that killed you.

"There's no reason to be scared of the dark. Now, come here, let me show you something." The sound of a light switch. A little girl's shriek. *"See that, in the corner? The big monster? Look,"* the sound of the light switch again, a little girl's voice in awe, *"see? It's just one of your stuffed animals with your blanket over it. That's the closest thing to a monster that hides in the dark."*

"Dad, there's so much more to the dark than that."

"I don't know what you mean."

"You should. You're the one that taught me that."

"What are you scared of?" the voice repeated.

"I'm sending in a couple applications this week, college applications. Grandma's making me. I mean, not making me, I want to. I just don't feel ready. The world hasn't been a very nice place."

The voice didn't respond.

Of course it didn't. I brought up the future. The voice only lives in the past.

I ran my fingers through the snow, letting the cold seep under my skin.

"Bye, Dad."

"Bye, Cassie."

I saw a figure at the bottom of the hill when I stood up and turned around. He disappeared, and I didn't go after him.

*   *   *

"Cass!" Grandma looked surprised when I walked in the door. "I thought you'd be gone longer!"

I shook my head, "It's cold."

"It is. Do you want hot chocolate, or tea?"

"Coffee, please."

"You know, coffee isn't really good for you-"

"Coffee, please, Grandma."

"Okay, coffee it is."

"Where's Mom?"

"Her room. She was sleeping last time I checked."

"Okay, thanks, I'll be right back."

I walked down the hall toward Mom's room and pushed open the door quietly. She was still lying in bed, but her eyes were open, staring at the ceiling. "Mom?" I said quietly.

"Cassandra?" her head turned, and her eyes locked on my face.

"Yes, it's me, Mom," I sat down on the edge of her bed.

She pushed herself up, leaning weakly against the headboard. "Cassandra."

"How are you?"

"I'm okay, Cassandra, I'm okay," she took my hand in hers, squeezing it tightly.

"Get some rest, Mom."

"I will." I started to get up, but she pulled me back toward her, "Sandra?"

"Yeah?"

"Have you submitted any of your college applications yet?"

"Not yet, but I'm going to."

"Where are you applying?"

"Boston University, NYU, Columbia, Yale, and University of Michigan. A couple others too."

"That's good," she sank back down onto her pillow, "I'm proud of you, Cassandra."

"Thanks, Mom," I smiled, "now, get some rest, okay?"

"Okay."

I let go of her hand and gave her a quick kiss on the cheek, "I love you, Mom."

But she was already asleep.

I closed the door behind me and went back to the kitchen. Grandma handed me the cup of coffee and asked me about my day, but I just shrugged and headed back to my room. There are only so many ways to describe a graveyard, and I didn't really feel like talking about it

I shut my bedroom door behind me, sitting down against my bed, next to the loose floorboard. I toyed with the edge for a while, popping it halfway up and then letting it fall back down. The coffee in the cup grew cold as I forgot about it, fixating on the floorboard. I didn't know if I wanted to revisit it again.

It's there. It's all there. Hidden under splintered wood and nails.

My throat started to close as my vision went blurry. I tried to keep my hands from shaking, but they rattled against the cold floor.

I left three times.

Everything I left behind is there. Under the floorboard. Everything I left behind and everything I'm still scared to go back to.

It's all there.

Every time I went back home everything was exactly the same as it was when I left. The only difference being the seasons and whether or not the trees had their leaves.

The house was always the same. The same dark blue siding, black shutters, porch with a small table, the back door, now with a wreath hanging on it for the season. A wreath we always forget to take down until long after snow has stopped falling. Lights on in Mom and Grandma's room, and darkness in Dad's office and

Claire's room. The gutter next to my window bent from when I would climb down it to escape.

The only difference was that the light in my room was out, and the door was closed. Like Claire's room. And Dad's office.

The rooms they stopped going in.

The same house. With lights that go off at night, when I would sneak out the window and watch it from the apple tree that grew in the back corner of the yard. The only place where the house and street lights couldn't reach me, where my presence could be hidden from the world.

One time, when I ran away, I didn't go far, and every night I would go back to that tree, and watch my little world get farther and farther away, until they would find me again, and drag me back.

My fingers traced the floorboard, feeling the ridges and splinters that have accumulated after so many years.

This house, it's not my home anymore. It hasn't been my home for a long time. I don't belong here. That's the simple truth. It's a foreign place in which I take shelter surrounded by familiar faces.

I popped up the floorboard.

Once, when I watched the house from the edge of the trees, I snuck back inside.

There wasn't anyone waiting, staring at the door, hoping I'd walk through it.

I don't know what I'd expected.

I went back into my room, then. It was the same. Exactly the same except for the places where furniture had been moved an inch or two to the left or right when they'd searched it. Everything was there, though, like it is now.

The bed was made and stood in the corner, solemn and empty, unused.

The window shade was drawn, shut tightly against the world.

The desk there, the note from when I left gone, but all the pencils, the pens, the sticky notes, the notebooks - they were there.

That day, I pulled open the top right dresser drawer and looked under my socks. They were missing, but I wasn't surprised.

After that, I switched to the floorboard.

The three craft knives and paper clips I used to hide there.

A shiver ran down my spine, and I let go of the floorboard.

I see myself, the way I saw myself that day. Sitting on the floor, my back to the wall. A cut on my left arm that refused to bleed.

I just wanted to know that I was made of more than skin and bone, that I was human. I wanted the voices to stop. I wanted it all to go away.

It never did.

Sometimes I got the confirmation I wanted. And I'd sit there, horrified.

Tears would roll down my face.

"See," the voices would say, "you're human."

"No," I'd say back, "I'm a monster."

Another night. Sitting against my bed. Just me. Voices in my head, fighting with each other. Ignoring my silent pleas. Pain. Just pain. Not physical pain. Mental pain. I couldn't move. I couldn't speak. I could barely think. The only thing running through my mind: three words. "Let me die." But they didn't. They didn't let me die.

That's the worst kind of pain.

The pain you can't make go away.

When you can't even move, when you just sit there shaking, your breathing shallow, fighting everything your body is telling you. Everything your mind is telling you.

Just sitting there wanting it all to end.

Knowing that it's not going to move.

I closed my eyes.

This place haunts me. This house. This room.

I don't know why I went back that day. I don't know why I ever went back.

There are ghosts here that should not be disturbed.

Ghosts of people I used to be.

Every face I wore to hide the broken pieces behind the mask.

And the broken girl?

She's here too.

I can see her. I can see here sitting against the wall, against the bed, crying, shaking, wanting to scream. Pleading with invisible ghosts. Whispering to herself.

I look in the mirror, and I can see her.

She's staring back at me. Her eyes meet my eyes. Her tears reflect my tears.

Her eyes are my eyes. Her tears are my tears. Her shattered pieces are my pieces.

Her scars are my scars.

She's still broken.

The floorboard fell back into place.

I can't even imagine what it must have been like for them to find all that. To find the notes I wrote to myself, to find all the hidden remnants around the room, under loose floorboards, under clothing in drawers, buried in the back of my closet, under my mattress.

I can't believe anyone would be so cruel as to do that to someone.

How can you just leave, and leave all that behind?

One of my picture frames was turned down, that day. When I picked it up, it was the one with Rachel, Gabi, and Maddy. And me.

I reached over and took the picture down from my nightstand, holding it close to me and wishing they were here to hug me, to reassure me and tell me that everything would be okay.

They don't know I ran away.

They didn't know then, and they don't know now.

They know, but they don't know that they know. They don't know that the little girl in the paper was me.

The wind rattled the window and I jumped.

It's midnight, and the world is quiet again. I took out my phone and texted Lily. She might not still be awake, but I'm banking on the fact that she is.

I pulled on a pair of boots, gloves, a hat, and closed my door quietly, trying to minimize the noise my feet made against the hardwood floor.

I stopped in front of Dad's office, at the end of the hall. I haven't gone in there in years.

I pushed open the door.

I wish I hadn't.

It was the same as I remembered it. Dad's army hat sat on his desk, all his papers arranged into neat stacks. His army jacket hanging over the chair. The picture of me, Mom, him, and Claire.

I miss her.

I miss him.

I picked up his army jacket and held it to my nose. It still smelled like him. Just barely. I pulled it on. I could feel him there with me, holding me, telling me that everything would be okay.

Then I left the house, locking the door behind me and returning the key to the top of the doorway. I didn't look back until I reached the end of the street. I stopped for a second, there, at the corner, and stared at the house. At the little world I grew up in. All the memories, and all the ghosts.

I pulled the jacket tighter around me.

And then I turned around.

And walked away.

Chapter Twenty

"Where are we going?" Lily met me by the park as the sky was beginning to grow lighter.

"I don't know," I shrugged, "but it's February break, so we don't have school or anything for a couple days."

"Are you planning on a day thing, or like a multi-day thing?"

"I don't know."

"Alright, sounds good."

"So you'll come?"

She hoisted her backpack up onto her shoulders, "Yeah, I'll come."

"Okay."

"So, again, where are we going?"

"I don't know, I just figured we'd pick a direction and start walking."

"Okay, which direction?"

"Uh... I don't care, you pick."

"What about east?"

"Okay, which way is east?"

"That way," she pointed in the direction the sun was rising, "remember, the sun, rising in the east!" and started belting the words to 'Tale As Old As Time', meticulously hitting every note off-key.

"Oh my god, stop, it sounds like you're murdering a cat."

"Haha I *know*."

"You sure about that?"

"Yeah, fun fact, I have relatively perfect pitch."

"Meaning?"

She turned around, walking backward so she could see my face. "Are you serious? You don't know what that means?"

"What, are you some sort of music nerd?"

She shrugs, "Sort of. I was going to be a music major."

"Were?"

"Yeah, but I don't know. Everything kind of changed when I moved here, and that was after I'd already ran away a couple times, so I don't know. Things change. Take today, for example, or tomorrow, but whenever we decide to go back into the 'real world', so to speak, we aren't going to be the same people we are now. It's not the same as running away, I mean, we'll still have the same opportunities, but especially after I ran away, everything changed. I have to find a way to explain why I missed a couple months of school on my college applications. That's not easy, and what do you think they're going to think? What am I supposed to say? 'Oh, I ran away on a life changing journey to find myself and to escape the shitty life I had', hell *fucking* no."

"I- I haven't thought about that."

"Well you don't have to."

"I do, actually. But I was just going to ignore it and pretend it didn't happen."

"You ran away?"

"Twice. I spent more time in the hospital afterward than I did actually running, though. I've never thought about having to explain it, or having it change my life in any other ways than it did then."

"Really?" she turned back around, kicking a loose stone out of place. "I think about it all the time. I regret it, sometimes, running away. There are so many other things I could've done. Once you leave, you can't stay gone forever. And big picture, there's nothing to go back for, usually. For me, at least, there wasn't. That's why I ended up coming here, not just because my parents kicked me out, but because after I went back I had nothing. I had absolutely nothing. So at that point, what was the point? Even now, I wonder, what's the point?"

"I wish I could answer that question."

She sighed, "Me too."

We didn't talk for a while after that.

I never thought about it like that before. Running away. It just seemed like something that could fix my problems, not something that would create a million more, even though I did it years ago. I *didn't* go back to a normal life. Nothing was the same. My entire life changed. Time didn't freeze and restart when I went back.

The only reason I'm not looked at differently is because no one knows. I'm the girl that used to be the "mute girl" and the "freak", but I've never been the "runaway". I've never been the kid that people have to treat like a glass vase hanging over the edge of a high shelf, about to fall.

I've never been normal, and I'll never be normal.

But running away made me less normal than I already was.

Normal is a stupid word. No one is normal. No one is normal because no one exactly fits the stereotypes we have set in place.

No one can be defined by anyone else.

And that's something we forget, and we forget it a lot.

I'm stereotyped as a normal high schooler. I couldn't imagine being stereotyped as the person I really am. The person that only a select few know. The person that they know, I'm sure has been stereotyped. She's been stereotyped as the scared girl who ran away and cried herself to sleep. She's been stereotyped as the girl everyone has to be careful around, the girl they have to put in a cage so she doesn't run away again, and she's been stereotyped because she was the scared girl. And she's the girl who missed school, the one who is stereotyped to not go to college. The one stereotyped with no friends, no family, no life.

And part of that's true.

But there's so much of it that's not.

But I'm a stereotype. And as long as I fit part of it, I am it.

I'm a statistic, too, I guess.

So, what's the point?

Because of the choices I made in my life, that's all I am.

A stereotype and a statistic.

* * *

"Where'd you get that jacket?" Lily asked.

"It was my dad's."

"Oh."

"It's not a bad thing, I actually wasn't sure we still had it. I... I went into his office this morning. I haven't gone in there in ten years."

"Oh, wow."

"Yeah."

"Well, I like the jacket, it looks good on you."

"Thanks."

My phone buzzed, and I shut it off.

"You don't want to check that?" Lily said.

"No," I shook my head, shoving the phone into my backpack, "not particularly."

"Are you okay?"

"Yeah," I pushed my hair out of my face, pulling my hat farther down over my ears.

"Are you sure? This was all just sort of out of the blue."

"I'm okay, I just needed to get out of my house."

"I get that."

"Yeah."

We walked for what must have been miles until we finally stopped to rest. Lily laid down on her back and closed her eyes, shielding her face from the midday sun. I laid down next to her, staring up into the clear blue sky, watching it grow darker as clouds blocked out the sun.

She rolled over, resting her head on my chest, and we sat there, watching the sky, enveloped in the silence that carried all of our tacit words.

*   *   *

Early morning.
5:27
It was still dark. The sun starting to rise.
Mom was still asleep, but Dad wasn't in their room.
So I walked down to his office.
It was cold.
I didn't have socks on, and my feet were frozen against the hardwood floor.
I knocked on the door.
There was no response.
I opened it.
I screamed.

Two years before:

Grandpa's funeral. I was five. Dad let me speak at it, he helped me figure out what to say and practice it until I could pronounce all the words.

I didn't really understand what was happening. It was my first funeral. At your first funeral at that age, you don't cry. You just sort of watch everything unfold, trying to comprehend it.

Dad introduced me when he was done saying his little bit, and when I stepped up onto the podium and looked out at everyone's faces it was silent. You could hear my grandfather breathe. That's how quiet it was.

I look a deep breath.

"There is a quote by Rich- Richard Bach that says, 'if you love someone, set them free. If they come back they're yours; if they don't they never were'. I loved Grandpa, and if you're here right now, you did too. We don't know if we'll ever see him again, but we have to set him free. I think- I think that we will see him again. He'll come back to us. At least, I want him to. I miss him. I wanted to tell a story about him and who he was, but you guys already know that. Why else would you be here? So, if you love him, please, for his sake and for ours, set him free."

It was short, but when I stepped off the podium I didn't pay attention to how everyone else reacted. I looked at Dad, and he was clapping, smiling.

He hoisted me onto his lap and hugged me. "Good job, Cassie. I'm proud of you."

"I love you."

"I love you too, darling. I love you too."

* * *

"Cassie," Lily was shaking me.

"Yeah?" I looked over at her.

"You spaced out for a while."

"Sorry," I sat up.

"It's okay! I was just making sure you were still in there," she grinned.

"Haha, yeah, I am." I blinked away the memory.

She pointed at the sky, "It's snowing again."

I watched as the white flakes began to fall from the sky. We sat there together, neither of us spoke. We just listened to the quiet breathing of the world and watched the quiet, frozen tears fall from the sky.

She laced her fingers in mine. I turned my head to look at her, and she stared into my face and smiled.

I felt myself smile back.

She gave my hand a squeeze.

I didn't let go.

*   *   *

I didn't talk at Dad's funeral.

There were no words I could have possibly said.

A flag was folded and laid on top of the casket. A bouquet of flowers placed over the flag.

When it was my turn to step up to the casket and say goodbye, I set an orange rose down on the casket. I bowed my head and whispered, "goodbye, Daddy."

I didn't cry. Not then. Not in that place. Not with everyone watching, expecting me to cry. The funeral wasn't for him. It was for us. He'd already been laid to rest by the world, he'd already left us all behind.

The funeral was for us, to feel like we did our job in letting him go, in setting him free.

We didn't let him go.

He set himself free.

I sat back down between Mom and Grandma, staring at the back of the chair in front of me. Mom was stiff and cold, she didn't say anything to me. She didn't hug me, didn't kiss me, didn't tell me it would all be okay. She had disappeared.

She became a living shadow of her former self. I missed the person she used to be. Once in a while she would let down her walls and I could still see that person, but not often. I don't know who she is anymore. I didn't know who she was.

I think she forgot herself.

It takes a lot to forget. It's not like breathing. Forgetting is like holding your breath; you can go without remembering for a while, but then your body remembers, like coming up for air.

I wonder if she's remembered yet.

I wonder if I made her remember.

The casket was lowered into the ground, tearing him away from me. Everything that I had left of him.

It was gone.

I stood up and pushed my way through the row. Then I ran.

I ran until I hit the layer of trees that lined the cemetery and I kept running until I tripped over a tree root and just laid there crying.

It was there, lying there on the dirt sobbing, that I realized that I wasn't completely human anymore.

*　　　*　　　*

It snowed throughout the afternoon, and we kept walking east, or what we thought was east, until we came across a wooded area and stopped. She'd been smart and brought a couple of matches, so we found some dry wood and did our best to start a fire.

We huddled around it, once it got going, and in the silence, I looked at the world around us. The little secluded area. It's not much different from anywhere else. The trees are the same, the dead grass is the same, the dead silence is the same, the stars are the same, the moon is the same, the clouds are the same.

Nothing's different.

But everything is different.

Nothing and everything.

Everything and nothing.

"Lily?"

"Yeah?" she rested her head on my shoulder

My heart jumped.

The something inside me twisted, a hundred knots becoming more and more tangled.

"Why'd you leave?"

She stiffened for a second. It took her a minute to respond. "I didn't belong."

"Where?"

"My home, my town, my- world. Isn't that why you left, or wanted to leave?"

"How'd you know?"

"I notice things."

"Like?"

"The way you act when anyone mentions home, when anyone or anything reminds you of something from your past, when you get too comfortable, you stare off into the distance. Like you're thinking of everything you used to have but at the same time everything that you didn't have. You had everything, but you had nothing."

"What?"

"Don't act like you don't."

"I- I didn't, I'm not-" I pulled away, she lifted her head. Her blue eyes met mine. "How-"

"I look at things the same way," she didn't look away. Her eyes searched me, looking for something. Something that wasn't there. Something that wasn't visible. Something so hidden that I'd forgotten it was there.

Something so hidden that I didn't *know* it was there.

"When someone says something that makes me think... it's hard. When you have to act like you understand something that they expect you to understand. When you have to ignore your own values and emotions to please someone else and their expectations. It's hard when you have to act like you understand, when you have to understand... and they don't."

I didn't look away.

I wanted to.

I couldn't say anything.

The knots inside me were twisting, tightening, tearing.

She looked away.

The knots didn't disappear this time.

The twisting something didn't fade.

"Sorry," she said.

I shook my head, "You're right."

"That's why I'm sorry."

We both stared into the flames, the white hot red and orange figures dancing in the darkness.

In it, I see everything. I see my father, I see my sister, I see my mother, my grandmother, my friends, I see them all.

I see the first snow when I was little, Dad picking me up, helping me make a snowman. I see him teaching me to throw. I see him and Mom teaching me piano, how to sing, how to draw. I see Mom and Grandma making cookies with me, letting me lick the icing off the spoons, yelling at me when I tried to eat the dough. I see her following me around, giggling at things I did. I see myself holding her when she came home from the hospital after she was born, her smiling up at me and then bursting into screaming tears before I yelped and handed her off to Dad. I see Grandpa bouncing me up and down on his knee, telling me a story. I see Dad sitting in the corner, holding her, listening and smiling to himself. I see us together as a family, everyone smiling and laughing, no demons lingering over our heads. I see Rachel and I meeting for the first time, her stealing my crayons, us hating each other for the first three years we knew each other. I see Rachel, Maddy, Gabi and me running around as kids, growing up into high schoolers, talking about gossip, grades, teachers, boys. I see us laughing together, making fun of each other.

Then I see me, sitting in the corner, not talking, barely smiling, not laughing, while they joke and goof off without me, while I feel sorry for myself, thinking about how shitty my life was.

I see the casket being covered with dirt, disappearing into a mound of darkness, Dad hugging me and Mom hugging him.

I see the small box, big enough for a child, sinking into the earth, lost forever. Dad and Mom and clinging to each other, leaving me to watch from the shadows.

I see the flag covered coffin being lowered, the orange rose slipping off, forgotten. Mom sitting with her head in her hands as I ran.

I see Grandma crying in my empty, abandoned room.

I see Mom, lying in bed unable to move.

Me, the only thing she had left. The only thing she had left that she lost countless times.

Gone.

Everything I had.

But I had nothing.

I made sure of that.

I made myself as distant as I could, and I blamed everyone else. I blamed them for not understanding, for not noticing, for not caring.

I used it to feel sorry for myself, as a reason for why I did what I did. For why I felt the way I felt.

I used it as an excuse, telling myself that I could leave because no one would care.

Disregarding how everyone I left behind would feel.

Owen was right.

I need to stop pitying myself for the shitty cards I was dealt.

It's not their fault. It's not my fault. It's what happened. And I can accept it and live with it, or I can let it destroy me and die with it.

It's my choice.

Not anyone else's.

I could have everything.

Or I could have nothing.

It's my choice.

Chapter Twenty One

"Good morning," she said, as I sat up and rubbed my eyes.

"Hey," I glanced around the woods, "how long have you been up?"

She shrugged, "I don't know. But sleeping in the woods isn't really my thing, so I didn't sleep that well."

"Sorry."

"Don't be! I'm having fun."

"That's good."

The fire had gone out.

"Are you okay?" she looked over at me, and she didn't look away. This time, I didn't either.

"Yeah," I gave her a small smile, "I'm okay."

I am. I'm done being sorry for myself. I'm done blaming everyone else. I'm done waiting for things to just change. I'm done expecting everyone else to understand when I don't even understand myself.

It *is* hard. It's hard trying to understand, having to understand when someone else doesn't understand you.

I don't even understand myself.

But I'm trying to.

The something inside me was writhing, twisting and fraying and so close to breaking.

I wanted to look away. I wanted to avoid those searching blue eyes, the eyes that saw everything, eyes that I couldn't hide from.

But I didn't. I couldn't.

I looked back, searching her eyes, trying to see what she was hiding. Trying to see what I was hiding from myself reflected in her eyes.

And it's there.

It's all there.

She looked away.

Her hair fell in front of her face and she reached up to tuck it behind her ear. Her eyes shined in the morning light, orange specks from the sunrise reflected in them, just like the pieces of myself I'm trying to hide. The ones she pulled out of the shadows and forced me to see. Forced me to accept. She made me see myself as the person I've been pushing away, hiding, locked behind a door, for years. The one I've been ashamed of, scared of, scared for, neglectful of, hateful toward, the one I shoved aside.

I didn't want to be her.

And by not being part of her, I neglected all the other parts. All the other truths. Everything that made me, me. All my demons and all my angels. All my flaws and all my perfections. By hiding half of me, I hid everything. And without everything, I wasn't me. Not even a little.

I wanted her to be me.

But she wasn't me.

She couldn't be.

That girl I hid is me.

The girl who got up every day and looked in the mirror as she plastered a smile on her face, she isn't me.

I wish I'd known that before I got my heart broken by someone I couldn't love.

I don't know what's worse.

Being scared to love the person you're in love with.

Or wanting to love someone that you know you can't fall in love with.

The worst part is, he didn't hurt me. I hurt myself by hurting him.

The only person I can blame is myself.

She raised her eyebrows at me when she looked over her shoulder and caught me staring at her. I looked down, but when I glanced back up, I saw her sideways smile for a second before her hair fell back over her face.

* * *

"So, what's the plan for today?" she asked, stepping over a log.

"Again, I don't know," I said, "I guess we could find our way back home, or we could just keep walking."

"Either sounds fine."

"You pick."

"Oh, don't make me pick! I'm extremely indecisive."

"That's why you should pick!"

"Alright, fine, how about we keep walking until around two and then we can start finding our way back, maybe find a bus. Sound good?"

"Sounds perfect."

"Alright," she started walking in a random direction. I followed. "You want to hear something crazy?" she said.

"Always."

"I'm excited for graduation."

"That is crazy."

"Okay, but hear me out. I want to get out. I want to get out of the small town, the limitations," she brushed a knot out of her hair with her fingers, "I get antsy quickly, I can't stay in one place. I want to see what's out *there*," she flung her arms out, gesturing at the trees on either side of her, "there's so much out there, Cassandra, and I want to see it all."

"All of it?"

"All of it. When I go back, I want to visit London, and Paris, and Ireland, and the Yukon in the Arctic Circle, and the Amazon Rainforest, and the Sydney Opera House in Australia. There's so much I haven't seen. The most I've seen is the Washington Monument in D.C. That's not enough. I've barely scratched the surface. I want to dive into it, to get the most out of life."

"Me too, Lily, me too."

"When we go back, we're going to see it all, someday."

"We?"

"Yeah, we. If you're in. Because I'm in, Cassie. I'm all in."

I took a breath and exhaled slowly.

"I'm all in."

She grinned.

"Lily?" I asked after a minute of silence.

"Yeah?"

"I don't want to go back."

"Me neither, but we have to."

"We don't *have* to."

"But we should."

"I know."

"Hey! Look!" she ran ahead all of the sudden, shouting with delight when she found that the ground ahead dipped down at a steep decline. "Come on!" she sat down in the snow.

"Are you *crazy?*"

"Are you *not?*"

"Fair enough," I joined her, "what are we doing?"

"This," she pushed off and started to slide down the hill, rolling most of the way and landing on her back at the bottom.

I followed her down, rolling and hitting bumps, getting snow in my face and boots, and finally landing next to her. "And what," I said, rolling over onto my back, "was the point of that?"

"Absolutely nothing," she pushed herself up onto her elbow and looked down at me, "but does everything have to have a point?"

"I don't know, it's just that at this point, I feel like if there's no point, then there's just no point. So why do it?"

"Oh, come on."

"What?"

"Cassandra James, do not let all the mundane concatenations in this world be for naught," said Lily Peters. "If there always has to be a point to live, you aren't living. Living just to live isn't living. And if you aren't living, you aren't surviving. If you aren't surviving, you aren't living. You can't live just to live. You have to live to live."

"Alright, fine, you're right."

"I know I'm right," she grinned.

I scooped up a handful of snow.

"Oh don't you dare…"

I chucked it at her, hitting her shoulder, "there was absolutely no point to that."

"You're so dead," she shaped a fistful of snow into a ball and threw it, hitting me square in the face.

I fell backwards, laughing, wiping the snow out of my eyes.

"Oh my god! I'm so sorry, are you okay?" she leaned over me, helping me brush the snow off my face, trying to hide her laughter.

"I'm fine! You, however, are also dead."

"Alright, fine, I deserve that," she grinned sideways.

The knots twisted.

The sun reflected off her hair, her eyes glowing from the light rebounding off of the snow.

"Cassandra?"

"Yeah?"

Her face was inches from mine.

"You're beautiful."

I sat up, and she leaned back a little, watching me.

"Cassandra?"

"What?"

She waited until I looked at her.

"I know you like me."

"I- I don't- what- no!"

"I always know when someone's lying."

"And if I am?"

She shrugged, "Guess we'll have to find out."

She pushed herself to her feet, a smug look on her face.

I watched her walk away.

"You coming?" she called over her shoulder.

"Yeah," I muttered, following a couple feet behind.

* * *

I've always had a point. A reason. A motive. When I didn't is when everything went to shit.

If I didn't have a point, I gave up. The point of running away was so I wouldn't give up. If I had stayed, there wouldn't have been a point. Living without a point seemed pointless. Why just live to live? If you weren't living for something, what was the point? But I guess that's the thing, there wasn't always a point. Sometimes you were just living to live. Lily's right.

If you're living just to live, there's no point.

You have to live to be living.

There's not always a point.

If you need a point to live, why live?

You live when you don't always need a point.

At this point, there is no point. We'll never be accepted in the real world, and we're hardly accepted by ourselves. We're two strangers in a strange place, we don't belong here. We don't belong there, either.

We don't belong anywhere.

So, at this point, there is no point. But that's the point.

We're not living just to live.

We're living to *live*.

The whole point is to live to get the most out of life. And that's what we'll do. No matter what happens, we have each other.

That's all that matters.

That's the point.

How am I supposed to get the most out of life if I'm constantly scared to live it?

"Lily?" I sat down next to her where she'd taken refuge under a tree.

"Yeah?"

"You're right."

"About?"

"I lied."

"I know."

"And?"

"Well, what's the truth?"

"I-" I swallowed the stupid excuses. "I like you."

A small smile crept across her face, "I know."

"And?"

She leaned in.

I didn't stop her.

Chapter Twenty Two

"How have you been, Cassandra?"

I looked at her, thinking. There aren't a lot of ways to describe quite how I've been. The past few months have been a blur. Lily and I went back, and school started up again, Mom went back to normal, Owen and I haven't talked, and other than that everything's been the same.

"Things have been good."

"Good? Not just okay?"

I thought about Lily, and grinned to myself, "Not just okay."

"That's good, I'm glad to hear that."

"Yeah."

The pen scratched against the clipboard. "And graduation's coming up in a few months, right?"

I nodded, "Yeah."

"Did you send in any college applications?"

"Yeah, I did, a couple months ago."

"Have you heard back from any yet?"

I shook my head, "But I'm supposed to hear back this week, actually."

"That's exciting! What's your top school?"

I shrugged, "I don't know, maybe Boston University, or Yale."

"What are you majoring in?"

"I'm pretty undecided, right now, but I'd enjoy doing something in writing."

"Do you write a lot?"

"A good amount."

"That's good!"

"Yeah."

"And how have your friends been?"

"They... they're good. One of them is going to Brown."

"Which one?"

"Maddy."

"That's exciting! And how's the boyfriend, are you two still together? You haven't been in in a while."

I skipped most of my appointments for the last few months.

"I broke up with him."

"How come?"

"It just wasn't right."

"That's too bad."

"Yeah."

She squinted at her clipboard, flipping a page over, "And your mother, is she still in her 'shock phase'?"

"No."

"Good, good."

"Yeah."

Awkward silence.

"Here," she put down her clipboard, walked over to a cabinet and pulled out a set of cards, "we're going to play a game."

"Game?"

"Yes," she sat back down, "a game. Here, so one of us will pick a card, and ask the other the question on it, the other person has to answer the question. Simple enough?"

"Yeah... sure."

"Alright, I'll go first," she leaned forward and picked up a card. The clipboard lay forgotten on the floor next to her chair. "What's your favorite season?"

"That's the question?"

"Mhmm."

"Okay, uh... I don't know, fall, I guess."

"Okay! Now you pick a card."

I picked one up and turned it over, "Okay, what's your birthday?"

"August sixteenth."

"Cool."

"Do you have any pets?"

"No. I had a fish when I was little, but it died a week after I got it."

"What happened?"

"I tried to feed it cereal."

"Oh no!"

"Yeah, that didn't work out too well."

"I'd imagine so."

"Yeah. Okay, what are your hobbies?"

"Um..." she looked up at the ceiling, "I play piano a bit, and I like to go on hikes with my girlfriend."

"Your *girlfriend?*"

"Yeah," she nodded.

"Oh."

She picked up another card.

"What's she like?"

"My girlfriend?"

"Yeah."

She grinned, leaning back in her chair, "Well, her name is Sarah, and she's a journalist, actually, so she travels a lot. She's funny, I think you'd like her, she has a sarcastic sense of humor. She's very adventurous."

I tucked a strand of hair behind my ear, "She sounds cool."

"She is cool," she laughed.

My girlfriend's cool too.

*   *   *

I didn't go home right away, instead I went to the little world I used to go to with Owen. I haven't been there since after we broke up.

The world has started to reawaken with spring, and the birds have returned to the trees. I'm not the only living thing anymore. I'm still human enough to be surrounded by living things.

I'm still human.

"*It's just a matter of time, Cassandra.*" I heard the cold voice. The one I hadn't heard in years. The "demons" I made up in my mind.

I closed my eyes.

"You know that. You're hanging on by a thread. It's about to break. You're hanging onto the side of a ship. It's about to sink. You're standing in the eye of a storm. It's about to break.

You're standing on the edge of a cliff."

I shut them tighter.

"It doesn't matter what you say, what you do, what you don't say, what you don't do. You can't control it. You have to die with it."

I have to live with it.

"You aren't living if you're just waiting to die."

I opened my eyes.

I looked up. The sky was grey, the clouds obscuring the sun. I pulled Dad's jacket closer around me.

What would he think of me, if he could see me now? Where I've ended up. The mess I've made of my life.

At least I haven't made the same mess he did.

"Not yet."

Not *ever*.

I wonder how Owen is.

Owen Taylor, with the curly blond hair that always gets in his face and those bright green eyes.

He's probably forgotten me by now.

I don't know what's going on with Lily and I.

Sometimes I wish it never happened.

Things would be so much simpler.

I'm sick of this place. This never changing, uneventful, boring place. It's the same as everywhere else. The town, the people, the house. Everything. It's not home.

I drew circles in the mud with a stick, round and round and round and round. Endless, continuous, tiresome.

Consigned to oblivion.

We all are.

We think we have control over our own lives, but how much control can we have? Everything is predetermined. Who our parents are, the kind of lifestyle we're born into, how smart we are, how athletic, how artistic. Our ancestry, our hometown, our opinions and biases and memories. It's all predetermined. And sure, people talk about "breaking away from the path" and breaking the "family traditions", but it all stays with you. How far do you really stray? A couple thousand miles, sure, but that's just distance. A new career path fueled entirely on your own, or a new lifestyle you have to support yourself because you aren't supported by others, alright, but that's just pretending to forget. Cutting yourself off.

It all stays with you.

It's predetermined.

We're all heading to the same place, anyway. We're all going to die. Different times, different places, different destinations, sure, but it's the same idea. It's complex, but it's simple. The foundation is the same, the only difference is the frame you build around it. We live differently, but in the end we die the same.

Maybe some die in a car crash, or a fire, or from a sickness, or naturally.

Some kill themselves.

But the actions and events that contribute to your death, it all happens when you're alive.

Everything afterwards happens when you're dead.

We all die the same.

When you die you're dead.

No one's special.

You aren't living if you're just waiting to die. But we're all just waiting to die, aren't we? So, if we're all just waiting to die, are any of us living?

I rubbed my head, burying it in my hands to shield my eyes from the sun. It's too bright.

A branch snapped.

I looked over my shoulder. There's no one there.

Lily's back home, probably asleep or off somewhere with her friends. She doesn't know half the stuff I've hidden. She doesn't even know I go to therapy.

She doesn't need to know.

She'd be better off without me. She knows that. I know that. But neither of us will ever say it. I don't regret having her in my life. I've become a different person because of it. I've become a better person. I know more about myself. I've stopped hiding as much.

At this point, I don't know who I'm hiding and who I'm not. I don't know who's just a face and who's real. I don't know if the person I want to be is the person I actually am. It's something I've been trying to figure out for months, but the closer I get to figuring it out, the farther away I get. The more confusing it becomes. The more tangled all the knots get, the ends fraying until you can't tell where it starts and where it stops and where it continues.

I'm consigned to oblivion.

Forever consigned to the idea that I can find who I am. That the person I'm looking for is out there somewhere. A pretentious idea formulated in books and movies, idealized and made realistic.

Forever consigned to the idea that all I have to do is pull aside a branch, venture underwater, look behind a tree, and there she'll be, waiting, smiling, congratulating me on finally finding her.

Forever consigned to the idea that I'm living for something more than the reward of dying, that my place on the Earth will not go unnoticed, that as long as I touch someone's life, I will have made my time here worthwhile.

Forever consigned to the idea that I'm not consigned to oblivion.

I drew a line through the circle. I made indents in the ground, little dots, surrounding the circle, within the circle, around the perimeter of the circle.

There.

I just broke the consignment to oblivion.

By breaking off the point of continuation, by creating tears and ripples in the soundness of the line forming a solid ring, unbroken, suddenly broken.

That's how simple it should be.

Have I broken my consignment to oblivion? Am I one of the dots within the circle? Instead of going around and around, revolving with the predetermined path, am I just standing there, watching it all go by and doing nothing? Watching my life pass by and seeing everything I could have had, watching from within, still able to touch and feel and remember it all. Still being a part of it, but not having any of it?

Or am I one of the dots outside the circle? Standing outside of the predetermined path, having successfully broken away from it, and watching it all go by and doing nothing? Watching my life pass by from afar and seeing everything I used to have, watching it get farther and farther away, unable to touch and feel and remember it all. Not being a part of it. Knowing that I used to have everything, and now I have nothing?

Or am I the line going through it, cutting it off at the source. Ending my consignment to oblivion.

That's what Dad did.

Life hit him a bit too hard, and it took him down.

He took all of us down with him.

I did that too, in some ways.

I always thought I was saving myself, saving everyone around me *from* myself.

All I did was make it harder for them to stay afloat.

All I did was drag them down with me.

A ship that sinks and takes all its passengers down with it.

I hate myself for that.

What's the point of breaking the consignment to oblivion if you break everyone else with it?

*   *   *

I can't break Lily. I can't break her too. And I break everything. I break everything *because* I'm broken.

I sat there, by the water, staring at the broken consignment in and around the circle. I didn't move for a long time.

"*Alright, get up.*"

The hairs on the back on my neck stood straight up and a shiver ran down my spine.

I knew that voice. It was the same voice that matched those eyes. That matched that hair. That matched that face. I'd know it anywhere.

There's no way...

"*Cassandra.*"

I folded into myself. I couldn't run, I couldn't hide, I couldn't escape, I couldn't do anything. I was trapped. I was trapped and he knew it.

"*Get up.*"

I forced myself to peek out over the arm covering my eyes, and there they are. The same shoes. Same pants. Same shirt. My eyes trace the outline, following it upward to the face. The nose, the freckles, the lips, the eyes, the hair, the ears.

"What are you doing here?" I said soundlessly. My voice failed me. While *I* couldn't run, my voice did.

"*Come on,*" he grabs my arm and hoists me to my feet. I yanked my arm away, stumbling backward. He raises his eyebrows.

"What are you doing here?" I said, the words cracking.

"*Where's Lily?*"

"It's been months and that's all you have to say?"

"*Where's Lily, Cassandra?*"

"She- she's back home."

"And where are you going?"

"Nowhere."

"We both know damn well that's not true."

"Okay, wait a minute," my voice returned with my anger. "What the hell are you doing here? You appear out of nowhere, no warning, no anything, it's been months, and why now? Why like this? What the *hell*?"

"All valid questions, but irrelevant as of now."

"Your point?"

"They don't matter."

"They don't?"

"No. Cassandra, you're leaving her."

It wasn't a question. It was a direct accusation.

If it were a question it would have been easier to deny.

"Why are you leaving her?"

"Stop- stop saying that."

"Saying what? Leaving?"

"Stop it, stop it, stop it," I grabbed the sides of my head. The words echoed through my head, haunting, torturing, demonizing.

"Look," he grabs my shoulders, grounding me, staring me down until I meet his eyes. *"You can't leave her. I don't care what's better for you, or what you think you're doing to help her, but she needs you. Lily needs you, Cassandra. You need her. If you walk away from her, fine, go, go live your life, alone. Do whatever the hell you want with it, but you'll never see either of us again. You have a choice. Choose your path. Pick your poison. It's up to you. Don't listen to the god damn voices in your head, okay? They aren't there, they don't matter, they don't control you. You hear me?"*

I nodded. Fingers shaking. Hands balled into fists. The palm of my hand burning.

"*Good.*" He lets go of me, the force of his hands leaving my shoulders sending me backwards a couple steps, giving me the choice to leave the ground, to let it slide out from under me.

Or keep my feet planted firmly on it. Grounded.

"Owen."

He looks down, "*What?*"

"Where are you going?"

He shakes his head. "*Nowhere, Cassandra. Nowhere.*"

A shard lodged itself in my heart when he said my name.

A shard of ice, of hatred, of regret, of desperation, of hopes that I killed long ago.

Slowly, I turned. I walked away, leaving him again. Leaving a path that I chose to stray from. Abandoning a poison I thought too strong to handle, a poison I couldn't pick, even though I wanted to.

I turned to go back, returning to her again. Returning to a path that I chose to wander. Returning to a poison I picked with my own fingers, my own hands, my own thoughts, of my own choosing. A poison too strong to handle, a poison I picked, even though I didn't want to.

Leaving a life that I could have had. A life that would have been simple. A life that would have been complicated. A life that would have been everything. But a life that would have been nothing. I would have had nothing. By leaving him I left a life that had everything I wanted staring me in the face, but forever out of reach.

By leaving him I left the ability to fool myself behind, the ability to tell myself I was someone I wasn't. By leaving him I left the girl I wanted to be.

I left her in the park, freezing on the ground next to a bench.

She died that day. Cold, snow covered, crying, heart broken.

The only funeral she got was the snow covering her in a soft blanket of possibilities.

The only person who mourned her was me.

She was forgotten by everyone else.

Returning to a life that I wasn't sure I wanted. A life that would be complicated. A life that would be simple. A life that would be nothing. But a life that would be everything. I would have everything. By returning to her I returned to a life that had everything I wanted staring me in the face, but I was blind to it. By returning to her I returned to the inability to fool myself, the inability to tell myself I was the someone I wasn't. By returning to her I left the girl I couldn't be.

I turned to the girl I could be, instead.

I saw her in the mirror, eyes broken but hopeful, face dirty but unstained.

She was recalled to life that day, in a place where she'd almost died, crying. Heart cold. Heart unable to be broken because it was already in so many pieces.

She was recalled to life that day, a girl with eyes broken but hopeful, face dirty but unstained, heart twisted but not yet broken.

The memory of the girl was allowed to rest in peace that day in the snow when she laid next to a girl she hadn't meant to fall in love with.

The snow no longer served as a blanket of possibilities, but a blanket of actualities.

She was welcomed by everyone and everything around her.

The only person she wasn't accepted by was me.

She was accepted by everyone else.

And the never fading voices swamped her mind, the same words forever echoing.

"*Why?*"

For the last time, I looked back.

The empty space stared back at me.

Chapter Twenty Three

"Hey," I said, sitting down next to her by the water. She was fiddling with a stone, eyebrows creased slightly, staring into space, looking at something I couldn't see.

"Hey," she said, looking up. Her face fell back into its normal composure, "Where've you been?"

"Wandering."

"Well, it's good to see you again."

"Yeah, it's good to see you too."

"You look exhausted."

I was, and my weak smile didn't do anything to hide it. Neither did my trembling hands and bruised palms.

"Is everything okay?"

"Yeah," I nodded, "everything's fine." A rock fell to the bottom of my stomach with a thud.

"Are you sure? You're never around anymore."

The rock lodged there.

The shard expanded.

"I know, I've just been stressed with school and everything."

"Yeah, me too," she ran her fingers through her hair, messing it up, "I haven't slept in weeks."

"Yeah, me neither."

She slipped her hand into mine briefly, giving my hand a quick squeeze.

I don't know why I can't let myself fully accept it.

I don't know what I'm scared of.

It's right. It's so right. It's her.

What am I scared of?

I hope she couldn't feel my fingers trembling beneath hers.

But I know she did.

She noticed everything. Even things that I didn't. Things I didn't want to.

"Hey," she said quietly, pulling away slightly.

I let my eyes travel up her face, lingering just below her eyes, scared to move farther.

"Cassandra…"

My eyes moved upward another half an inch. She was searching, scanning, pulling information, thoughts, emotions, things I couldn't even describe, bringing them to the surface, making me see them as she saw them, making me acknowledge that they were there. Making me face them.

"It's okay," she kissed me.

It was different than how I'd ever been kissed before. It wasn't passion, want, hope, unobtainable love, a fire sparking out of control, desperation in the fear that there won't be a tomorrow.

It was a gentle, slow burning flame, growing steadily brighter, fueled by a spark but not controlled by one. It was hope, possibility, obtainable love, a forever beating heart, forever breathing lungs, living and breathing as one, consolidated by the knowledge that there will be a tomorrow, a tomorrow in each other's arms. An infinity of not questioning it.

It's not her I question. It's not even her and I together that I question.

I question me.

Why is it the one thing I'm so sure of is the one thing I can't accept.

She pulled away slowly, leaving me breathless, my heart racing at the speed of light, toward a star billions of light years away that it can never reach.

"It's okay."

And for once, I believed those words. Simple words. Complex words. Everything words. Nothing words. Words that, no matter who spoke them, if they were true or lying, an ideology or a reality, a want or a possibility, I didn't believe. After Dad… there was no point. Nothing was okay. Nothing was supposed to be okay. Nothing was allowed to be okay. Nothing could be okay.

But now, when she says those words, I believe them.

Everything is okay.

Everything is supposed to be okay, not always, but eventually.

Everything is allowed to be okay, it's not always just consigned to oblivion.

Everything is okay.

*   *   *

We didn't talk for a while. She looked over at me, and her eyes scanned my face.

When her eyes finally met mine, her walls were down, and I could see everything she'd hidden from me. Just for a second, before they went up again.

Mine are always up, brick walls, covered by steel and guarded by barbed wire. I don't know how she knocks them down, every time. They were built to protect, to keep everyone and everything out, armed with weapons to attack if necessary. Laden with tons and tons of words, emotions, neglect, rejection, fear, anger, hurt; laden with thoughts, thoughts that can easily become words, everything needed to push people away. There was only so close anyone could get. Even Owen couldn't break them down. He tried, and like so many before him, he failed. Even I've failed. I've built them so strong that I can't break them down, I've hidden myself from me, I've protected myself from me, I didn't let myself get too close.

It only takes her a second, one look, one touch, one word, to disintegrate them. The walls. My boundaries. My protection. I've tried to keep them strong, but they don't listen to me. At some point, they became so strong that they became independent. I have no control.

They listen to her.

And now, hers have listened to me.

In the silence, I have the space to think.

Owen Taylor.

He was there.

He touched me.

He spoke to me.

He disappeared again.

If he hadn't turned up, would I still be there, sitting by the water, or somewhere else in the world, without Lily Peters in my life? I'd tried to fight my instincts, everything telling me to go, and without him, would I have failed?

The thought sends shivers down my spine. It makes the hairs on the back of my neck stand up.

I don't want to think about it.

Where is he now?

Where was he then? He showed up out of nowhere, knowing exactly where I was. There's no way he could have been there. I don't know how long it's been, but it's been long enough since the snow first fell to know that it's been a long time.

Time is so different now, though.

Time has shifted into a blur. Days have become weeks and weeks have become months. An eternity could have passed, and I wouldn't have noticed.

I don't understand it.

Any of it.

It's all a jumble of things, a mess of pieces, some that fit together and some that don't. Like mixing two puzzles together, and then you just keep adding pieces. Pieces that have no match, pieces that have a single match, pieces that have two or three or four matches. Hoping that they'll all fit together, but knowing they won't. You'll never have a completed puzzle because you can't change the pieces. If they don't fit together perfectly, they'll never fit together perfectly. You'll have to make do with what you have, and hope that it will fit enough to connect them all, even though no matter what you do, the end result won't make sense. It will never make sense.

You want to believe that the pieces will fit together in the end.

So, you believe it.

But in the end they don't, and you're thrown into a whirlpool, going round and round but never sinking, wondering where all the missing pieces are. Wondering if you're ever going to find them. Watching their possibility passing you over and over again in the endless cycle as you go around and around and around.

Once you throw yourself into the whirlpool, once you let yourself fall in, you can never get back out.

I don't understand it.

Was he ever really there?

Could he have possibly been a figment of my imagination, my last chance at escaping the choice I was making? A last lifeline to cling to? A fraying rope that had just enough left to help me escape the hell I was falling into?

Was I so far gone that I imagined him? Am I so ridden with guilt and regret that he made his way into my life, without ever really being there?

Was he ever really there?

Could he have possibly been standing there in front of me, my last chance at escaping the choice I was making? A last lifeline that held out a hand for me to cling to? A fraying rope that had just enough left to help me hang onto the edge of falling and climbing back out, giving me the choice?

One of the many ghosts from my past come back to haunt me.

I let my thoughts tangle around the thought of him.

If he was real, then he knows that by seeing him again I will never forget. If he was real, I let myself fall into his arms as a last reserve, I let myself rely on him to keep me safe, to keep my sanity, to keep my control.

If he was an imagination, he doesn't know, I'll never see him again, and I will never have to remember. If he was an imagination, I let myself cling to the idea of him as a last reserve, I let myself rely on the remembrance of his touch, of his voice, of his face, to keep me safe, to keep my sanity, to keep my control.

He was there, in some form. And because he was there, I will never forget, I'll always remember. I still need him, I still rely on him, even if I never see him again. He'll always be there.

He's not going anywhere.

But he's nowhere.

He's nowhere and he's everywhere.

* * *

I looked up at the cliff.

A girl stands on top of it, over the waterfall, looking down at the surface of the water.

She steps closer to the edge, still looking down. Her toes hang off the edge, and she rocks back and forth, balancing on the edge of life and death.

She steps off.

I blinked. And she was gone.

There were no ripples in the surface of the lake.

I ran down to the edge of the water, looking out across it, looking for any sign of life.

It was completely still.

I sank to the ground, staring across the glass surface.

There's a face reflecting off the surface. A little girl with sandy hair and blue eyes. Another face. A man, with sandy hair and brown eyes. A third face. A woman, with brown hair and blue eyes.

A body rises to join the faces. Long brown hair covering her face, arms spread eagle, face down, floating on the surface.

The woman's face dissolves back into the water.

The face of the girl fades shortly after.

The man's face looks down at the girl, floating in the water next to him. He doesn't shed a tear, doesn't look pained.

He gives her one long, sad look, and backs away, disappearing back into the water.

I closed my eyes.

When I opened them again, she was gone. The water was still. The sun was shining. The sky was clear.

I looked up at the cliff again, at the little run-down structure ridden with relics.

There was no one there.

Everything was the same.

"Hey," Lily returned from her car and sat down next to me, wrapping her arms around my neck. She kissed my cheek, "You okay?"

"Yeah," I laid my hand over hers, resting my head against her, "how 'bout you?"

"I'm okay."

We sat in the wake of a long silence, watching the world around us succumb to darkness as the stars came to life above our heads.

"You know," she said, looking up at the sky, her eyes reflecting the millions of little lights shining there, "how we talked about not having a reason to live, knowing our lives are forever changed?"

"Yeah."

"I never knew why there would be a reason. To live."

"And?"

She looked at me, searching, not desperately for answers, but for answers that lie on the surface. Answers to questions that have never been asked. Questions that she already knows the answers to.

"And what?"

"Isn't there an 'and' to that sentence?"

"There is."

"And?"

She looked back up at the stars. "That's the Big Dipper, isn't it?" she asked, leaning back on her hands, "I think that's Orion, that's his belt, um… and that's Ursa Major, and Cassiopeia, and Polaris. The north star. You know, if you follow that star, you'll never be lost."

"Lily?"

"What?"

"What's your reason?"

She tried to hide her smile. She sat up, running her hand along my cheek, resting her fingers under my ears, her thumb along the side of my face. I wrapped my hand around her wrist, my thumb on the back of her hand.

She kissed me.

When she pulled away, she stared into my eyes, our noses less than half a centimeter apart. She didn't look away. She didn't blink. Our foreheads touched.

"*You.*"

Chapter Twenty Four

My eyes flew open.

A turned back. No last look. No letter. No last words.

I sat up, gasping for breath.

Footsteps that fade with the echoes of the last words spoken.

My hands were shaking.

Footsteps that fade from view but never fade from remembrance.

The world was spinning.

Footsteps that leave roses broken and scattered beneath heavy feet.

Cold sweat dripping down my body.

Footsteps that melt with the snow but leave cracks in the ice.

I couldn't shake the cold shiver running down the back of my neck.

Footsteps that, no matter how quiet, make a sound.

My head felt like it was splitting in two.

Footsteps that make stable boards creak and wobble.

I closed my eyes.

Footsteps that leave thorns from trodden roses in trodden hearts.

My room melted away under my fingers.

The echoing of footsteps running over hallowed, haunted ground.

The voice comes from every direction. Calls to come back, to turn back, to look back.

Just one word. Just one look. Just one second.

But the footsteps keep running.

They never stop.

They can always be heard.

In the morning, before the sun rises when the world longs for the arrival of the light to break through the scattered remains of the darkness, and fears the loss of the quiet neutrality hidden in the coverage of the moon.

In the day, when the sun hangs above the heads of those who sit and watch it, a protector and an overseer, judgmental and unbiased, warning and uncaring.

In the night, after the moon has begun to appear when the world fears the loss of the light to which it clings for sanity, and longs for the return of darkness to which all things good can hide all things evil that remain within them.

They can be heard.

The same words forever echoing.

The same words sending earthquakes through my heart.

"Don't leave."

But I left.

"Please come back."

But I didn't come back.

Everything around me becomes a blur. One single stream of water that has flooded into an array of color on an undried canvas.

I looked down at my hands. The lines scattered across the palms, the fingers that shook.

Hands I don't know anymore.

In learning to accept myself, I forgot to learn how to accept the one thing I know I can't live without. The one thing I know I can't forget, I can't ignore, I can't turn away from. I can't live without. The only thing that I've known consistently, the only thing that's been with me even when I pushed everything else away, the only thing that stayed when I was most alone. The only voices I welcomed over my own. The only words I listened to over my own. The only touch I didn't flinch away from. And while I hate it, what am I without it? I'm nothing. I'm nothing with it, but I'm nothing without it. I'm a nothing of something with it, though. Without it, I'm just a nothing of nothing.

The truth is, there are some parts of our lives, whether they're good or bad, that shape us beyond anything else. Things that, no matter how much we may hate them, no matter how much we want to be rid of them, we can't live without. We don't know how to. No matter how far away we get from them, no matter how free, how happy, we return to them at one point or another. They're not even a happiness, or a reliance, or a need, or a want, or a care, or a friend, or a conscience, or a condolence. They're not even something that helps us survive.

Sometimes they're our worst enemies, our deepest sadness, regrets, our biggest fears, our biggest hatred, our strongest chain, our demons, our darkness.

Sometimes they're the very things that make us desperate to not survive.

The things that make us walk off the edge of the cliff.

Sometimes they're the things that reside inside our heads, creating the ghosts we see in our past, in our present, in our future. The ghost we see when we look in the mirror, searching for our own faces, our own eyes, our own noses, our own mouths, our own reflections to reflect back at us, reminding us that we haven't become the darkness we're sinking into.

For a while, there's a time when you look in the mirror, and you see all those things reflected back at you. You see your reflection. There's enough light within you for the mirror to reflect. Enough light to create the image standing before you. The image that hints of haunting, of pain, of darkness, of ghosts, but you can't see it.

Then there's a moment, when you look in the mirror.

And all you see is black.

Maybe you see a ghost.

But you can't see your reflection.

Because the light the mirror needs to reflect the image isn't there anymore.

There's nothing left.

Not even a single ray, dim but there, fading but visible.

It's gone out.

All you see is black.

You see the darkness that you've disappeared into.

The darkness you were terrified of becoming.

And in that moment, when you can't see your face, your eyes, or your nose, or your mouth, or your reflection, you know. You get that sinking feeling in your stomach as the ground opens beneath you, and you fall. And you fall. And you fall.

And in that moment, you're lost.

You've lost your grip on the world. On the ground beneath your feet.

You've been lost by the world.

You've been forgotten by yourself.

You no longer have control over your own life. You just have to hope that you never stop falling. That you are consigned to oblivion forever.

Sometimes, when you get desperate, you just have to hope that you stop falling. That you break your consignment to oblivion. You don't care how, when, why.

Sometimes, when you give up, you just have to close your eyes and wait for your feet to hit the ground.

Sometimes the only reason you don't break the consignment is because you're scared of everyone you'll hurt by breaking it.

Sometimes, when you're most alone, you don't think you'll be hurting anyone. You'll be doing them a favor. You'll be relieving them of a burden they never asked to carry.

Sometimes there is no reason to stay. Sometimes there are only reasons to go. Sometimes you don't care about the reasons there are to stay.

Sometimes, when you get so tired, so desperate, so lost, so forgotten, there's no part of you that cares.

The thing is, once you start falling, you never stop.

Even if you learn to control it, to regain control, to not be so lost, to see parts of your reflection again, you'll never see it in full. There will always be at least one part that's missing.

You can fall more slowly, even almost stop falling for a while.

But you're always going to hit the ground, to hit the bottom, at some point.

It doesn't matter how hard you try.

You may not break your consignment to oblivion, the darkness may not break it. It may break entirely on its own.

But when you hit the ground, it breaks. It shatters.

It doesn't survive the fall.

Once you're broken, you're broken. Like a vase that was knocked off a table and shattered. You can glue the pieces back together, but there will always be gaps, cracks, imperfections. You can paint over the cracks and gaps, erasing them from view. But they're still there, hidden beneath. Everyone else might forget them. You might forget them.

But they can always be remembered.

I'm never going to see the entirety of my reflection again.

Just like I'll always see the ghosts in the corners of my room, just like how the scars covering my body will never fade, the darkness will never go away.

I'm made of it, now.

As much as I want to live without it, I can't. It's engrained in me, in my way of life. I'm addicted to its presence. Without it, I'll lose sight of the only pieces of my reflection that I can see.

It's a part of me.

I can't imagine living without it. I can't imagine not seeing the scars in the mirror. I can't imagine not seeing tear streaks left from the war I fought at three in the morning. I can't imagine not seeing the broken pieces hidden behind my eyes.

I can't imagine it.

Any of it.

And when I do live without it, in the moments when it disappears, when I am alone with myself, no darkness, no demons, no thoughts, just me, I feel it. I feel the weight of what used to be there hanging over my head, an empty void, a missing piece.

A missing piece that outweighs all the weight of all the other missing pieces.

One piece that outweighs a million other pieces.

And I'm condemned to it. It controls my life, now. Now and forever.

An empty room.

A closed window, shades drawn tightly. No light allowed in. Everything still. Nothing moved, nothing touched, nothing different.

A woman sitting on the bed, a small piece of paper in her hands.

I watch as she reads it over and over again.

Her mouth shaping the only two words left on it.

'I'm sorry.'

Her eyes filling with tears over and over again, like a glass left under a faucet, overflowing over and over and over.

A man's hand on her shoulder, gripping her gently. He sits down next to her, trying to take the paper out of her hands. She grips it tighter.

"There must be a reason," she looks at him, "she can't have just left."

He shakes his head, "but if there is a reason, she didn't tell us. How would we know?"

She gets up, walking around the room, running her fingers lightly over the surface of the furniture, of all the last things she had touched before she left. Retracing her steps. Around the room. Over and over and over again.

She stops at the dresser, pulling open drawers, starting at the bottom, shifting through folded clothes. At the top drawer, she gasps and steps away, slamming it shut.

"What?" he asks, his forehead creasing.

She shakes her head.

My stomach sinks.

Her tears turn into sobs, sobs that turn into dry heaves, dry heaves that turn into gasps, until she can barely breathe. Words that she tries to speak, but can't. Body that shakes until she sinks to the ground because it can no longer support her weight.

The man takes her up in his arms and holds her, rocking her back and forth.

"She can't have just left," the woman whispers.

"I know, I know, but she did."

The woman looks up at him, touching his face lightly, "And so did you."

He kisses her forehead, holding her tightly as his grip begins to loosen, "I'm so sorry."

He disappears.

Leaving her alone in an empty room full of ghosts.

I walk over to the piece of paper, which she's dropped on the bed.

The words stare back at me. The rushed, tilted handwriting. How could someone do that?

I walk over to the drawer and pull it open. She doesn't move, staring at the wall in front of her, not seeing it.

They stare back at me. All the scars that they made reflected in their rusted metal faces. All the ghosts they brought to life watching from the shadows.

I pulled little pieces of paper out from between floorboards, between clothes, book pages. The words echo around the room.

'I can't do this anymore.'

'I hate hurting people. The one thing I try to never do is hurt people. Especially the people I love. But I find myself hurting them anyway. And most of the time I don't even know how.'

'Just smile.'

'I'm sorry I hate myself.'

'Why am I like this.'

'Maybe not today... maybe not tomorrow... maybe not next year... but maybe... just maybe... someday.'

'I'm fighting a battle with myself.'

'I think I'm losing.'

'The worst feeling is being happy knowing that you're being tricked into thinking you can be happy just so it hurts more when you're not. It hurts when you're happy one second and then the next you're wondering what the hell is wrong with you. It only takes a second... and your world turns upside down.'

'The remains of my broken soul are shattering and deteriorating... and I can feel it. It feels like something within me is breaking. And it hurts. It's killing me.'

'I skipped from happy, to numb, and now I'm sad and depressed. And I'm scared of what's going to come next.'

'I'm fading away...'

The words of all the things I thought had disappeared. Words I forgot I wrote. Words I forgot to remember. Words I left for other people to find and forget and remember.

'It's funny looking back to when I was younger and wondered how it was possible to be so unhappy... how it was possible to think those things... it's funny how quickly things can change.'

'A smile can hide the demons.'

'Just smile.'

'When my life feels perfectly normal I wonder why I've ever thought the things I have, or done the things I've done, or felt the way I've felt. I wonder if somehow I conjured it up in my head... if it was even real... but then when it hits again, I know that nothing else could be more real.'

'I'm not winning anymore.'

'I'm sorry.'

'Everyone thinks they know me... but they don't. I'm the girl who's had a rough life, doesn't talk enough, but smiles, who's managed to survive despite

the horrors, the unthinkable. I'm the girl who's okay with who she is… but the truth is, I'm not. I'm not that girl anymore, if I ever was. I smile, I laugh, I talk. But I'm breaking. Every time I talk, I want to stay quiet. I want to look down and walk away. Every time I laugh I'm trying to ignore the demons screaming in my head. Maybe this is something I made up in my head. Maybe I did do this to myself. But that doesn't mean it hurts less… Every time I smile… I'm hiding the milüon tears I am too numb to cry. I'm tired of forcing myself through every day. I want it all to end. I'm struggling… and there's no one there. I'm at the point where I don't know how much longer I can do this. Why do I have to be me. Why do I have to be so fucked up. I could be getting better… but I'd rather fall off the cliff than step away from it.'

'I want to be happy.'

'I'm a monster.'

'How can I live… I've already lost.'

'It comes in waves. I'll be doing fine. I'll be happy. And then the first wave hits… and then the second… until I swear I'm losing my fucking mind.'

'Hating yourself is easy. It's like hating other people. Instead, you're the other people. And you hate yourself.'

'I drive everyone away.'

'The thing about falling apart in the middle of the night is realizing there's no one there for you to turn to. And you're completely alone.'

'I'm losing my fucking mind.'

I left everyone the way I didn't want them to leave me.

So many words.

'I'm so done.'

'I'm so ashamed of my thoughts. They're selfish. Because I know that I would hurt everyone I left behind but at the same time I know no one would care.'

'Someday I'm going to be "that girl" with a suicide note.'

'I won't leave a note. I want to just disappear. And hope no one finds me.'

'I don't want to be the one people feel bad for feeling bad for.'

'I'm broken.'

'I'll never be good enough.'

'I'm losing my fucking mind…'

'I don't want to be me anymore…'

And then, the one at the bottom. The most terrifying one.

'I'm fine.*'*

*　　　*　　　*

How could anyone just leave, and leave all that behind?

*　　　*　　　*

I watched as the girl stands on top of the cliff again, looking down.

She steps closer to the edge, still looking down. Her toes hang off the edge, balancing on the edge of life and death.

She steps off.

And she's gone.

There are no ripples in the surface of the lake.

I watched the surface from the base of a tree as the moonlight reflects off of it. Lily's head resting on my shoulder, her breathing light and unburdened.

There's a face reflecting off the surface. A little girl with sandy hair and blue eyes, with the same nose as me, the same face as mom.

Another face. A man, with sandy hair and brown eyes. A third face. A woman, with brown hair, like me, and blue eyes, like the girl.

A body rises to join the faces. Long brown hair covering her face, arms spread eagle, face up, floating on the surface.

The woman's face dissolves back into the water, followed by the girl, who glances at the figure in the water before disappearing.

The man looks down at the girl.

I closed my eyes.

They're gone.

Chapter Twenty Five

"Dad, I find out about college applications today," I kneeled on the soft earth, no longer frozen and snow covered in spring.

No voice answered me this time.

"I'm kind of scared, to be honest," I replaced the dead flowers with new ones. "I don't know what to think. I mean, I think I have a good chance, but who knows. Maybe I didn't get in to any of them. Grandma keeps checking the mail, and even Mom is anxious. They're both excited. Probably more excited than I am. I mean, I don't blame them. I actually made it to college. That's farther than anyone thought I'd make it."

I paused, then stood up. There wasn't really anything else to say. "Bye, Dad."

I turned around, and my heart stopped.

Someone's standing down at the bottom of the hill, by a tree, watching me. I'd know them anywhere.

They waved. I hesitated, then made my way toward him. He didn't disappear this time.

So much has changed since I last talked to him. I've seen him in school, in class, but we haven't talked. He hasn't looked at me.

I don't know what to say to him.

But I'm more me today than I've ever been. So that's a start.

Everything seems so long ago, I don't even know where all the stops and all the starts are, they're untraceable. Was there even a start? And if there was a start, was there a stop? There's a start and a stop to everything, even those consigned to oblivion have a start and a stop. They start their consignment to their oblivion and they end their consignment to oblivion.

There is always a start and there is always a stop. Every letter, word, sentence, paragraph, page, chapter, and novel starts and stops somewhere. Every life starts and stops somewhere.

Every time a door slams, a story, a chapter, a page, a paragraph, a sentence, a word, a letter ends. Every time a door opens, a story, a chapter, a page, a paragraph, a sentence, a word, a letter starts. There are spaces between each start and stop, and sometimes they overlap. There was a space between the time I left and Owen came into my life, when that part of my story started. Lily's chapter started before Owen's could end, and Owen's ended when Lily's was just beginning. Owen's started after Lily's had been going on for pages, for thousands of words, for chapters, and ended halfway through. I don't know if Owen's chapter will ever find its way into my novel again, or if the few he managed to write himself into are the only ones that will ever exist, the only words that will ever be remembered. I don't know when Lily's chapter will end, if it ever will. I don't know how many stops and starts there will be until the final period makes its way onto the page. I don't know when my final chapter will be, when my final page and paragraph and sentence and word and letter and period will be. There could be so many more chapters, an infinite number of pages. There could only be three chapters left, and then everything ends, with nothing but a sentence in an epilogue to complete my story.

I could see his face, now. Tall, blond hair, green eyes fixated on me. Everything the same. He really hadn't changed at all.

"Where are you going?"

"Nowhere, Cassandra, Nowhere."

He's nowhere.

But he's everywhere.

And now, he's here.

A stranger. A stranger I used to know. A stranger who has ghosts surrounding him; ghosts with blurred faces, ghosts he hasn't told anyone about, ghosts that he refuses to remember, ghosts that will haunt him as long as he tries to forget.

A stranger who has become a ghost in my world.

He stepped toward me. A tremor raced through the earth under my feet.

"Hey," he said. Those green eyes met mine. My heart no longer did the dance it used to when he looked at me. It's lost its wings.

They're Lily's, now.

There's no fire. No flame. No spark.

Just two people who used to know each other.

"Hey," I said back.

"So, you came back here again?"

"Yeah. You did too?"

He nodded slowly, "Yeah, I did too."

"I-"

"Don't apologize."

"Okay," I didn't look away from him, "how have you been?"

"Okay."

"Why..."

"I just needed to talk to you."

"Okay." We stood there in silence, staring at each other.

"Cassandra," he looked away.

"What?"

"I know."

"You know what?"

He reached into his pocket and pulled out a piece of paper. A newspaper clipping. My heart dropped. "I know this is you."

"How?"

He shook his head, "I wanted to know more than you'd tell me. I found out about your Dad. I just knew he died... I didn't know he... you know."

"Why are you telling me this?"

"Because that day, I threw my past in your face, and didn't tell you what it was. I didn't give you any warning. I treated you terribly."

"I deserved it."

"No, no one deserves that."

"So what are you saying?"

"I just wanted to apologize, for everything."

"There's no reason for you to apologize."

"There is, and I'm sorry. That's all," he turned around, starting to walk away.

"Wait," I said. He paused. "Do you... do you want to talk about it?"

"About what?"

"Your past."

He shrugged, "There's not really anything to talk about."

"You showed up out of nowhere, in a *cemetery,* and I've seen you here before. We haven't talked in months, and you bring it up, just to apologize?"

"Yeah."

"Would you tell me if I asked?"

"There's no reason for you to ask."

"I'm asking as a friend. Because I care about you. Because of all the things you did for me," I blinked back tears, "please, I owe you so much more than I can give you. Let me give you this."

After all, I owe my life to him.

"I..." he turned to face me, "okay."

"Thank you."

He gave me a weird look, then sat down against a tree. I sat down next to him.

After a second, he started talking.

"I didn't find out that my dad existed until I was eight. Whenever I asked about him, my mom's response was always 'he left a long time ago'. She never liked to talk about him, but after eight years, he called her. I think it took her off guard, really, because she agreed to meet up with him. She didn't let me come, she said he didn't want to see me. But a month later, he showed up at our door, and she was forced to introduce me as his son. He didn't know I existed. They started dating again, and he made his way into my life. One of the problems, I think, was that they didn't actually love each other. They felt obligated to be together because of me. When they split up a year later, it hurt me more than it hurt them. He disappeared, sleeping on someone else's couch until he could get his own apartment. He called me every night for a while, and then it was every other night, and then once a week, once every other week, and then once or twice a month at most. He bought a new apartment, and when he got his life together I was allowed to reenter it. That was the thing, between Mom and him, I was either a convenience or an inconvenience. If I would benefit them, I was there. If I wouldn't, I wasn't. I got close to my dad, I mean, I'd never had a connection with someone as much as I did with him. I had an older brother, but we'd never gotten along very well. We got along like brothers well enough, but he was older than me, had a different father, and wasn't around much. She didn't pay much attention to me, my mom. Half of it was her trying to make a life for us and half of it was her not knowing how to make a life for us. With my dad, I had no competition. I was his only kid, he spent time with me, and he wanted to get to know me. At first, fatherhood was just a game for him, something he could do without trying. Once it got serious, he started dodging out on me. He moved again, farther away this time. He remarried and had another kid. I wouldn't have cared except for the fact that he completely abandoned me. I was irrelevant. I didn't benefit his life, I was an inconvenience, so I wasn't needed. He broke all of his promises. Every single one. Mom was busier than ever taking classes at a community college, she remarried, and slowly all my family ties fell loose, either by fraying to the breaking point or being cut clean through the middle. My dad moved again, to a house this time, even farther away. He was barely within the same state, as far away as he could get without leaving altogether. He was unreliable, inconvenient, couldn't pay rent half the time and was lucky if he could pay his phone bill without needing a loan from some unwilling friend or family member. He had an unstable career and an even more unstable temper, and I couldn't even talk to him without a fight breaking out. I stopped staying with him as much, and even when he would scrounge up enough money to take me places, it was just compensation for all the things he couldn't give me. He was my father, but he wasn't a father figure. A lot of the time I would've much rather never known he existed and listened to my mom's line 'he left a long time ago'. The thing is, knowing that she'd never told him I existed made me question her, and knowing him made me wish I never did. I didn't know what I wanted or what I knew anymore. I felt abandoned, a lot of the time. Then he moved a thousand miles away, cutting off all communication. At that point, I'd given up. I never wanted to see him again. He didn't care about me, and he couldn't even afford to act like he cared about me. I could have let it go then, focusing on rebuilding everything I'd knocked down. But a year later, he sent me a letter. I didn't want to read it. I should've torn it up when I got it, but I shoved it into a drawer and tried to forget about it. But every night I'd pull it out and open the top by a millimeter, until finally there were no more millimeters to open. I read it. I've never hated anyone more in my life," Owen looked down at his hands, "after that, I stopped caring." He looked up at me, "And then, I found out he died. He got drunk and crashed his car," he gestured to a grave in the distance, "he's buried there."

I looked in the direction he pointed. "Wait," I turned back to him, "when you said your uncle..."

He nodded.

"I'm sorry," I said quietly.

"Don't be, it's in the past. It doesn't matter," he stood up.

I grabbed his arm, keeping him from walking away. "Hey."

"What?"

"I'm glad you talked to me, I've missed you."

"Yeah," he smiled a little, "I've missed you too."

"Maybe this time," I said, "we can try being friends? Just friends."

"I like that idea."

I held out a hand, "Nice to meet you, Taylor."

He grinned, shaking it, "Nice to meet you too, James."

*   *   *

The girl falls.

I watched her hit this time.

There's no sound. No movement of the water. With my ankles still in the water, I should be able to feel the shockwave.

The faces appear again. A little girl with sandy hair and blue eyes, with the same nose as me, the same face as mom. Another face. A man, with sandy hair and brown eyes like mine. A third face. A woman, with brown hair, like me, and blue eyes, like the girl.

A body rises to join the faces. Long brown hair covering her face, arms spread eagle, face up, floating on the surface. Her features are blurred.

The woman takes the little girl's hand, looking down at the figure before dissolving back into the water.

The man takes the hand of the girl floating in front of him. He gives it a squeeze, mouthing words. The same three words over and over again.

Then he let's go, and I watch the fingers fall back down into the water.

*   *   *

"Sandra!" Mom rushed me when I walked through the door, "Cassandra!"

"What?"

She held up a handful of envelopes, "You got them."

"Oh my god," I grabbed them, sitting down at the kitchen table. I looked up at her.

"Open them!" she said, clasping her hands together.

"Wait for me!" said Grandma, rushing into the kitchen and standing next to Mom. They both had tears in their eyes as they watched me, especially Mom, who covered her mouth with her hands when I picked up the first envelope.

It was from NYU.

My fingers shook as I slid open the envelope, and held my breath as I pulled out the piece of paper.

I read the first line and looked up at Mom, stunned.

"Well?" she asked.

"I got in," I said, looking back down at the paper.

"Yay!" she screamed, jumping a little. "Open the next one!"

I did.

I got into Boston University. And the University of Michigan.

"I didn't get into Columbia," my face fell, and I looked back up at her.

"That's okay!" she said, hugging me, "you've got great options. I'm so proud of you."

"Wait, don't you have one more envelope?" Grandma nodded toward one on my right.

"Yeah," I said quietly, "that's from Yale."

That's the one I don't want to open. Because, even though I didn't tell anyone, that was my top school.

I don't want to be disappointed.

"Open it!" Grandma said.

I shook my head, and handed it to Mom. "You open it, please."

She took it gingerly, "Are you sure?"

"Yeah."

"Okay," she slid open the envelope. I waited as she read it. She looked up at me. I couldn't read her face. "Cassandra?"

"Yeah?"

"You got in."

"What?" I stood up, knocking the chair over behind me.

"You got in!" she screamed, hugging me tightly. She was full out crying, now. "I'm so proud of you, Cassandra."

"Thanks, Mom."

"And you know what?"

"What?"

"Your father would be so, so proud of you."

Chapter Twenty Six

"Hey, so Owen and I are on speaking terms again," I said, blowing on my coffee.

"Really?" Rachel asked, pulling her keys out of her pocket and balancing her coffee on top of her car. "How'd that happen?"

"I don't know, honestly," I pulled open the passenger side door, "it was kind of weird."

"What'd you guys talk about?"

"He apologized for all the things he said to me the day we broke up, and then I asked him about like his past, because he threw that in my face then and brought it up again. So he told me. He told me everything."

"Wasn't that a little random?"

"Yeah, maybe, but I don't know."

"Okay."

"Yeah."

"Alright, well aside from him, how are things?"

"Good, I got into Yale."

"Congrats! Wow, that's amazing!"

"Have you heard about college yet?"

She nodded, "I didn't get into Juilliard, shocker, but I did get into the Manhattan School of Music."

"That's amazing!"

"Yeah, I don't know if I'm going to go, though."

"How come?"

"I can't really double major in music and something else if I go there."

"You wouldn't have been able to at Juilliard, either."

"Yeah, but it would have been *Juilliard*, I wouldn't have had to double major."

"True. So what are you thinking of doing?"

"Well, I got into Oberlin, and Boston University, so I'm debating between those."

"I got into BU too!"

"Oh my god, could you imagine if we both went there?"

"That would be a little insane," I laughed.

"Yeah," she turned on the radio, "but it would be *fun*."

"It would be. I think I'm going to commit to Yale, though."

"That your top school?"

"Yeah."

"You never mentioned what your top school was."

"I know."

She drummed her fingers on the steering wheel, "Any reason for that?"

I shrugged, "I didn't want to get my hopes up."

"Fair enough."

"Yeah."

"And how's Lily?" she raised an eyebrow.

"She's fine," I grinned.

"Still just friends?"

"Yup."

"Of course."

"What, you don't believe me?"

"You're talking to *me*, of course I don't."

"Alright, then don't believe me."

"I don't think I should."

I shrugged. "Can you believe we're graduating in like a month?"

She shook her head, "Not at all. It just doesn't feel real."

"I know, it's crazy."

"I'm not sure I'm ready to leave."

"Me neither, even though I've been ready to leave for years."

"It's weird."

"It sure is."

"And, are you *sure* you and Lily are just friends?" she pulled up in front of my house. Lily was sitting on my front steps.

I rolled my eyes, getting out of the car, "Thanks for the ride, I'll talk to you later."

"Okay, talk to you later."

I walked toward Lily as Rachel drove away, and she stood up, running to me. She had a piece of paper in her hands.

"Cass!"

"Hey! What're you doing here?"

"I got in!" she said, breathlessly.

"Where?"

"UCLA."

"Congrats!"

"Thanks!"

"Are you planning on committing there?"

She nodded, "They offered me enough money, and with scholarships and work I'll be able to pay for it myself. How about you? Where are you committing?"

"Yale."

"Oh, congrats!" her voice was enthusiastic, but her face fell a little.

UCLA and Yale aren't really all that close to each other.

"Hey, hey, look at me, we still have months before we leave!"

"I know," she forced a smile, "I know."

"So let's not worry about that right now. We're both going to some pretty great places."

"We are, I'm proud of us."

"Yeah, me too!"

"Do you want to go celebrate?"

"Sure!"

"Where do you want to go?"

"Do you want to go swimming?"

"Where?"

"That little wooded area you go to a lot. With the lake and the like run down building or whatever it is."

"Sure! Can I grab a bathing suit real quick?"

"Nope, come on, I'll drive."

"What?"

"We're already running out of time, so let's make the most of it while we still can."

I watched her run to her car, eyes alight with a kind of determination I haven't seen in her. A determination to beat time, once and for all.

"Okay."

*   *   *

I swam out to the middle of the lake and let myself sink to the bottom. My bare feet hit the soft sand and I hung there, suspended in nothing, until my lungs screamed in agony, and even then I stayed, taking in the peace of the still water. The only things that stirred were the currents that played quietly around me. It was a different world. One where nothing could reach me.

No demons. No angels.

They can't swim.

They can't swim and they're scared of drowning.

In this world, I can be me, just me, no demons and no angels and all the hopes and worries that come with them. They're gone. Everything has disappeared.

I opened my eyes and watched as my hair floated around me.

I sank until my feet hit the sand.

Then I pushed upward, springing off the bottom and gasping as my head broke the surface. I took a couple deep breaths before my breathing returned to normal.

I floated on my back under the sun, letting myself relax.

I've forgotten what it's like to escape, even just for a moment, into a world where nothing can reach me. A place where everything is so distant that even time is far away, blurred and disoriented.

I like it.

For once I don't have to be continuously reminded that I don't have all the time in the world.

Water splashed over me. I jumped, sinking back under the water, flailing until I caught my bearings and started to tread.

"Hey!" I splashed her back. She's laughing, and if our feet were on solid ground she would've been bent double.

It's been a while since I've seen her laugh like that.

Every now and then I see her like I did that morning after I wanted to leave. I see her, sitting on the ground, against a tree, a log, at the edge of the water, in the grass, staring down at her hands. Sometimes passing a rock back and forth, sometimes continuously skipping stones, sometimes studying the lines in her hands, as if she were trying to determine her predetermined fate.

It only takes her a matter of seconds to recompose herself, but it's started to take her longer and longer to look me in the eye, smile, and become herself again.

She's haunted too.

But we're all haunted. Owen's haunted. I'm haunted. Lily's haunted. Everyone is haunted. No one has lived a life so pure that they aren't haunted. There are so many ghosts. Ghosts of people who've died, who's bodies and minds have long since parted with their existence.

Ghosts of people who're still living. Part of living people that have died and returned to haunt us in our eternal living until they can haunt us in our eternal death.

The ghosts will always be there.

Will they ever stop haunting us?

If we fixed the things they haunt us for, would they fade?

But we can't fix the things they haunt us for. They haunt us for things from our past, things that are staring us in the face, things that we have buried so deep we almost forgot they were there. Things hidden in desks and dresser drawers and floorboards. We can change how they evolve into our future, but we can never change how they shaped our past.

They're ghosts for a reason.

We don't get to go back and re-live every day. We don't get to fix our mistakes, erase them from existence. We don't get another yesterday, but we get another tomorrow. We get another tomorrow so long as there is another tomorrow, until we reach the point where there's no yesterday and there's no tomorrow. At that point, we have to hope that we did everything we were supposed to do, everything we wanted to do, with each tomorrow that we got.

The person I used to be hasn't become a ghost yet, but she stays at the bottom of the lake. She isn't gone for good, yet, and sometimes she has to come up for air.

I've missed her.

*   *   *

The sun glared off the glass-like surface.

The girl has already fallen.

I could see her face more clearly this time.

The little girl with brown hair and blue eyes, the same nose as me, the same face as Mom. The man, with sandy hair and brown eyes, like mine. The woman, with brown hair, like me, and blue eyes, like the girl.

They're all there.

The body rises to join them, face up, hair obscuring her features.

The woman takes the little girl's hand, gives the body one long, sad look, and they disappear together.

The man looks down at the girl, floating in the water next to him. His expression is melancholy. No tears, no pain, no happiness, but a sort of subtle hope and relief, trying to mask his happiness at her joining him after all these years, guilty because she should have had decades before she joined him again.

He reaches out a hand and runs it gently down her arm in a fatherly way. He brushes the brown hair away from her face. Her eyes are closed. Her features are relaxed. The same nose as the little girl.

The scars visible on her arms, turned toward the sun, shine white.

The bruises around his neck are purple and black in the reflection, a continuous circle of torn, broken skin.

Consigned to oblivion.

He leans over her, kisses her forehead gently, and disappears.

* * *

We sat by the water, as usual, watching the sun shine off the surface. I kept pushing my wet hair out of my eyes, waiting for my clothes to dry in the sun.

I wonder where the faces are now.

The clouds blocked the sun, and the water grew dark.

A rope.

A dark hallway.

A closed door. No light under it.

A little girl's voice. "Daddy?"

No response.

A small hand reaches out and turns the door handle.

A dark figure next to the desk. The light flickers.

"Cassandra?"

"Yeah?"

"Can you believe we're graduating in a month?"

The light flickers.

"Nope."

The girl stands there, gaping.

"Me neither."

Then she screams.

"I'm not sure I'm ready to graduate."

Footsteps on the stairs.

"Me neither, but just think, we're free. We can leave this town. We can get *out*."

She can't move.

"True."

A woman's scream in the doorway. She grabs the girl, covering her eyes and holding her close to her chest.

I am excited to leave. I'm sick of this town. This place.

Screams echo through the room.

I'm ready to leave all my ghosts behind.

All of the ghosts I left farthest behind me, the ones I buried so deep nothing could unearth them- they've clawed their way out.

My fingers started to shake against the sand.

A rope tied to a light, half torn out of the ceiling.

A pair of feet suspended a foot off the ground.

There's a rope hanging from the side of the worn down building, probably where they used to hang flour bags or something. It shifted in the wind.

I saw a face as it spun toward us.

The sandy hair.

The brown eyes.

My brown eyes. The ones I got from him.

Staring, bulging.

Face purple and swollen.

Bruises and blood blossoming around his neck.

"Cassandra?"

I looked over at Lily, "Yeah?'

"What's wrong?"

"Nothing."

"I know you're lying. Please, come on, tell me."

"It's nothing."

"*Cassandra.*"

I blinked away the stinging behind my eyes.

"What happened?"

"Just a memory," I shook my head, "it's stupid."

"No it's not. What was it?"

I bit my lip, wrapping my arms around my knees, creating a wall between me and her. "You know how my sister died?"

"Yeah."

"I was there when she drowned."

"Oh my god."

"And then my dad died."

"What happened?" she hadn't taken her eyes off of me, and she didn't, but her eyes were wide with terror and pity and worry.

All the things I never wanted to make her.

"He was a war veteran, he'd always had issues because of that. Most of the time he was fine around me, but sometimes he'd sit there staring off into the distance, remembering something terrible, and he'd become someone else for a while. Then... my sister drowned. He blamed himself. I think that's what really destroyed him. Mom didn't blame him, at least, she didn't eventually. It was an accident. After that he became two completely different people. He stayed locked up in his office for three months after. After that, around me and around other people, he was fine. He had a permanent look in his eye that hadn't been there before, but other than that, he was normal. Mom was worse, she cried all the time, could barely leave the house, most days she could barely get out of bed. But it- it was just... just one of those things you expect a family to get through."

"Cassandra…"

"He hung himself, in his office. A year after she died."

"Oh my god."

"I found him."

The words were quiet, quivering, and shaking, but somehow they managed to echo off the walls off the cliff, louder than the water rushing past the relics.

"Oh my god, Cassandra…" Lily stared at me, horrified. I couldn't look up at her. I've never told anyone that before.

I never told anyone.

"Cassandra, I'm so sorry."

"Don't be," I said. I wiped away the few rogue remnants of tears. "I'm sorry, this isn't really celebrating, is it?" I forced a smile.

"Can I ask you something?" she ignores my last comment.

"Sure."

"Why did you run away?"

I hesitated, "I was scared. I was scared of the person I was, and all the things I couldn't escape."

"What do you mean?"

Slowly, I pulled up my left sleeve. She grabbed my wrist, looking at my arm.

"Did you…"

"Yeah."

"Why?"

"I don't know. I couldn't see a point to live most of the time. I get these thoughts… dark things that I don't want to think, but I can't help it. There are so many things from my life I'm scared of,

I'm haunted by, I'm ashamed of. I'm ashamed of the- the thing I've become, the thing I used to be. I was scared of what I could do to myself, and what it would do to people who found out. So, I didn't tell anyone. My life was bad enough, what was the point making it worse for anyone else? I withdrew, and I blamed everyone else for me forcing myself out of humanity."

"Did you ever want to kill yourself?" she said quietly.

I looked at her, meeting her eyes before looking away, and nodded. "Yeah, I did."

"Why? Didn't anyone tell you that you were loved? That they cared?"

"Yeah."

"Then why?"

"Because it wasn't that simple. No one got it. I was standing on the edge of a cliff. People kept telling me that I was wanted and loved, and I knew that I should step away from the edge. But it didn't matter who told me to step away. Because what I wanted someone to understand was that it didn't matter what they said, it didn't matter if I understood how I was feeling or what I was feeling or why I was feeling it. The only thing that mattered was that I didn't want anyone to tell me it was okay, that I shouldn't want what I wanted. I just wanted them to really understand the things going through my head, and let me stand on the edge of the cliff. I wanted them to let me stand there, and instead of telling me to back away, I wanted someone to understand… and shove me off."

"But they didn't."

"Nope."

"Do you still want to?"

"Sometimes. But you know what I've learned?"

"What?"

"Dying is a lot easier than living. And life wasn't made to be easy."

She smiled a little, "Yeah." She took my hand in hers, "Cassandra?"

"Yeah?"

"I hope you know that, no matter how much you want me to, I'll never shove you off. Even if you hate me for it forever, I'll be the one to grab you and pull you away, to catch you before you fall."

"I know."

"Good."

"Lily?"

"Yeah?"

"Why did you run away?"

She paused. The finger she was quietly drumming rapidly up and down on her knee froze in midair.

She looked at the water in front of us. When she finally answered, she looked at me.

"I- I came out to my parents. Well, not exactly 'came out', I more of fell out and got the door slammed behind me."

"What happened?"

"My mom, um, caught me with a girl."

"Wow."

"Yeah."

"What'd she say?"

"Nothing, her face turned red and she slammed the door."

"Oh."

"I guess I should've led with this- my family's fucking homophobic."

"Really?"

"Yup."

"All of them?"

"Well, the aunt I'm living with is gay, but that's pretty much it. Other than her, they're all a bunch of fucking homophobes."

"And that- that's why they kicked you out?"

"Yeah. They didn't want my siblings to 'catch my illness'."

"Where'd you go?"

"I stayed with a friend for a while, but I was still in the same town as them. I ran into my mom in the street one day, and I tried to be mature and say hi to her. She ignored me. It was like I wasn't there. That's when I left. I didn't want to be anywhere near them. So I asked my aunt if I could stay with her, and then I left."

"I'm sorry."

"Hey, no being sorry, remember?"

"Yeah," I said, "no being sorry.'

"Are you okay?"

"Are you?"

She let out a short laugh, shaking her head, "I don't think anyone's ever okay."

"Yeah, me neither."

"But, yeah, I'm okay. I didn't use to be, but I'm more okay than I was."

"Me too."

"As weird as this place is," she looked around, "I have to say, there's something almost magical about it."

"Yeah, there is. Maybe it's not so much the place as just being able to escape from the people we used to be."

"That's probably a lot truer than 'it's magic'."

"Maybe just a little."

She rolled her eyes at me.

"So, you're gay, are you? When were you planning on telling me?"

"Oh, shut up."

"I thought you *trusted* me."

She shook her head, laughing. After a while she stood up, "I should get going. You need a ride, right?"

"No, I'll walk."

"You sure?"

"Yeah."

"Alright, well, I'll text you later."

"Okay."

She started to walk away, and I got up, watching her leave.

"Lily?" I called after her.

She turned around, "Yeah?"

"I love you."

I didn't plan on saying it.

But I'm sure. I'm sure of the words. I'm sure of Lily.

And I'm sure of us.

She stared at me, new tears forming in her eyes. Then she ran at me, throwing her arms around my neck. She kissed me.

"I love you too."

We broke apart, smiling and laughing and crying.

"I thought Owen and the world had fucked you up so badly you'd never..." she kissed me again, "never say that."

"Honestly, me too."

Our foreheads met. "I'm sorry, for everything. For the cards you were dealt, for everything you've had to deal with, for putting all my shit on top of your shit. I love you, I love you too. And I'm sorry."

"Fuck being sorry," I said.

"Fuck being sorry," she smiled.

Chapter Twenty Seven

"This is the last session you have scheduled, I believe," she said.

I nodded, "Yeah. I graduate tomorrow."

"Oh, wow! That's exciting!"

"Yeah, and a little nerve-wracking."

"Yes, it is," she smiled, "is there anything you'd like to talk about?"

"Not really," I thought for a minute, "everything's been pretty good."

"I'm glad to hear that."

"I'm going to see Dad and Claire's graves tomorrow, before graduation, and this time Mom's coming with me."

"Does she usually not?"

I shook my head, "She never does."

"How have you been holding up, with your dad not being there for graduation?"

I bit my lip. Honestly, that's the one thing I've been trying not to think about, because every time I do I start to cry. "I mean, I'm going to miss him, but there's nothing I can do about it."

She tilted her head, looking at me over the rim of her glasses like she always does. "Is that all?"

I nodded.

"Cassandra, it's okay," she reached across and took my hand. I didn't look at her.

"I just..." I started, "I wish he could be there. I want him to see me. When I was little I expected him to be there, you know? And whenever I thought about graduation after he died I just skipped over the part where he wouldn't be there. And it's not fair, but I'm mad at him. I'm mad at him for leaving. He had a choice. And he decided not to stay."

"I know, and I'm sorry he didn't stay, but it wasn't because of you."

"It was," I said in a quiet voice.

"Why do you think that?"

"Because," I blinked hard, "because it was my fault."

"What was your fault?"

"Claire."

"How?"

"I rocked the dock. I made it move, and I made her lose her balance. I made her fall. Dad never got over her death. He killed himself because I killed her." The sobs broke free, sobs that had been pent up from years and years, sobs built over the words that I'd never said. Never aloud.

"Cassandra, you didn't kill her. None of that was your fault."

I stared at the floor.

"Cassandra." She waited for me to look back up at her. "Please, believe that. It wasn't your fault. None of that was your fault. They were accidents and mistakes, and you couldn't have stopped any of it. It wasn't your fault."

"It was someone's fault."

"No, it wasn't. And it wasn't yours. It's time to stop blaming yourself. It's time to stop putting that weight on your shoulders. You have more than enough to be responsible for, but you don't have to be responsible for their deaths. Claire did not die because of you. Your father did not die because of you."

I didn't say anything. I couldn't. My body had been overtaken by sobs and tears. Sobs and tears from the past ten years.

And then she got up from her chair and sat down next to me, wrapping her arms around me and holding me tightly. She didn't say anything else, she just let me cry.

"It's not your fault," she whispered.

The clipboard lay forgotten and blank on the floor across from us. The array of bullets dead and quiet in the no-man's land she had just crossed.

"It's not your fault."

"Okay."

*   *   *

I went back to the lake the morning of graduation. I got up early, before Grandma or Mom, and snuck out. I wanted to watch the sunrise by myself, one more time.

I pulled a notebook and a pencil out of my backpack. I've barely written anything in the past few months, let alone the past year.

There's been too much to write. But then again, some words are better left to be forgotten, I guess.

I touched the pencil to the paper.

Mom,

It's me. Cassandra. I don't know if you'll ever read this, because I may never give it to you, but there's so much that I need to tell you, so much I need you to know. I'm so sorry, Mom. I'm sorry for everything I've done. You never deserved any of it. All those times I ran away, I wanted to call myself in. I did, once, but they'd already found me. I don't know if you knew that. I miss you. I've changed, Mom, and it's not right, it doesn't make up for all the pain I've caused the people I left behind over the years, the people I pushed away, but I've changed. I'm happy. I've been running for eleven years. I've been running since Claire died. I've been running since Dad died. I just wish I'd stopped running before I ran so far away that I couldn't come back.

I owe you an explanation for all the times I did actually run.

I didn't leave because of you, I need you to know that. I know we didn't always get along that well, but I never blamed you for that. Aside from the fact that I didn't make it easy for anyone to get close, I know you were scared. You were scared of losing me. I was scared of losing you. Of course, my leaving only meant that we lost each other. We had to face our fears because I made them a reality. And I kept making them a reality.

I'm sorry for that.

I wish you didn't have to find what you found in my room all those years ago. It was never meant for anyone but me to see. It was my way of coping with everything I couldn't acknowledge or comprehend. I know it wasn't right, but it's how I got through the hard parts of life. It's how I avoided remembering things I didn't want to remember, things I wanted to forget. Instead of facing the pain that came with remembering, I covered it with new pain.

Sometimes it got to be too much, and I got scared.

But I couldn't tell anyone. I think a part of me was scared of being treated differently, of being singled out. I didn't want people to think that I was different or weak or a 'freak'. I should've said something, I know.

I think a bigger part of me was scared of being forced to stop. Because stopping would mean that I would have to face the things I'd spent years trying to forget. I let myself depend on it. By the time I finally became sick of myself, disgusted, and wanted to stop, I couldn't.

I was so used to it. It became a part of me.

I'm sorry.

But I did stop. And you helped me do that by making me confront everything I didn't want to.

Mom, I miss Dad. I miss Claire. I miss you. I miss who we used to be.

I've become a different person, and I'm happy with that person.

I don't know what's going to happen after I graduate. I'm scared. Fear is one of the strongest things that drive us as humans. It's ironic, sometimes.

Mom, it was my fault Claire fell off the dock and drowned. I rocked it when I jumped, and she stumbled off the other edge and slipped out of her life vest. She could barely swim.

I was her older sister. I was supposed to protect her.

I was supposed to take care of you and Dad.

I failed Claire. I failed Dad. I failed you.

I'm sorry.

I need you to know that I love you. I hope that someday you'll forgive me. Because I'll never forgive myself.

Mom, I was selfish. I ran away and acted the way I did because I knew that it was the only way I could ever change. I took my life into my own hands. But by taking it into my hands, I took it out of yours.

I took away the last child you had.

I'm sorry.

I can never say that enough.

I love you.

    - Cassandra

I ripped out the paper and folded it, tucking it into one of the inside pockets of Dad's jacket. I could feel the ghosts and demon's icy breath on the back of my neck as they watch from over my shoulders. They swarm me.

They kill me.

And then I breathe.

This has been my life for ten years.

This will be my life forever.

No matter what I do, what I say, how much I change. The darkness always stays with you.

It never leaves.

I placed the pencil to the paper again.

Owen Taylor,

I don't know what to say. There's been so much between us, so many different dynamics and levels. Things I'm sorry for, and things I'm not. Things you're sorry for, and things you're not. I'm sorry for all the things that have gone wrong between us. I didn't treat you as well as I should've, but I hope you know, I really wish I could have loved you.

I wish that at that point, I'd realized why I couldn't.

Everything you said that day was right. I never told you that. It would've hurt my pride too much to say it.

I want to thank you. Even if, in five, ten, twenty years, we're still in touch, or if we're not, I want to thank you. You helped me in ways I can barely begin to describe. You taught me how to let someone else in. You taught me to learn to trust. You taught me that I could survive on my own. And when I needed you most, you were there. You kept me from making terrible decisions. You kept me grounded.

When I wanted to leave her, you were there.

I still don't know if it was really you.

Regardless, you helped me. It was you, in one form or another, who reminded me that I was in control, not the voices I made up in my head. The voices that were my voices. The voices that were my thoughts. The thoughts I was so ashamed of I convinced myself it was another voice so I wouldn't have to accept the fact that it was me.

But it was. And you reminded me of that.

I can never repay you for that.

I love you, maybe not in the way you wanted me to, but I love you. You're one of the people I trust most. I depend on you, and I know that with you, I'm safe. Without you, I wouldn't be where I am now. I wouldn't be who I am now.

Because of you, I am.

So, thank you, Owen Taylor.

Thank you for everything.

    - Cassandra J.

I ripped out this one too, tucking it into the same pocket as the other.

My hand moved automatically.

The fingers weren't shaking.

They were steady, sure.

Even though I wasn't.

The pencil touched the paper again.

Lily Peters,

You're insane, you know that? But that's what makes me love you. You're so different from anyone else I've ever met. I don't know why I'm writing this, and I don't know what to say, but I'm going to see what happens when I let myself write these words.

I love you. You're the first person I've ever truly fallen in love with. The first person I never questioned being in love with. You forced me to accept myself, and it took a while, but I did. For so long I'd been trying to convince myself I was someone else, someone I'm not. If I hadn't met you, I would still be convincing myself. There are still parts of me that don't know who I really am, parts of me trying to convince myself I'm someone else. Trying to convince myself that I am the person it would be easier to be, the person who wouldn't stick out in society, whether or not because I'm gay or just 'different'. It would be easier to just be the same as everyone else, to be normal.

But what's the fun in being normal?

There's a point, a reason, to be normal. Being normal lets us blend in, it keeps us safe, and it keeps us sure.

There's no point to not being normal.

That's what lets us live.

We need more people who are different. So much of being human is learning how to fit into society, following trends, keeping up with the stereotypes, questioning anyone who breaks the linearity of human nature.

I'm okay with being different.

I wasn't always okay with it, though. Part of what I ran away from for so long was the person I wasn't okay with being, the person that made me different. The person that set my consignment to oblivion on a different orbit than the consignment of everyone else.

You helped me accept myself.

You showed me what it was like to live.

I had this idea that living was always because of purpose, that if there wasn't a reason there wasn't a point.

You took that idea and broke it into pieces.

Thank you for that.

You are the person I trust most. I've told you more about myself than I've ever told anyone. You've helped me face things I've been scared of facing for years.

You broke down my walls.

No one else has ever done that.

No one else has ever been able to do that.

That's why I love you.

You're everything I'm not, and with you I've become everything I wanted to be.

    - Cassie

I folded that one and placed it into the pocket next to the other two.

One last time, I touched the pencil to the paper. One more letter, to one more person.

Once I finished it, I set the pencil down.

I ripped the paper out of the notebook.

I folded it.

I tucked it into an inside pocket. A separate one. Away from the other letters.

I watched the lake glitter in the wake of the rising sun. The glass like surface reflecting the colors the sunrise paints the sky every morning.

I watched the girl, one more time.

Then I stood up, turned around, and walked away.

I never went back.

*   *   *

"Oh my god, it's the big day!" Mom screamed, rushing around the kitchen putting together last minute things, trying to keep from crying again.

"I'm so proud of you," Grandma hugged me, handing me a cup of coffee.

"Thank you," I smiled, giving her a quick kiss on the cheek. "Mom, are you ready to go?"

She stopped, nodded, and smiled, still fighting back tears, "Yeah."

"And Rachel's picking you up before graduation?" Grandma asked, tucking a strand of hair behind my ear and handing me my graduation cap.

I nodded, "Yeah."

"Okay."

"Mom?"

"I'm coming," she said, dabbing away some of her running mascara, "I'm coming."

We walked out of the house and got in the car. We didn't talk the whole drive there, and when I got out of the car it took her a couple minutes to get out.

"Are you okay?" I asked, helping her up.

"Yeah," she nodded slowly, pausing before walking up the hill toward their graves. I grabbed the flowers out of the backseat and started walking after her. I took her hand in mine, and she gripped it tightly.

She froze every so often, and I had to tell her it was okay before she would start walking again.

After a long walk, we made it to the top and stopped in front of their graves.

Kenneth James

Claire James

The two of them, side by side.

I started to kneel to the put the flowers on the little mound of dirt, but Mom stopped me, "I'll do it, don't get your gown dirty."

"Are you sure?"

"Yes," she said, tears welling in her eyes. She placed them on the graves, and then stood back up. We stood there together, looking at the two headstones, side by side. The two people we both want back in our lives, and the two people we'll never get back in our lives.

"I love you, Mom," I whispered.

"I love you too, Cassandra," she whispered back.

* * *

After Mom drove away, I walked back up to Dad's grave and knelt in front of it, being careful not to get my gown dirty.

I pulled the note I wrote to him out of my pocket and read it. "Dad,

I miss you. I miss you so much.

Everything's changed without you. We're all different. Mom's different, I'm different. We miss you.

I don't blame you. I wish what happened hadn't happened, but it did, and no one can change that.

I hope you're happier now.

It's been hard without you. Everyday we're reminded that you're not there. But we've managed. We've made it this far. Every day it gets a little easier.

You're with Claire, now. I know she needs you. Maybe now you can finally forgive yourself.

I see you every day. I think about you all the time. I'll never forget you. I don't try to forget you.

You're the one thing from my past I've tried to remember.

Well, you and Claire.

I've tried not to remember everything else.

Can you blame me?

I miss you, Dad. It's been ten years. It's been so long. But at the same time, it seems like yesterday.

I hope you're in a better place now. This world can be hell.

What if we're all living in hell, all the people on Earth, all of humanity. What if we've already died in some other life, and we're paying for everything we did wrong before?

I hope you're not paying anymore. You don't deserve to.

I love you. I miss you.

I'll see you again, someday." I paused to regain my composure and wipe away a few of the tears. "I'm sorry, Dad. I'm so sorry. I should never have blamed you, for anything. And I don't blame you. I miss you, I miss you so much. And I wish you were here. But you're not, and that's okay. I still love you."

I pushed myself to my feet, and ripped up the note, scattering it across the grave. I stepped away. "Bye, Dad."

Rachel honked at me from the bottom of the hill.

I took one look at the headstone, and then I left. I didn't look back after that.

"Hey!" Rachel said when I got in the car. Gabi and Maddy were in the back, talking.

"Hi," I closed the door.

"Are you okay?"

"Yeah," I brushed away some of my running mascara, making sure not to further ruin my makeup, "I'm okay."

"Okay."

"Cass!" Maddy reached around the seat to hug me, "are you ready?"

"I guess I have to be!"

"Well, we still have some time before we have to be there," Rachel glanced at us in the rearview mirror, "so I was thinking we could make a stop on the way. Play a little game."

"Could we?" I asked.

"Yeah!" Maddy grinned.

"Alright, Gabi?"

"I guess that's okay."

"Alright, sounds good."

*   *   *

We all got out and walked up to the railing, letting the spray from the water hit us.

The four of us sat there, and for once, we didn't talk. I don't think any of us could quite process the fact that it was almost over. I know I couldn't.

Gabi checked her watch, "Hey, guys, if we want to make graduation, we might want to head back."

Rachel checked the time on her phone, "I guess you're right. Okay, come on, guys. And Cass, get in the back with the other two."

"Why?"

"Just do it."

We all stood up, and as I did I felt the three letters left in the pocket of Dad's jacket, which I wore under my gown. "I'll meet you guys at the car, there's something I have to do," I said, sliding under the railing.

"Alright, but please, be careful," Rachel gave me a look, but didn't question me.

"I will."

I stepped closer to the edge, digging the first letter out of my pocket. I ripped it half. Then into quarters. And then I did the same with those, until the letter lay in little pieces in my hand. I let them drop into the water below me, watching them spiral as they fell.

Then I did the same with the second letter. And then I did the same with the third, except this time, I blew the little pieces away from me, letting the wind take them far away. Not quite the miles that will be between me and her in a few months, but far away. Somewhere they won't be found.

I stood there for a minute, watching all the pieces of my life float away from me, at the same time they all came together.

"Hey, come on!" Rachel called, sticking her head out the window.

I took one last look at the pieces. Then I got in the car and let Rachel drive away, leaving them all behind.

They're a part of my future, that became the present, and is now the past.

Rachel opened the sun roof, and I could feel the wind in my face as she started to pick up speed on the empty roads we traveled so long ago.

The world flew by, and in a moment of irrationality, I stood up, balancing myself, and pushed my shoulders up through the opening, letting my head out into open air. I heard Maddy scream, but it got swept away in the wind rushing past my ears.

Then I let go of the car, and held my arms out like wings, feeling the wind pour through my fingers.

I let out a scream, letting the wind carry away the sound.

I heard Rachel laugh somewhere below me.

"Live a little," she used to say.

I'm living more than a little, now.

By simply living, we break our consignment to oblivion.

"*Do not let all the mundane concatenations in this world be for naught,*" said Lily Peters.

Which was just her way of saying, don't live for nothing.

Epilogue

She steps up to the edge of the cliff, the spray of the water making her image falter. The colors bringing her gray figure to life.

I watched her fall.

The water doesn't change. No ripples, no splash. Everything is still.

I saw her face this time.

Claire's face appears, the little purple and green life vest pulled over her shoulders. Mom's face, eyes sad but hopeful. Dad, looking down at her.

Mom takes Claire's hand, and they watch the girl's body as it rises to the surface.

Dad reaches out and brushes the hair out of the face. Her eyes are still closed.

But I know who it is.

They watch her, floating there in the water, silent elegies sending ripples out around her body.

Dad scoops her up into his arms, holding her close to him. Mom kisses her forehead and Claire takes the lifeless hand in hers.

The scars on her body are visible.

The bruises around his neck are faded, but still there.

Then they fade for good. The ghosts of the past finally returning to their graves.

Together, they turn their backs on me. They walk away, fading back into nothing.

And then they're gone.

The consignment to oblivion is broken.

CONSIGNED TO OBLIVION

B.C. Hedlund

Acknowledgements

I would like to thank everyone who has been involved in this process. It has been a long, five-year journey with many ups and downs, and there is no way to properly thank the people who have helped me through it.

First and foremost, I would like to thank…

…My parents (and sister), who have been there since the first draft. They've always encouraged me to pursue my passions, and I don't know where I'd be without them. They've put up with the late nights, the constant writing talk, and countless other things.

…My friends, of whom have never tired of my endless babble regarding my writing, and have always been there to support me, whether it's reading and commenting on my work or simply keeping me sane.

…Kate Griffin, the first person to ever read my book, cover to cover. She has never failed to be there for me, and has listened to my countless rants and ramblings. Without her, I would not have written the third (and final) draft of my novel, and without her, I would not be where I am today.

I would not have been able to complete this project without the support of all my friends and family. Thank you all so much for your constant encouragement and inspiration.

B.C. Hedlund

About the Author

B.C. Hedlund is an emerging novelist and short story writer. She currently lives in Connecticut with her family, and is a busy high schooler, college student, and musician. She is fascinated with inspiration derived from the small things in life, and her work focuses on turning the ordinary into the unordinary. *Consigned to Oblivion* is her first novel. You can learn more about her and her work at https://bchedlund.journoportfolio.com

Printed in Great Britain
by Amazon